The Good Man

The Good Man

A NOVEL

Edward Jae-Suk Lee

BRIDGE WORKS PUBLISHING COMPANY
Bridgehampton, New York

Copyright © 2004 by Edward Jae-Suk Lee

Published by Bridge Works Publishing Company, Bridgehampton, New York, an imprint of The Rowman & Littlefield Publishing Group, Inc.

Distributed in the United States by National Book Network, Lanham, Maryland. For descriptions of this and other Bridge Works books, visit the National Book Network website at www.nbnbooks.com.

FIRST EDITION

The characters and events in this book are fictitious. Any similarity to actual persons, living or dead, is coincidental and not intended by the author.

Library of Congress Cataloging-in-Publication Data

Lee, Edward Jae-Suk, 1975–
    The good man : a novel / Edward Jae-Suk Lee.—1st ed.
        p. cm.
    ISBN 1-882593-94-4 (hardcover : alk. paper)
    1. Korean War, 1950–1953—Veterans—Fiction. 2. Korean American women—Fiction. 3. Mothers and daughters—Fiction. 4. Suicidal behavior—Fiction. 5. Nogaeun-ni (Korea)—Fiction. 6. Sheep ranchers—Fiction. 7. Massacres—Fiction. 8. Amnesia—Fiction. 9. Montana—Fiction. I Title.

PS3612.E3428G66 2004
813'.6—dc 22
                                2004016433

10 9 8 7 6 5 4 3 2 1

♾™ The paper used in this publication meets the minimum requirements of American National Standard for Information Sciences—Permanence of Paper for Printed Library Materials, ANSI/NISO Z39.48-1992.
Manufactured in the United States of America.

For my wife, Carly, and my mother, Sook

The Good Man

ONE

He walked west along the county two-lane, looking up at the familiar ridge of the Bridger Mountains, the last light of the downed sun casting a pink refraction just above the low peaks, and that halo bleeding through some woolen altocumulus clouds in the western sky.

It was a good time to return, the warmer days come about with the Chinook breeze, calling the cyclical migrants back to the myriad camping grounds and the isolation of the place. To the residents of Thalo Valley, he appeared to be one of those migrants—just another broken old man, carrying his life in a worn leather satchel that was missing a strap, and his once-muscled body now eroded to the bone, so that the clothes he wore draped loosely around him like the last best suit of a dead man.

Forty years had passed since he'd been home, but Thalo Valley was one of those places excused from the momentum of the world, a place where a person could come and go and not miss much with the passing of time.

Despite his minimal memory, he still knew the valley in all its incarnations—all its colors under vernal equinox, all its monotones in the Montana winter. He still knew the animals, eaters and eaten both, and their migrations south to the park grounds and back, sometimes fuller in number, sometimes less. He knew the break of grazing land from wilderness wood, and the deer runs gone dry in scorching summer and mudded after the thaw. He knew the trees, the lodgepole pines and Douglas firs and the orange tinting of their bark, and the boughs short and leading to the sky. And he knew himself among them, walking hand in hand with Emily Cottage, hidden away under the canopy and only the needles underfoot. Only the chilly air in Null Gully, where the water ran fast, carrying the cold down from the mountain, and carrying the mountain itself in the guise of fine silt and sand.

From the corner of his good eye, he spied a shift of copper miners marching along Rural Road J toward the hewn-log roadhouse that stood where J intersected the two-lane. The air was crisp but not cold, the ground seeping the warmth soaked up from the day heat, and he took a deep breath and ran his fingers along the strap of a black patch that covered the scar flesh grown over his empty right eye socket, the dark hole two layers removed from the light of day. Save for the eye patch, there was no malice in his face, his nose soft and his lips full to closing, and his skin weathered and leathery like a saddlebag flap, with symmetrical wrinkling around the mouth and just a little droopiness of the fatless folds around his jowls and neck. And the one good eye, the left eye, round and blue and ever soulful, as if all the stored luminescence from his lost right eye had found that other egress.

The copper miners traversed a roadside drainage ditch to gain quicker access to the parking lot of the roadhouse, and then picked up their pace as they came back to ground level where the dirt lot met the ditch flora, all their booted feet kicking up dust as they marched to the entrance, and the dust cloud just hanging there at eye level, no breeze blowing at this junction in Thalo Valley.

The dust and the miners reminded him of another march he had witnessed along another dusty tread, a war tread he knew from a time he didn't care to remember. And as the miners approached him, their gilded faces became those of Asian peasants, and the roadhouse lot became a jutted dirt road that ran parallel to a rail line hidden by wild wheat. He imagined hundreds of peasants marching, draped in soiled white, their expressions dumb like quagmired sheep. Marching like automatons, all those feet trolling through the dust and the prettiness of the place under that pink, post-dusk sky.

He closed his eye and breathed deeply, and the smell of the airborne dirt triggered more images—rice paddies terraced along a hillock and that same pink sunset and the tall grass hiding grouse and some sparse scrub oaks providing small blinds for the hunting of elk. Was it for the hunting of elk? Or was it cover from the enemy? And the peasants still marching, always marching, the same sun-dark faces looping over and over in his imagination, the same ones carrying swaddled babies on their backs and leading the oxen and hauling A-frame packs over their shoulders. The same dumb expressions. But there was no illumination beyond the fact that his name was Gabriel Guttman of the 7th Cavalry, and it was war.

When he opened his eye again, he found himself within the crowd of miners, swallowed by their wheezing and the smell of loamy sweat, and the herd of them just in front of the wooden wraparound deck that surrounded the roadhouse. The miners filed up its triple step and then through the open front door, their eagerness for drink pushing them two abreast through the jamb, and leaving Gabriel no more time to dwell on his memories.

The interior of the roadhouse was stark and dank, with no windows and walls of open log and old plank floors, and weak light shining from yellow bulbs hung down from the rafters. Gabriel eased his way to the bar and sat down on a stool, resting on his lap the dirty leather satchel with its two-buckle flap. He looked over his shoulder and surveyed the crowd. The miners had pulled tables together and sat in the center of the room, and a skinny barmaid had brought them cracker baskets and pitchers of beer. Stetson-wearing ranch hands stood along the walls, and some older men sat alone, staring into drams. The few female patrons loitered in the darker corners, looking plenty used.

–Bourbon. Straight up, said Gabriel to the bartender, the timbre of his voice a strong and slow tenor, and his speech polished and with no accent.

The chestnut-headed bartender nodded and set a shot glass on the bar and poured two fingers from a bottle of amber swill. Gabriel downed the shot and hard-knuckled the bar, and the bartender poured two more fingers, which Gabriel downed with one hand as he hard-knuckled the bar with the other. The bartender looked at him cockeyed, and Gabriel pulled a crisp hundred from his back pocket and dropped it on the bar and hard-knuckled the green-back. The bartender snickered, pocketing the bill, and then poured Gabriel's next shot to the brim.

Gabriel sipped the meniscus from the shot glass until it was a half inch down, and then felt a heavy hand on his shoulder.

–Who the hell are you supposed to be? asked a woman to his left. John Wayne?

John Wayne. The name was familiar, and he kicked it around in his head until he located the broad craggy face and the slit mouth and familiar bent-back walk, and the title of a movie, and a cowboy hat too small for that chucked head, and yes, the eye patch. The black patch also too small. John Wayne. *True Grit.*

He smiled, pleased with himself, and touched his own patch and then looked over at the woman, examining her loose face and bleach-blond hair, which was feathered around the crown and long in the back to curtain her thick neck. She wore a white ribbon shirt draped over her wide shoulders and stout torso, her head and body uniform in girth, wide and white like a thumb. She did not stir him, so he swam his arm away from her and went back to sipping his bourbon.

–Don't recognize your face, she said, sitting down on the stool next to him. You from the valley?

–No, he mumbled.

–Passin' through?

He shook his head.

–Well where you headed? she asked.

–A place I remember, he said.

–So you're a drifter?

–If that's what you want to call me.

–You look like a drifter. Look like trouble.

–Too old to make trouble.

–Never too old to make trouble, said the woman and cackled, revealing a gum line missing its front four teeth on the top and bottom. Gabriel looked into her mouth and saw her sick tongue in the darkness between her lips. He pegged her for a whore.

–What's your name? she asked.

–Gabe.

–Drink up, Gabe. Make me look prettier.

Gabriel looked at the chestnut-headed bartender, and the bartender laughed and topped off Gabriel's bourbon.

The woman leaned over, wavering for a moment, and then spoke in Gabriel's ear, her breath hot and footy.

–Well, if it's trouble you're lookin' for, this is as good a place as any, she said and then pointed sloppily toward the billiard tables along the far wall.

Gabriel breathed through his mouth and looked over his shoulder to where the woman was pointing. There was a bearded man leaning down over one of the tables, lining up his cue. A handsome, horse-faced boy stood against the wall nearby, a beer in one hand and a cue in the other and a black Stetson on his head worn low across his tanned brow.

–Bet you them two have it out before night's over, said the woman.

Gabriel watched as the bearded man banked the eight ball in the near side pocket and then slapped palms with the fellow to his left. The handsome boy flared his nostrils as he tossed his cue onto the table, and then removed some cash from his front pocket and slammed it down hard on the bumper rail. The bearded man snatched it quickly and walked bandy-legged up to the bar. The boy cursed at the bandy-legger and then walked out the front door, followed closely by a dark giant, a half foot taller than anyone else in the roadhouse and black straight hair down his back.

–One with the hat's Jude Finn, said the woman. Ham Finn's grandson. The bowlegged bastard is Uncle Duck. Finn's main hand.

–And the tall kid? asked Gabriel.

–Val Rey, another of Finn's.

–Finn a cattleman?

She nodded. –Owns most the land in Thalo Valley. All the way north to the government forest and west to Road K. Got grazin' rights northwest of that.

–What about the old Cottage ranch? asked Gabriel.

The woman paused. –Thought you weren't from around here, she said.

–I lied, said Gabriel, no expression on his face.

The woman squinted and made a half grin, unsure of what to make of him, and then lit an unfiltered cigarette and blew the first drag above Gabriel's head.

–Finn bought it up about twenty year ago, she said.

Gabriel nodded. –You know where the Cottage woman went off to? he asked.

–Nowhere, said the woman. Stayed here. Ham Finn let her stay on as a sharecropper. Gave her a parcel south of Null Gully for her sheep.

–So she's still there?

–She would be if she wasn't dead.

Gabriel felt the left half of his body begin to tingle, from the top of his scalp above the left eye down the neck and shoulder and branching down the left arm. Then his left hand began to shake.

The woman stared at Gabriel's tremoring hand. He gripped the wrist with his right and brought both arms into his torso and stood up from his stool and whistled at the bartender, who was talking to Uncle Duck. The bartender came over and set the bottle of cheap bourbon on the bar within Gabriel's reach.

–How? asked Gabriel as he let go of his left arm and watched it for a second to make sure there would be no more spasms before he poured himself a drink.

–You all right? asked the woman, tilting her head like a curious dog.

–Fine, said Gabriel and then took the bottle firmly with his right hand and slouched his shoulders in heartbroken fashion. How'd she die? he asked.

–Died three year back in the spring storm of '89, said the woman. Bad storm. Wiped out a lot of animals. Put a lotta folk in a bind. Chinawoman's boy died too.

–Chinawoman? asked Gabriel and then closed his eye tight and felt his left hand twitching again. He focused on the baseline noises of the bar, the clacking of billiard balls and bulbous laughter. It was too much, too many triggers all closing in on the dark place where his lost memories lived, trying to illuminate that darkness. As he poured himself another shot to deaden the senses, the woman held out her own empty glass. He filled her offering halfway deep.

–I figured she'd be long gone by now, he said, unable to block out the face of the young peasant girl he'd brought back with him after the war. He did not remember her name. Only that she was lovely, and that the thought of her made him uneasy.

–She's still there, said the woman. Same as she ever was. Lives with her daughter. A real pill that one. Got the men round here blue-balled, that's for sure.

Gabriel sat still, not really looking at anything, the pupil in his good eye dilated and his mind visiting a particular clearing on the west face of the mountain behind the Cottage compound where the bitterroots blossomed early.

–Anyway, said the woman, swirling the whiskey and trying to regain Gabriel's attention. He got a wicked temper, that Jude Finn. Which is a bad thing for a man with a gamblin' problem. He's into the Cat's Paw for a few thousand I hear. Borrows against his granddaddy's name and keeps getting his ass kicked in Texas Hold'm.

She turned and pushed out her chest, and Gabriel looked down at it, at the sad breasts pulling down from her ribs to her waistline. The woman reached up and touched him on the cheek and then curled her fingers and combed them across the side of his head.

–You a gamblin' man? she asked.

Gabriel closed his eye and let her stroke his head. The whiskey had settled affectionately in his empty stomach and her fingers felt good. Not good from a woman's touch, though. A different good. A guiltless good. Like a mother's hand upon a child's aching belly.

–No, he said.

–Where'd you get the money, then? she asked.

Gabriel opened his eye.

–I seen that hundred, she said. A man carryin' cash like that's either a gambler or a thief.

Gabriel did not answer.

–What's in the bag? she asked, looking down at his lap.

–Nothing, he said.

–You got more money in there?

–None of your business.

–I ain't expensive, said the woman.

–I figured.

–Ain't askin' for much.

Gabriel nodded and reached under the satchel flap with his left hand. –Defend this child in the name of the Father, he whispered, and removed a worn vinyl-bound Bible and handed it to her. All you need's in here. Take it.

The woman looked at the Bible and then punched Gabriel in the nose. He fell backward off his stool, landing on the floor in a puddle of old beer.

–Bastard, she said and tossed the Bible to the ground. Gabriel reached up to wipe his mouth and felt blood running down onto his lips. He pinched his nostrils shut and picked up the Bible and his satchel, tipping his head back as he walked to the rear of the roadhouse toward the washrooms.

Inside the men's room he knelt down and stared at the Bible's cover. He looked at the maroon vinyl finish, and the two big gold-flake words centered plainly. *Holy* and then *Bible*, it read, but he was unable to make the connection of the arrangements of the letters within the words to the sounds they produced on the tongue, only knowing that the two of them together named the journal of the Word of the Lord, and he knew that only because it was his Bible, the same one he'd had for the last two decades. A gift from somebody meaningful whom he did not remember.

He wedged the Bible tightly in the folds of an old twine-colored sweater, spine down so the gold leaf of the pages was facing skyward. Next to the sweater was a tightly sealed envelope whose unflapped side was scrawled in dark ink with his own handwriting. He removed the envelope and stared at it and ran his fingers along its surface, smearing the white stock with a streak of blood. His lost memories were in there, that much he knew, but he could not decipher the words scrawled upon the envelope.

He slid the letter into the gilded pages of the Bible and then closed the satchel flap and went to the rusted sink to let the last of his nose blood drip into the basin. The whiskey had made quick work of him, the warmth and the euphoria already gone and leaving just the lamenting. He imagined the pale face of Emily Cottage, as he had often done of late, and he chased her swirling figure as they had chased the summer fireflies in the years he remembered best.

Emily, the one who had loved him, the one who had said yes to him four decades ago among the primrose of the valley floor. He remembered the nights they spent rolling along the hillside and the wild wheatgrass, and how pretty she looked after she'd been rained upon, the water soaking into her summer dress, pressing the curves of her shoulders and hips closer to those places he'd wanted to know.

Emily Cottage. Dead.

The bleeding in his nose abated, and he rinsed his hands and face and looked at himself in the mirror, at all of his sixty-one years, and then he cried a little and slumped down to the stained floor of the bathroom. He thought of his lost love, that corrosive love that had left its mark like his scars of war, eating into him and affording no filler when it was gone, leaving only a hole, a hollowness to remind him of what he had missed, to remind him how it felt to be consumed by such a thing, to be fulfilled by such a thing.

The door to the washroom swung halfway open and he saw the thick head of the surly whore peer around the edge. She grinned at him tooth-free, and then the door opened fully and she strolled into the bathroom. Behind her followed two burly men, brothers they looked like, chested like bulls and wearing too-small flannel shirts and canvas overalls, and sporting reddish beards and thick necks like Vikings.

–Get his bag, said the whore.

Gabriel cradled the satchel tightly as the flanneled brothers came upon him.

–Come on, now, he said, scooting backward by his heels. I don't want trouble.

–Give me the bag and there'll be none, said the whore.

–There's nothing of value in the bag, said Gabriel.

–Then you should have no worries partin' with it, she said and nodded at the brothers.

They split out, one to Gabriel's left and one to his right, and each took a handful of the loose cloth around Gabriel's poorly tailored shirt and hoisted him up.

–You know, I never did catch your name, said Gabriel, standing now and still clutching the satchel tightly to his chest.

–Late to be tryin' to win favor, said the whore.

–I'm not trying to win favor, said Gabriel. But seeing as how you're in a position to harm me now, I'd like to know how to address you.

–Name's Sweet Crude, she said.

–Is that your given name? asked Gabriel.

–You don't like it?

–Didn't say that.

–My daddy was an oil man, she said, looking away from him.

Gabriel nodded. –All right then, Sweet Crude, if it's money you want, I'll give you all I've got and we can part ways. It's not much, but it's better than nothing, and it's all I have to give. There's no need for your meaty friends to get worked up over a misunderstanding.

Sweet Crude shook her head. –I gave you the chance for charity and was left wantin', she said and removed a cigarette from behind her ear and lit it with a wooden match struck on the cement wall. I'll be takin' that bag of yours now.

The brother to his right pummeled Gabriel in the gut. Gabriel doubled over, short-winded, and watched his satchel fall to the ground before him, and the lack of air had the hole in his face awakened and trying to re-create itself, trying to illuminate the seminal moments from the last forty-some years of his life. The streambed in Chu Gok Ri. The hospital in Pusan. The foothills of Thalo Valley. The birth of the child. A drunken sunrise alone. Casper to Ogden. Ogden to Omaha. Omaha to Oklahoma City.

From the run of those memories he found strength, becoming Gabriel of the mid-century, Gabriel of the soldiering and hay-baling and bar-fighting days, when his body was fleshed and his limb junctions coiled and quick.

12

That younger self wrenched free from the brothers' grasp and grabbed the satchel from the floor and took Sweet Crude by her hair and threw her down in front of the brothers. Then he sprinted out of the washroom and through the roaring miners, and as he passed the chestnut-headed bartender, he snatched the bourbon bottle he had left on the bar, and then he was out the front door onto the wraparound deck and the monochrome of deep evening.

As he jumped down to the ground-level lot, his eye met with Val Rey's, the tall Indian boy who had been with Jude Finn. Val pointed across the highway into the lodgepole forest, and Gabriel ran in that direction, scrambling up the slope, and turning around only when he was twenty yards up the mountain.

VAL REY WATCHED THE DRIFTER DISAPPEAR into the forest, and then turned around just as the big brothers came huffing out of the roadhouse, Sweet Crude a step behind them. Sweet Crude paused for a moment in the parking lot, looking up and down the road for movement, and then walked up to Val, her face flushed and milky sweat beading around her hairline.

–Where is he? she asked.

The brothers came to her flank, squeezing their huge hands in the air to loosen their knuckles. Val stood his ground and folded his arms across his chest. He had brawled with the brothers before and had come out no worse than they, even though he'd been outnumbered two to one.

–Ran off, he said.

The brothers clenched their jaws and hands, and stepped forward within swinging distance.

–We fightin'? asked Val.

–Not if you tell me where he went, said Sweet Crude.

–What'd he do to you?

–He's got somethin' I want.

–Somethin' he stole?

–What difference does it make, Val, said Sweet Crude. And why you comin' to his aid anyway? You know him?

–No. Just wanna know why you're chasin' him.

–Okay then, said Sweet Crude. He stole some money from me.

Val nodded. –He ran into the forest, he said.

Sweet Crude smiled and reached up and patted Val on the cheek. Val watched as she and the brothers began walking along the road on the forested side, venturing a few paces into the trees now and then. He especially watched Sweet Crude, who was about the same age his mother had been when she'd died, and had the same stink of liquor and body rot.

He tried his best not to remember his mother. Tried not to think of her dying in their dying town outside Spokane, dying from the inside out, always drinking the Canadian whiskey from a glass tumbler, until the hair fell from her scalp and the skin grew taught against the bones in her face like plastic.

As a child he thought the more he ate, the less she could drink, because she loved him and would never let him go hungry, not even if it meant stopping the flow of whiskey. He grew into a bear of a boy, but as hard as he tried, he could not eat enough, and his mother died like that, thin-haired and yellow of skin, and it had been slow and he had seen every day of her dying.

He was ten when they buried her, and for the next three years he bounced around state care facilities, until he ran away, east, away from his mother's memory to the Black-feet reservation in Montana, the land of his father, who had left them before Val was born. It was on the reservation that he met Ham Finn, who would come by every now and then to look at the women. Even at thirteen, Val had had seen eye to eye with Ham, the only man or boy in the valley tall enough to do so. Finn had taken him back to the ranch, and it was there that Val caught a glimpse of the neighbor girl, the dark-skinned girl—skin like his and hair like his, and he knew he would never leave.

In the distance he saw Sweet Crude and the brothers turn around dejectedly and head back toward the roadhouse. He looked up the mountain and wondered where the drifter would be headed next. Maybe south to the park grounds. Maybe west to the Bitterroot Mountains. There was something about him that made Val hope to never cross paths with him again. Something about the way he ran. As if wherever he went, bad luck chased him.

GABRIEL RESTED ON HIS HAUNCHES FOR A MINUTE, pulling a quick one from the bourbon bottle and pouring the remainder into a leatherbound nickel flask that was clipped to his waistband. He tossed the empty bottle to the ground and stood up and began following an animal run that sloped gradually up the mountain, parallel to the road. He walked with a whiskey belly and a mind of chaff until he came to a familiar scree at the base of a mountain ledge. He knew the lay of the land from his childhood days, and he sat down on a rock berg and closed his eye and the darkness came, and from the darkness a dirt road that led to the Cottage ranch and the years he'd lost in a slow, meltwater stream. And he traveled that dirt road in his mind and felt the days peel away and he became a young man again, a young man in love.

The drowsiness overwhelmed him, and he began seeing memories in the darkness, himself on the ranch just before he left for the army, waving good-bye to Emily Cottage and her image fading in the distance. Then everything slow, and him walking along the dirt road away from her, looking back and forth across the valley, the white Rambouillet following him in a steady stream, lambs blatting and jumping upon their mothers' backs to be carried.

And the white sheep became Korean peasants dressed in white frocks, bundles on their backs, chattering, and the sound of crying babies. He kept walking, and the hot sun made him think of hot thoughts, like the hot tea in which the panpan girls had bathed, and the warm fog that descended to the base of the Korean country hills as they strolled along the fields of rice at the base of a hillock whose sides were terraced with paddies.

A WHITE HERON GLIDES above the green fields of rice paddy rows, then swoops down to a low puddle of water trapped in a swale, searching for fish. A dense column of peasants marches east, away from the fighting near Yongdong and the advancing communists. The dirt roads have dried out and the dust kicked up by the peasant throng saturates the air, clinging to any semblance of moisture.

It is early evening, and the 7th Cavalry has reached its position on a hillside just above a long rail tunnel that runs parallel to the main north-south road stretching from Seoul to Pusan. Some of the men linger around the railroad tracks, waiting for orders, while the light artillery and mortar units dig into the hillside. Peasants walk the parallel road along with a few scraggly-looking cattle and the few oxcarts that pull larger items like stoneware and long-handled farming tools. The older men carry A-frame packs on their backs, loaded high on their shoulders with wrapped bundles, so it appears they might tip over at any moment, their short and skinny bodies tenuous under the weight borne by their legs.

The sun is low in the sky, but still burns in full. The whole country is hot. Hotter than he has ever known. He thinks of the mountain summers in Montana and the high dry sun that covers his bare skin with light downy heat, and the sun showers that come through almost every day to keep the heat honest.

He looks around at the grassy hills along the valley, cleared mostly of trees, and the higher peaks on the horizon to the south. They resemble the foothills back home and the mountains covered with Douglas firs and pines that hide the elk and mule deer.

It is almost like home. Almost like home and almost perfectly alien. The dusty haze of sunset resembles the air during the Montana summer, when the wildfires fog the sunlight, casting lines of purple and crimson at dawn and dusk, colored like the petals of the bitterroot blossoms in the clearing behind the Cottage house.

The rice paddy rows hide puddles of old low water.

He has never seen rice paddies before, or the mud huts that make up the villages along the rail line. There are scrub oaks across the mountainous areas, and low ridges that remind him of the Crazy Mountains, but it is different. Lonelier.

They have orders to dig in among the hills to provide cover along the dirt highway and the rail line for the retreating infantry that has been pushed back from the Yongdong front. They are in a narrow valley now, the hillsides steep immediately where the incline begins, a perfect spot for an ambush should the communists chase the retreating 24th Infantry east across the valley floor until the road and the rail line turn south again. He removes his canteen, guzzling the warm, metallic water, and notices some of the peasants watching him as they pass. He wonders what it would be like to be displaced like that, to be herded away from their homes and farms, their land slipping through their fingers like topsoil collapsing under heavy rain. They carry whatever they can, some of the oxcarts loaded with large clay pots and iron kettles and caged chickens, and the few cattle interspersed with the slowly moving crowd. The rest they leave behind, to be burned when the village burns.

His eyes squint against that stream of white, the frocks flecked occasionally by exposed brown skin and the babies swaddled in dirty clothes across their mothers' backs. Some of them have cloth-wrapped bundles balanced on their heads, bobbing up and down. He watches the oxcarts trundling slowly along the rutted, pockmarked road, and the bare-skinned children running to and fro along the massive stream of people and farm animals, chasing one another in games through the middle of the herd, occasionally making their way outside the boundaries of the road.

His eyes settle on a dark, young girl with short hair. Had he not seen the small swell of her breasts rising from her loose-fitting shirt, he would have thought her a boy. He looks at her, the girl, the first time he has looked deeply at any of them, and he sees that timelessness that secretes away their ages. She is unlike anything he has ever seen, and yet familiar. Her clothes are covered in streaks of fine silt, her straight hair bunched in short tresses, the grease and sweat from her scalp pulling the strands together with the gravity of desperation.

She is unlike the girls back home, who have shown their shapes since they were twelve. She is unlike the girls back home in every way, unlike even the panpan girls, those Ginza whores with their faces painted in the colors of tropical bird feathers, calling to the men with the promise of the exotic first taste. She is a girl, straight and narrow of body, a long cylinder of clay molded in angles along her ribcage and pelvis. She is unlike any woman he has seen, and yet she is familiar.

He knows her. He knows her from a future time. Knows who she will become. And he realizes he is within a dream, and her face evolves, the angles of her cheeks changing, maturing, and the hair grown longer and the eye sockets shrinking so the whites are fully eclipsed. The tableau of the hilltops blurs so that all he sees is her face and black pearl eyes. He tries to look away, turning his attention to the other peasants, but they are all the same. All her. All her eyes on him. He tries to dream within the dream, to dream of home and the crispness of mountain air. He tries to dream of the foothills where he and Emily lie upon the primrose and clover in the late summer nights, whispering lovers' anthems to each other amidst the coyote baying. He reaches for them, the images, but they remain only words. He sees only her. Only the peasant and those black pearl eyes.

She tells him her hair is cut short so that men like him will think she is a boy. She tells him there are enemy among the refugees, wolves among the sheep. She tells him he will never know peace, and then she laughs and within her laughter he hears the squeaking of oxcart wheels, babies crying, and the godless sound of jet fighters strafing in the distance.

TWO

Within the shallow gully bordering the Cottage ranch flowed a moderate creek that carried the excess of an alpine lake down to the valley floor. The water's run was invisible from the ranch, hidden by a bend in the mountain base and a thicket of firs, but Yahng Yi could always sense its presence, as if it watched her from the gully, moving as she moved, mimicking her rhythms.

It was a warm spring day, a good day to beckon the spring lambs, and the creek was running fast again. The year's thaw had arrived early, and Yahng Yi's skin had already coppered to its warm-weather hue. A spade-blade shovel in hand, she walked along the log fence that paralleled Rural Road K, heading toward a band of Shetland sheep. She was tall at sixteen, and her body soft in line and gentle, like the curve of water moving slowly over rock. She wore a plain white T-shirt and blue jeans, the denim streaked where she'd wiped her hands. Her long black hair hung down in tangled waves, buttressed by high cheeks.

She stopped before a pile of wet sheep manure and bladed the shovel into the soft ground, letting the handle stand upright on its own. There was high music coming from a red pickup truck parked at the base of the gravel driveway. A woman was singing a sad song, and it reminded her of when she and her brother Jihn would sing the old sad songs their mother had taught them. Those folk songs they would all sing during the first week of warm weather, when the three of them opened up the windows in the house and let the new air come inside to bully out the old. Their voices against the running water from the gully as they wiped down the furniture and swept the plank floor. And then outside to the heat, the sun rays stern on their open skin as they beat the detritus from the rugs, Auntie Emily up on the mountain somewhere painting her watercolor landscapes.

She looked up the mountain, at the comeliness of the colored swatches on the rise near the house—the blue larkspur, and the patches of sagebrush and chokecherry bushes and the green shoots of new grasses. Above the western ridge was nothing but wide blue sky and cloud scraps that moved in the expanse like watchful ghosts. At the foothills below the tree line were grass moguls that fed the returning herds of elk. There were dozens of them now, tiny dark flecks on the open slope, the high antlers of the bulls moving across the hills.

A warm breeze blew, and she held her hair down with her hands, pressing her palms against her temples to keep the tresses from snapping. Pregnant ewes loitered around her near the fence, sticking their heads through the slats to reach the willow shoots that had sprouted in the roadside ditch. She surveyed them as they craned their necks toward the road, examining the swells of their underbellies to guess which would be the first to drop.

This year there were just thirty ewes, only six of which were pregnant. Ten of the ewes were just yearlings and hadn't been bred. And fourteen were grannies, too old to lamb. They had sold a half dozen yearling ewes and the two rams to a breeder in Canada the year before. Without the rams to pen, Yahng Yi had torn down the cross-fencing and the barnyard fence up on the plateau to fuel the heat stove over the winter. She'd always wanted the band to roam anyway, to access the wildflowers and sweet grasses up the slope. But the band stayed near the valley floor even without the fences, waiting in that feeding spot. With the meltwater flowing into the arroyo and the fresh pond south of the drive, the band didn't even need to come to the water troughs by the barn.

The manure had been getting thick by the fence line, so Yahng Yi tied her hair back and retrieved a rusted wheelbarrow from next to the truck, then freed the shovel and began scooping black pellets into the wheelbarrow. The blonde Pyrenees guard dogs came to her side, sniffing at the fresher dung and eating some of the pellets as if they were biscuits. She scolded them, waving the shovel at their muzzles until they sprinted away, one chasing the other and then the other chasing it back until they both sat down near the fence and began sniffing at the manure again.

She filled the wheelbarrow and trundled it to the pickup and unloaded the cargo into the bed, her arms burning from the work and the smell of the urine-soaked feces making her eyes water. She thought about Jihn, and how the two of them used to have manure fights in the barnyard. How she would taunt him as he shoveled, throwing the pellets high in the air so they plopped down on him from above like cones from the evergreens. He would chase her around the barnyard, the two of them winding through the ewes, and her laughter riling up the spring lambs so the lambs would butt around and hop

22

upon each other and then upon their mothers' backs. And then Jihn would catch her and dump her in the manure pile.

She missed him. Missed their play and the security she felt when he was near. Missed his broad face and big features, wide eyes and bulbous nose and fat lips, and his high voice that sang the witless stories he told. She especially missed those stories of his navy days before Vietnam. He'd told her of his visits to Japan, the port cities and the great buildings erected after the inland bombs, and the coastlines along the European continent, the white sand beaches of the Mediterranean, and the girls with Moorish blood. He told her that she resembled them, the beautiful Moors, with her olive skin and dark thick hair and that sultriness about her. She would consume his every word, imagining those places, and herself within them. Even as a child she had understood the mundanity of ranch life, with all the days like the weeks, and the weeks like the seasons, and the seasons like clockwork.

Jihn hardly spoke of his time in Vietnam, sidestepping the subject whenever Yahng Yi brought it up. He told her once that he had taken no part in the fighting—his ship used only to keep the waterways passable. She had asked him about the people there and he said that the Vietnamese looked a lot like he did, and that it would have been hard to fight them face-to-face.

Yahng Yi finished unloading the wheelbarrow and bladed the shovel again, looking across the valley and taking stock of the natural borders of the land. For all her sixteen years there had been only the valley. Only the valley and the earthen walls of the mountains and the tufted piney hills, and the veiling thickness of groundfall during the snowbound months. All of which pressed upon her from all sides, keeping her apprised of only the expanse of the valley itself and its emptiness. She had grown especially restless this spring, and the horizon had been calling her no longer in whispers, but in a deep and devilish voice that she heard often in her dreams, daring her to clear a path through the fir trees and mountain boulders and cross the low ridges once and for all.

As she opened the door to the truck, she saw her mother walking the driveway down from the house. Her mother looked angry, but Yahng Yi waited for her, watching her mother's little steps on little legs and how her mother's head did not move, her back straight and neck taut, and her black greasy hair pulled back tight into a bun. Her mother had lost some height over the years, but her frame remained lithe and supple so that a stranger would have guessed her age at a decade younger.

–Who is he? her mother asked as she came within earshot.

–Who? asked Yahng Yi.

–Whoever it was that soiled your underwear.

Yahng Yi shook her head. –Don't know what you're talkin' about, she said.

–I know who he is, said her mother.

–Then why'd you ask?

–You are too young to be lying with men.

–Too young? asked Yahng Yi.

–Yes.

–What about you? When Jihn was born, you were a girl. Younger than I am now. What was that? A miracle?

Her mother tried to slap her, but Yahng Yi was too quick, ducking so that her mother's hand caught only air. Her mother lost her balance and fell to the ground on her backside, her tightly bound hair whipping back into a cluster of sheep pellets.

24

YAHNG YI HELPED HER MOTHER UNDRESS as the bathtub filled, trying not to stare at her naked body, at the small breasts and dark nipples the color of chocolate, and the line around her neck that divided her skin—pale sunless yellow and the darker peasant brown, like two worlds on one body. Her mother put on an old terry bathrobe and cinched the tie around her waist, and then sat down with her back to the tub. Yahng Yi rolled a towel and placed it on the lip of the tub, and her mother leaned her head back, resting her neck on the towel. Yahng Yi knelt to the floor and undid her mother's bun and combed out the greasy locks with her fingers. The smell of the ewe feces was pungent, and she rinsed her fingers in the warm water and then tossed some dried rose petals into the bath from a wicker basket. Yahng Yi's Mother crossed her arms over her chest as Yahng Yi used a large wooden ladle to scoop water over her scalp, rinsing out the feces and soiling the water to the color of weak tea.

–Drain it before you wash, said her mother.

Yahng Yi unplugged the stopper to let the dirty water run. When the tub was clear, she plugged the drain again and turned the faucets. Her mother stopped her, reaching over and grabbing her elbow.

–You must rinse it first, she said.

Yahng Yi made a childish growling noise and her mother pinched her on the arm. Yahng Yi unplugged the stopper again and rinsed the tub with clean water before refilling the bath. Yahng Yi's Mother did not move, and the two of them listened to the tub fill.

–Why do you hate me? she asked.

–I don't hate you, said Yahng Yi, turning down the faucets and leaving a slow drip from the spigot.

–I see the way you look at me, said her mother. With hate.

25

–Quit being dramatic, said Yahng Yi and squeezed a palm full of shampoo into her hand.

–Well if it is not hate, what is it? What causes you to scowl at me the way you do?

–I don't know, said Yahng Yi, and began to work the shampoo into her mother's scalp.

Yahng Yi's Mother closed her eyes and let her daughter rub her head with those strong, labored hands. –It is a slow poison, she said. This hate you build within you.

–It ain't hate, Umma, said Yahng Yi.

–Tell me what it is then. It must be mended, whatever it is.

–It ain't any one thing.

–Then tell me all of them.

Yahng Yi stopped massaging her mother's head and wiped the sweat from her brow with the back of her wrist. –Never mind, she said.

–You keep speaking of *things*, said her mother, letting Yahng Yi rinse the soap out of her hair. What things? What kind of thinking is that, that you can hate your mother for these so-called things?

–I don't know, but I don't want to talk about it with you. And for the last time, I don't hate you. Jesus, you're starved for affection.

–Yes, I am starved. You think an old woman does not need affection? You see me as a stone. No feeling. No blood. I was once a girl. I know about love.

Yahng Yi finished rinsing the shampoo from her mother's hair, wringing the excess water from the tresses. She handed her mother a clean towel. Her mother took it and dabbed away the moisture from her face.

–Do you remember when I used to bathe you? she asked.

–Yes.

–That is still how I think of you. As a little girl.

26

–Umma, I run this whole ranch on my own, said Yahng Yi, standing up from her kneeling position and stretching out her legs. I ain't a child no more.

Yahng Yi's Mother sighed. –I was your age when I saw my sisters die, she said. I remember I did not know how I would go on. I was so helpless. So alone and scared. When I see you, sometimes I see myself at that age. How scared I was. I forget how you are more worldly than me.

–You never told me what happened, said Yahng Yi.

–It is not something to repeat in words, said her mother, looking down at her lap and breaking the vision. I can see it clearly enough in dreams.

Yahng Yi knew her aunts had died in the Korean War, and had often imagined the circumstances, especially when she was younger and her relationship with her mother was built on doting. But her curiosity had waned with the years, as did her interest in her mother's history in general. She could not remember the last time she had asked her mother something about her past.

–You're never going to tell me, are you, she said, no disappointment in her voice.

Her mother closed her eyes and shook her head, and Yahng Yi detected a delicate quiver in the lips.

–Did Jihn know what happened? she asked. Did you ever tell him?

–No, said her mother. Why would you think I would have told him and not you?

–Because you favored him, that's why, said Yahng Yi and sat down on the edge of the tub and leaned down and grabbed the small chain that hooked onto the stopper. Some rose petals clung to the tub walls and she peeled them away and rolled them into a ball, letting the red-brown juices run down her hand, like rehydrated blood.

–That is not true, said her mother.

–You don't have to lie, Umma. It don't bother me no more. I know it's the truth.

Her mother stood up and sat down next to her daughter on the tub's edge.

–You cannot compare my love for you and him, she said. There were too many years between the two of you. I was a girl when he was born. I was an old woman when you were born. I was two different people. Your mother, yes, but not the same mother I was with him. They are different loves, but one no less strong than the other.

Yahng Yi's Mother took the stopper from her daughter's hand, plugged the drain and began running new warm water. –Leave me, she said. I might as well bathe now that I am already undressed.

As Yahng Yi stood to leave, her mother grabbed her hand and turned her so that they faced each other. A quick storm had blown through, raindrops pattering softly against the windows, the wind whistling through the chokecherry outside.

–It is no use to dwell on the past, she said to her daughter.

–I could have saved him, muttered Yahng Yi.

–You would have died as well.

Yahng Yi snatched away her hand and left the bathroom, slamming the door behind her. Her mother did not flinch as the door closed. She reached into the bath to test the water's temperature and closed her eyes and listened to the strong wind, the voice of the mountain spirit, that deep and assuring voice that heralded the changing of seasons.

The organic smell of the sheep feces still lingered in the moist air, and the stench reminded her of her earliest home, Gaduk Island off the Korean coast. She thought of the stinking fish entrails rotting within the coastline rocks and the seafoam grown old on the shore. Kelp drying in the wind and pickled vegetables from clay jars, ripe from a winter sleep. It had been so long since she had set foot on the island that the memories seemed secondhand, as if she knew them only through the hearing of a story.

She had been forty-two when Yahng Yi was born, and now, as her daughter had entered into pubescence, she had been reflecting on the events of her own youth, the events that had determined her fate. She would have always done what she did, always fled to the mainland with her two sisters to escape their father and the earthen mud huts of the village and the rocky shores that imprisoned them, that walled them in like all the women of Gaduk Island—victims of something so arbitrary as place and time, given the enormity of the world and its history.

It was *palcha*. Fate. And she had accepted it. It was the way of her people. The way of the *mudang*. It was *palcha* that had brought her to this country in the arms of the American, freeing her from the wounded story lines of her homeland. It was *palcha* that had dictated she fall in love with him, and it was *palcha* that he should someday return.

She rubbed her hands together and thought of the spirits that might try to find their way back to the house. The spirits of stillborn lambs and the ewes who had died in birthing. The spirits of her son Jihn and Emily Cottage, escaped from the bodies that were frozen in the blizzard. She opened her eyes and looked around the room at the mahogany paneling that covered the walls and then down at the plank floor, chipped and stained with water marks and grease spots from soiled boots. From those floors, she imagined ghosts rising up, and she wondered if her beloved Jihn would ever return to this house as a new mountain spirit, to stare out at the same vista he had as a boy, at the valley and the clear-cut mountain faces. Or if his spirit would seek the old world. Seek the land of his conception.

How she had loved him. She remembered the first summer after he had joined the navy, and how she had cried for him every night, and in those nights when she bathed she would save some of the bathwater in a jar and in the morning she would water her pepper plants with those bathwater tears so that when she ate the peppers she would remember her love for him.

She imagined his spirit wandering in the wilderness, in the forest near Gallatin Creek, or maybe east of the ranch, walking the badlands with his back to the rising sun. She imagined him and the longing he would know from walking alone, west across the central buttes to the mountains, emerging in the valley under morning calm. She remembered them dancing together under the harvest moon and watching him ride his horse along the banks of the river. She had stroked his black-blue hair under blue moonlight. Her son, the only thing she had brought to this country from her native land.

A strong wind whistled the chokecherry, and there was a low hum in the air, as if just before a lightning strike. There were spirits in the house. Already arrived. She could hear them moaning under the floorboards. She could see them dancing in wind and rain.

FOUR RAVENS STOOD over a dead snake in the road, watching Gabriel as he removed the canteen from his satchel. His head ached from whiskey and sun, and he struggled to keep his one good eye open, raising his hand in a salute to cut down the sun's glare. There was a stinging sensation along his left cheekbone and he reached up and felt the puffiness of his skin, a sunburn that covered the entire left side of his face. He ignored the pain and saw that a quarter mile away the dirt road angled inward toward the mountains around a foothill covered with pines. He thought about his grandfather, and the happy days he'd spent hunting game in the mountains and fishing for cutthroat in the Bighorn, and then when he was older, working alongside his grandfather at the Cottage ranch.

After his grandfather had died, Mr. Cottage had taken Gabriel in like his own, boarded him and fed him and loved him, taught him the ways of the ranch—how to keep the riparian areas ungrazed so the coulees wouldn't erode, how to trick a ewe into thinking an orphan was its own, how to catch coyote by trap and by foot. Having sired no son, Mr. Cottage had thought that Gabriel would someday take over the ranch. Emily was his only child, and he saw how she had watched over Gabriel with kind eyes as he showed his sullenness during the long summer days, and how she had cried along with him when she heard the late-night whimpering Gabriel made in his pillow. It was always everyone's belief that Gabriel and Emily would marry and carry on the Cottage ranch, the outcome of their fates predestined, like water taking the easiest route down the mountain.

The brief rain had expired and the sun shone unobstructed and the day was hot. Gabriel took a drink from the canteen and wiped his brow. He had been walking through the night among the foothills, and then along the county two-lane again to Road K, the turn-in that led to the Cottage ranch. He squinted his good eye and looked north down the road. A tiny head poked through the willow shoots that lined a small coulee, a squatting girl, her black hair thick from wind-dried morning rain. He watched her splash water on her face and then turn her head to look around, skittish like a winter-lean doe. For a moment he was taken back to the year of his return from Korea, watching from afar as the peasant girl bathed her dark body in that same coulee.

The girl rose from her squat and wiped her hands on her jeans. Gabriel looked up the mountain base toward the faded, porchless red house that rested on a small plateau just a couple of hundred yards up from the valley floor. There was a large unpainted barn fifty yards to the north of the house, the tree line beginning just behind the barn and angling upward to the south, past a clearing and a slow rise with high grass and then a forest not yet clear-cut at the south border. A wooden fence ran perpendicular to the gravel drive that led up to the house, and another followed the dirt road, a quarter mile from where the mountain began.

He rubbed water into the skin of his bone-thin arms, then knelt down and filled the empty canteen with clear ditch water, wondering where the years had gone, as if he'd misplaced them in the back pocket of an old pair of jeans. He turned his face away from the sun to catch his breath and looked for the lost years in some smooth pebbles along the side of the road and in the patches of leafy spurge that had grown across the valley.

There was a dull ache at the base of his skull, and he stood up to let the blood drain from his head. He watched the black-haired girl moving up toward the house, fast and steady like a prairie fire, her hair flickering like the fire's shadow in the breeze. The dizziness came, and he closed his eye and spread his feet apart to brace himself for the pain. He saw colors swirling in the blackness, and the colors became images and he saw himself as a young man on horseback, riding past animal skulls bleached white in the sun.

As the pain and the memory waned, he heard the sound of a vehicle approaching. He turned around and watched a black pickup pull slowly alongside him. Inside the cab he saw Jude Finn.

–You all right? asked Jude, a fat wad of dip snuff wedged in his lower lip and making his lower jaw jut primitively. He spat neatly into an amber beer bottle.

–Yes, said Gabriel.

–Need some help?

–I could use a ride, I guess.

–This road goes to a dead end three miles north of here. You headin' back to the highway?

–No. To where that driveway turns in.

–The Cottage ranch?

Gabriel nodded.

–If you're lookin' for work you might try my granddaddy's ranch, said Jude. Yi's ain't gonna last another season.

–Is your granddaddy's place down the road? asked Gabriel.

–Yeah. Name's Jude.

–I'm Gabe.

–Your face is all burnt up, Gabe.

Gabriel reached up to touch the swelling on his cheek.

–Staring at it isn't going to help any, he said.

Jude snickered.

–You wanna come inside the bunkhouse and put some cold on it? he asked. Our compound's just around the bend here.

–Is that log house still up? asked Gabriel. The one built by the Cottages?

–We live in it. You know your way around here?

–I worked on the Cottage ranch when I was young.

Jude nodded. –My granddaddy owns it now, he said.

Gabriel pointed toward a cluster of ewes near the fence.

–I've never seen sheep like that, he said. Wool all different colors.

–Shetlands, said Jude. Fancy wool they got's pretty pricey.

–There can't be more than a hundred acres of grazing land.

–Don't matter. They used to feed'm hay through the summer. Old Emily Cottage didn't want'm eatin' the wild-flowers, so they haul the hay down from the barn and the band all gather there waiting for it. Got'm trained like dogs almost. Stay down near the valley. Yahng cut down the cross-fencing, but they still don't wander up near the house. Laziest animals I ever seen.

–I'll be damned, said Gabriel.

–Yup.

–She can afford to feed them hay year-round?

–Nope.

Gabriel nodded and clutched his satchel and opened the passenger door.

–I appreciate your offer, he said as he entered the cab. But I'd just as soon get dropped off where that driveway turns in. I'll tend to the burn later.

–Ain't no difference to me, said Jude and floored the gas pedal, sending the truck skidding on the dirt road, and tossing up some loose pebbles against the undercarriage.

YAHNG YI GRABBED A CLUMP OF WILLOWS and held them through the fence to a musket-colored ewe on the other side. The ewe wagged her tail and took the willow into her mouth. Yahng Yi scratched her on the head and watched as the ewe chewed the willow into a ball of cud. A cloud of dust kicked up in the distance, and she saw a white strip of metallic light flashing in its midst. The truck slowed, pulling up next to the swing gates that blocked the gravel drive. After the truck had stopped, a man exited the pas-senger door, carrying a leather bag. She tried to peer into the cab to glimpse the driver, but the truck drove away.

Gabriel walked over to her, holding out his hand. –Afternoon, he said. Name's Gabe.

Some of the ewes had gathered around the fence to greet the stranger. The dogs had wandered down from the house as well, and walked up to him, wagging their tails. Yahng Yi shook his hand quickly. The dogs lowered their heads and sniffed around Gabriel's ankles, but when he knelt down to scratch their long, coarse coats, they backed away and went to Yahng Yi's side.

–Can I help you? she asked.

–I came to see your mother.

–Why would you wanna do that?

–I knew her at one time.

Yahng Yi sized him up with squinted eyes. –She never spoke of you, she said. Woulda remembered hearin' about a one-eyed man.

–We were good friends once, said Gabriel.

–Mother ain't never had any friends.

–What about Emily Cottage? She wasn't her friend?

–You knew Auntie?

–Auntie?

–Emily Cottage.

–Yeah, said Gabriel. I knew Emily Cottage.

–She never spoke of you neither.

Gabriel shrugged his shoulders. –I knew her, he said. Knew her pretty well. I swear. Knew the Cottages like family.

Gabriel swiveled his head around to catch a panorama of the valley and brushed some loose gravel and dirt with his boot toe. –Land looks about the same, he said. House is new.

–Mr. Finn built it, said Yahng Yi. Built the barn too.

–How come the barn's up by the house instead of down here?

–Auntie kept her horses in there. Mother never liked horses, so since Auntie died we been usin' it to store supplies. There's still some tack in there, but we turned the stables into paddocks to pen up the lambs.

–What if a storm blows through? asked Gabriel. How would you round up the band and take them to shelter all the way up there in the middle of a blizzard?

Yahng Yi shrugged her shoulders and turned away from him, and then walked toward the driver-side door of the pickup. Gabriel watched her, the symmetry of her lean body artful against the backdrop of the mountain base.

–You plannin' on staying? she asked.

–It's lambing season, said Gabriel. I can help.

Yahng Yi opened the door of the truck and got in. Gabriel looked up the driveway at the house squatting low on a plateau, and the barn to the left, its dark wood cutting a gap in the mountainside. He slung his satchel over his shoulder and walked to the truck.

–I'm sorry about her, he said as he entered the passenger side. Your auntie.

–You know your face is all burnt on one side, said Yahng Yi.

–So I hear.

–You fall asleep in the sun or somethin'?

Gabriel grunted and said nothing. Yahng Yi shifted the truck into gear and drove up the gravel driveway, parking the truck on a flat spot near the house. She exited quickly and walked toward the back door, her head over her shoulder, watching Gabriel as he stepped down from the truck and wiped the sweat from his face like a preening bird, his thin body hidden by the loose shirt, and the blue jeans frayed at the seams, white with wear around the groin and knees.

Yahng Yi opened the back door, which led into the kitchen. Gabriel followed her inside.

–Nice and cool in here, he said.

Yahng Yi went to the kitchen sink and filled a glass of water and drank it, offering none to Gabriel.

–I'll get Mother, she said, setting the glass down. As she walked toward the front room, her eye caught movement from outside the kitchen window. A dark gray ewe had wandered up from the valley. It was loitering around the barn, its water bag poking out from its hindquarters. Yahng Yi motioned toward the window, and Gabriel saw the ewe and smiled. They went back outside and headed toward the barn. As they approached the ewe, it began twirling around, two small legs poking out from its vagina, and then a little black head as well.

–This the first lamb? asked Gabriel.

Yahng Yi nodded. The lamb's shoulders were out, and the ewe went to the ground, its head reaching back toward her hindquarters to clean the membranes from the lamb's mouth. Yahng Yi went over to the ewe and it blatted softly and reached its head up to meet Yahng Yi's hand. Yahng Yi rubbed it behind the ears, and stroked the soft down around the neck. The lamb was halfway out and breathing normally. The ewe stood and the force of gravity dropped the lamb to the ground. It wobbled on little brown legs, the birth sac still covering its hindquarters, and searched for a teat while its mother licked it. The ewe walked off a little way, the lamb trailing it and rubbing its small black head along the top of the ewe's udder.

–You and your mother been tending the ranch on your own? asked Gabriel as they watched the lamb search for its first meal.

–Mother don't do much, said Yahng Yi.

The ewe turned suddenly and expelled her bloody afterbirth onto a patch of clover. The lamb jumped away as the ewe reached its head down to nibble at the splayed mess on the ground. Yahng Yi walked over to the lamb, picked it up and held the warm supple weight in her arms while the ewe continued nibbling at the placenta. She bent down and let the ewe smell the newborn's coat, and then walked toward the barn where there were some paddocks for the new mothers to rest and bond with their lambs. Gabriel followed them.

–You know how to do the taggin'? asked Yahng Yi.

Gabriel nodded, his eyes focused on the lamb, which Yahng Yi held to her breast.

–I gotta get rid of the leftover afterbirth, she said and handed the lamb to Gabriel and stepped back out under the sun.

–Why? asked Gabriel.

Yahng Yi ignored him and grabbed a shovel from next to the barn doors and went back outside. The ewe was just finishing up the placenta, and Yahng Yi waited until it went off to look for its sire. When the ewe was gone, she dug a small hole in the ground and dumped the remaining afterbirth in the hole and covered it up. Then she made her way through the thicket of pines behind the barn and rinsed her hands and face in a cool meltwater brook that led into the gully creek. Years before, the snowmelt from high on the mountains followed a different course a few miles to the south. Over time, water from the mountains grew in volume until a new stream formed, eroding its path in the years thereafter, washing with it some silt and pebble from the mountainside, until bare rock showed from under the clear water, naked and exposed.

She squatted on her haunches and stared at the brook, the water flowing viscous with cold, and then dried her hands on her jeans. Gabriel came into the forest and squatted down next to her and rinsed his hands as well. Yahng Yi watched him as he stripped the water from his forearms and closed his eye and mumbled to himself, cupping his hands to drink from the brook.

–*He would have given you living water*, he said in a low voice and then cupped some more water and held it to his burnt red cheek.

Yahng Yi looked over at him. –Come again? she said.

–Living water, said Gabriel, wiping his mouth and face on his shirtsleeve. Jesus said, *Whoever drinks the water I give him will never thirst, for the water I give him will become in him a spring of water welling up to eternal life.* Book of John.

–You a preacher or somethin'?

Gabriel paused for a moment and filed through the appellations he'd been called in the past, and from that quick audit he found none that called him clergy. It dawned on him that he had no memory of a covenant with God during his childhood years, nor the years leading up to his departure for the war, and by that knowledge he understood that he had found the Lord somewhere in his wanderings, and also that his relations with God lived in the parts of his brain that were impervious to the damage done to other parts. But he could not identify the impetus of his faith and that troubled him.

–Wouldn't call myself a preacher in name, he said meekly. But I spread the Word to any that'll listen, I guess. Help those in need of help.

Yahng Yi nodded. –Yeah, she said. You don't sound like a preacher.

Gabriel raised a brow. –Why's that? he asked.

–Don't sound sure of yourself.

Gabriel laughed and held out his hand. Yahng Yi did not take it, rising from her squat on her own. Gabriel turned and walked out from the shade of the forest canopy into the open sun. Yahng Yi watched him walk for a few steps, and then got down on her knees and drank quickly from the brook as he had done. The water felt good and harsh as the cold entered her, and she got back to her feet and jogged through the pines.

YAHNG YI'S MOTHER STOOD by the kitchen window, looking through the double panes and wondering how she could access the inner surfaces, where the condensation had dried and left some dirt behind. Her father would have scolded her had he seen that dirt, dainty as he was. She thought of him, her father, wondering if he were still alive in that small fishing village west of Jinhae Bay that the Yi family called their ancestral home. She had been dreaming of the village the last few days, dreaming of the ocean breeze and the fog that lingered in the hot months around the tops of the low mountains like an ashen veil. That primitive fog that ensured the people would never venture away from the coastline, never neglect the bounty of the ocean's fertile womb. She had been dreaming of her mother as well, the two of them hunting for crabs together along the coastline and jumping together into the ocean off Turtle Rock. Helping her mother repair the fishing nets laid out on the beach, and making preparations for the *kut* as her mother's first assistant, the apprentice *mudang*.

But no matter how good the dream, it always ended the same way, with her and her sisters on the mainland in the midst of war, and the last images of them as they lay lifeless among the mounds of bodies, all those holes and the blood blossoms on their backs.

She watched through the kitchen window as Yahng Yi approached the rear of the house, followed closely by the visitor. She recognized him immediately, and was not surprised to see him though it had been forty years since she'd seen him last. The old feelings were still there, that comfort she had always felt when he was near. She walked to the kitchen door and waited for them to enter, her daughter first, and then the one she had once called her beloved.

He smiled sweetly as he approached her, and she whimpered as if in mourning, shaking uncontrollably as they embraced, and then she began to strike him on the shoulder with an open hand as she continued her song of tears, soft at first, and then harder and quicker until she wailed out in anger at him for leaving her.

–Ohpa! she yelled.

His smile subsided, and he tried to restrain her. As he did so, she felt how brittle he was.

–Easy, he said, and squeezed her hard until she let her weight go limp and slid to the ground. He descended to the floor with her, and she leaned her head forward into his and he took her neck with a curled hand and let her cry into him. Yahng Yi interrupted them with a mocking sigh.

Yahng Yi's Mother wiped away her tears with the back of her hand and pushed Gabriel away. Then she stood up and went to the sink and ran cool water from the faucet to splash on her face.

–I can't watch this, said Yahng Yi and went back outside.

Gabriel watched Yahng Yi leave, and then went over to where Yahng Yi's Mother was drying her face on a kitchen towel.

–Been a long time, he said and smiled, wanting to leave her name at the end of the sentence, but unable to do so, her name still lost somewhere in the clutter of Korean names and cities he had absorbed from his war days, one indistinguishable from the next.

–I have not forgotten, she said.

–Me neither, he said.

–Sit, she said. You look like you have walked a thousand miles.

Gabriel sat down at the kitchen table as she ignited a gas burner on the range and put on an old iron teakettle, his viable memories of her returning. He had not forgotten her face or form, her body language the same, and the body itself not so different either, just grown fuller with age. She was lovely. Lovelier now than she was as a girl, her skin still taut and her features that were once so sharp grown softer with the years, the bones tempered, more beautiful, the angles soft like the rim of a low fire.

–I can't believe it's you, he said. You sure you're the girl I used to know?

She laughed. –I look different to you, do I? Fatter?

–No, said Gabriel. Prettier. You've aged well.

She blushed and turned away. –You have grown skinny.

He smiled. –Don't eat much these days, he said. But I'm used to it.

–We are linked, you and I, she said. You grow smaller as I grow larger.

–Come on now, said Gabriel. You look amazing. Honestly.

She grinned and then went to the pantry and opened it. Within the pantry she found a small glass canister and pulled out a pinch of dried leaves. She placed the leaves in a plain white ceramic teapot that was sitting on the kitchen counter and then poured the hot water from the kettle. She brought the pot and two matching teacups to the table and set the pot down to steep. The two of them sat for a moment at the table saying nothing, Gabriel just staring at her, and she looking up occasionally to check the tea for its color.

As Gabriel was about to speak again, she rose suddenly and went back to the pantry and rooted around until she found a small jar of balm. Then she removed two dried bitterroot blossoms from another glass canister and placed the jar of balm in front of Gabriel.

–For your burn, she said, pointing at her own face and then sitting down again, still holding the two dried bitterroot blossoms in her small hand.

Gabriel opened the jar and dipped his finger in it. –I heard it's going to be a mild spring, he said as he applied the odorless balm to his face, the moisture stinging him at first, but softening into numbness as the skin absorbed the medicine. That'll be good for the crop, he said. Make it easier on you and your girl.

–The weathermen are wrong, she said. The spring will be a difficult one.

Gabriel chuckled. Yahng Yi's Mother looked up quickly into his good blue eye and reached across the table to pour the tea, placing a dried blossom in each of their cups. –I'm sorry, she said.

–For what?

–You laugh at me. I speak with too much familiarity. I forget it has been so long.

–No, no, he said and reached over and patted the top of her hand and then took the teacup and watched the shriveled, pink and white blossom floating atop the wide brim, filling out as it soaked in the liquid so that it appeared to have been resurrected. The tea itself was bitter with a dirty aftertaste, but the hot liquid felt good in his empty stomach.

–I was sorry to hear about your boy, he said, not knowing what else to talk about.

She sighed.

–I remember him, he continued, surprised that the image had come so quickly, the birthing and the sprouts of ink-black hair, and his flat face and big eyes and orange skin.

–He was just a baby when you left us, she said.

–You know, I don't think you ever told me who the father was.

–It is not important.

–And your daughter? asked Gabriel.

–Also not important.

–She was born late.

–Am I so old?

–No. It's not that. Was just surprised to see you with another child.

–You find her pretty, she said. I can tell by the way you seek her.

Gabriel felt the blood rush up to his cheeks. –Sure, he said. She's pretty. I've just never seen anything quite like her. She's different.

–You looked at me like that once. I was once a pearl in your eye. Do you remember?

Gabriel nodded and took her hand and squeezed it softly, her bony fingers icy to the touch. It shocked him at first, how little warmth there was there, how little life.

–And where have you been these forty years? she asked. You could not return to visit?

Gabriel shrugged his shoulders.

–Then why do you come back?

As she waited for his answer she released his hand and blew on her tea to create a small eddy that moved the blossom around the surface. Then she picked the blossom out of the cup and set it on the table, watching as the tea puddled around the petals.

Gabriel sighed. –I don't know, he said.

44

Yahng Yi's Mother looked away as if pained he did not name her as the reason for his return. –You do not know much for one so old, she said.

He did not want to tell her that he had wandered upon this place because it was the only place he remembered. All the other places he'd once lived had become merely generalities, perhaps a tableau and a smell, perhaps a mood, or a play on words of a street name. Thalo Valley was the only place that he could close his eye and visualize, both its geography and its spatial representation on a map.

But at the same time there was something attractive about losing himself completely. There were times when he saw his forgetting as a gift from God, a great gift that would allow him to live out his earthbound days in peace, forgiven of those sins that tortured him, those sins he knew existed by virtue of an uneasy itching from time to time. Sometimes the itching was so torturous that he would decide once and for all that he could not go on living without knowing the things he'd done, without knowing whether his sins had been expiated. How could he ascend to the Kingdom without forgiveness? Or had he already been forgiven? Was this his forgiveness, this forgetting? He did not know what he wanted, whether to live out the remainder of his days as he was now, content save for the itching, no longer tortured as he suspected he once was, or to play it all over again, let himself be reborn with the knowledge of what had made him who he was, tortured and all.

It was all in the letter that he kept in his satchel, and it was comforting to him, knowing his life still existed on paper, despite not knowing whether he wanted to remember that life. He was sometimes thankful that he could no longer read, because he had more than once examined those pages at some pique in his curiosity when his will was weak and he was living in the moment. And always he had failed. Had it been as easy as picking up the pages and reading, he would have finished it by now. But because it would require another's help, it could not be a spontaneous moment, and he decided it was better that way. Because once he remapped all those memories, good and bad, there would be no forgetting them again until death.

–Well, I'm here now, he said.

–And do you plan on leaving me again?

–No, he said. I don't plan on leaving.

She smiled. –You have spent too many years away from home, she said. We must have a *kut*. I will prepare the food.

–I don't know what that is, said Gabriel. But if there's food involved, I won't argue.

–You don't remember the *kut*? she asked.

–Guess not.

–When you see, you will remember. It will purge you of wandering spirits.

Gabriel stared at her, squinting a little to let her face come into greater focus. His vision in that eye was acute, having been sharpened by the loss of the other, and he saw something beneath her smile, beneath her loveliness. There was a desperation within her, and he saw the woman she had become because of it. He sensed that her pain, her burden, was on his shoulders, a weight that was thick and full and reminiscent of the worst weariness he could remember, when he'd left the Cottage ranch the first time, left Emily behind though they were in love and life was good and the only discontent he had was an unfulfilled and imaginary duty.

THREE

Gabriel watched as the fire danced upon the logs and the cinders blew out from the burning wood, cracking fast and filling the room with the smell of good smoke. His belly was full and he was glad for it, and he sat on a reading chair with a cup of chicory and a saucer resting on his lap. Yahng Yi's Mother sat in a chair to his right, Yahng Yi to his left. He turned his head and looked around the room, at the heirloom furniture that he remembered from his younger days—reading chairs and an unused spinning wheel and a familiar Victrola in the southeast corner, the bell of the gramophone pointing toward him. He imagined the music coming forth, sounding old and tinny, and brought the teacup to his lips, letting the warm liquid go down easy, his insides chilly from the night cold that came in through the window glass.

–A lot of beauty in this place, he said, tracing the wood grains in the armrest of the oak chair with his left index finger and then running the knuckles under his chin to feel the day's end stubble.

–Even at night, you can tell, he said, not directing that phrase to either Yahng Yi or her mother, speaking the words simply to hear the words.

–You don't even need to see it, he continued. You can just tell it's pretty out there.

–How can you tell, Ohpa? said Yahng Yi's Mother, staring into the fire and not inflecting her voice in inquisition, but to lend texture to Gabriel's monologue, a show of her deference.

–Because it's pretty in the light, he said. Darkness doesn't change a thing's prettiness.

–Ain't pretty on the other side of the gully, muttered Yahng Yi.

–What's that? asked Gabriel.

–I said it ain't pretty on the other side of the gully. Land's been overgrazed.

–By Finn?

–Yup. And I don't blame him, the way the cattle business is these days. Meatpackin' companies all having their own captive supplies. When the prices are up, they flood the market with'm to drive the price back down. Lotta ranchers end up doing contract work for the meatpackers straight up instead of sellin' their own stock on the open market. Can't afford to live otherwise. I guess Finn's got an agreement as such. They tell him what to do, and he does it. It's the best use of his land these days, so I don't blame him.

–You know a lot about ranching, said Gabriel.

–Why wouldn't I?

–I don't know. Young girl like you I figured would have other interests.

–Seein' as how Ham Finn owns the land under our feet, I think it'd be wise to keep my eye on his affairs, said Yahng Yi.

Gabriel smiled at her and Yahng Yi's Mother saw his smile and stood up impatiently. –It is late, she said. You will sleep in the barn, Ohpa. Yahng will show you.

–We've still got catching up to do, said Gabriel, making a halfhearted attempt to keep her in his company.

–Later, said Yahng Yi's Mother. Tomorrow. There is plenty of time.

She bowed to him and then disappeared into the dark hallway. Gabriel looked at Yahng Yi.

–I'll show you the barn, she said.

–After I finish my tea, he said, unclipping the flask from his waist and doctoring the tea with the last of the roadhouse bourbon.

Yahng Yi smirked, having already suspected him to be of the boozing ilk.

Gabriel finished the last of the whiskeyed tea and set the cup down on the mantel. Then he knelt down and picked up a quartered log and set it on the fire. Silence continued as the new log heated and flamed, the shards of pine jutting off the log crackling as they combusted. One of the sparks came through the fireplace and landed on the floor near Gabriel's feet.

–How old are you? he asked, grinding the spark into the plank with his boot.

–What?

–How old are you? he asked again. Fourteen?

–No.

–How old then?

–Old enough to be bored shitless talkin' to you.

Gabriel laughed. –You in school?

–Don't need school. Auntie taught me all I need to know.

–You can read then?

–Course I can read.

–Maybe you can read to me sometime.

–Why should I?

–To help a man in need of help.

–You can't read for yourself?

–Not anymore, said Gabriel, looking down at the planking.

–How come? she asked.

–Can't see the words, he answered, looking away from her.

Yahng Yi furrowed her brow. –You're lyin', she said. You're a bad liar.

–That may be, said Gabriel.

–You can't read cause you can't read, dumdum.

Gabriel stared at her for a second, frozen by her candor. He saw an innocence in her eyes that told him she knew no other way to behave, that she'd picked up that smart-mouth persona from some influence, and then he realized that it was the way Emily used to speak. It's what Emily would have said. He clasped his hands together. –You're right, he said. I can't read.

–I knew it, she said.

–But it's not because I'm dumb.

He closed his eye and ran around in his memory for a while, trying to find the starting place of the story. A dark dirty motel in Billings. Himself hunched over a desk. The untidy stack of paper. His wrist cramped from writing. A spider hanging five inches down from the water-stained ceiling, dangling at the end of its silken tether. Just dangling there by that invisible thread, dangling so tenuously with all its legs writhing, trying to gain purchase, trying so hard just to remain. He remembered watching that spider, remembered that at the time it seemed relevant, but he could not remember why it moved him.

And then the hospital, inside a room he could not remember entering, sitting on a padded chair and running his fingers back through his hair, staring out the window at a smokestack across the street, and then his self-awareness returning. He had wanted so badly to cry, but did not know how, or why, like an infant born aware of what he cannot do, what he cannot know.

Then the doctors. The nurses. Telling him he would just have to live with it, that bullet in his head. Learning how to talk again. Learning how to walk again. Learning to be human again, and then that humanity taken from him. He had left without telling anyone, tired of all the experiments.

–Took a bullet to the brain a couple years ago, he said abruptly as he returned to the moment. Haven't been able to read since.

–No way, said Yahng Yi.

–It's true. Got shot in the head with a .22.

–How?

–Don't remember what happened. Just woke up one day in the hospital. The doctors at the VA told me I got shot in the head. Guess the bullet's still in there, too. I wouldn't know one way or the other. I sure can't feel it.

–Shit, Patch. You're tellin' me you got shot in the head and the bullet's still in there somewhere, and here you are walking and talking and the only thing wrong with you is that you can't read no more?

Gabriel nodded. –The brain's made up of two halves, he said. Left and the right. Your left eye is wired to the right half of your body and the right eye is wired to the left half. When I got shot, the bullet cut the line between the two halves so they couldn't talk anymore. And because I lost my right eye, my left half went blind, since it couldn't talk with the right half. My right half is connected to my left eye, which can see, but it can't tell my left half what it's seeing, and the left half is the half that knows how to read. Follow?

Yahng Yi paused, the complexity of his explanation making it impossible to believe. She squinted her eyes and glared at him, trying to get him to tip his hand. –But other than that, you're all right? she asked. You ain't retarded or nothin'?

–No, said Gabriel, chuckling weakly. My memory's not so good anymore, but I've still got my wits. I had to learn a bunch of things over again. Simple stuff like what to do with a spoon and fork. How to open and close a door. Even had to learn how to talk all over again too. I guess I talk like the guy who taught me how to talk again. He was a city boy.

–If your memory's so bad, how'd you find your way back here? she asked.

–Just came to me.

–Where were you livin' before you got shot?

–Don't remember. There's a lot of years I don't see at all. Sometimes I even forget how old I am.

Yahng Yi rolled her eyes.

–You don't believe me? he asked.

–It's a whale of a tale, Patch. You're tellin' me you got a brain that's cut in half and all that's wrong with you is that you can't read and your memory ain't good. Of course I don't believe you.

–It's true, said Gabriel. You can't tell the difference between a split-brain person and a normal person on the surface. We can get along just fine.

They locked eyes, both of hers on his one, and held the exchange as if in a child's staring game. She looked into the pale blue iris, the flicker of the fire's reflection illuminating the outside corner where it was slightly wet and red with whiskey. After a ten count, Yahng Yi looked away.

–That how you lost your eye, too? she asked. From the bullet?

–Yes.

–You must of got shot right in the face.

–I don't remember what happened, but I do know who shot me.

–Who?

–I did.

–You shot yourself?

–That's what they told me, he said, looking down again at the floor. I used to carry a Colt Huntsman around with me, .22 cal. That's the gun that did it. Accident, I guess.

–How do you know it was an accident? How do you know you didn't try to kill yourself?

Gabriel paused. –I don't, he said. But if I did try to kill myself, I don't remember why.

–Ain't you afraid you'll remember one day and try to kill yourself again?

He shook his head immediately. Yahng Yi noticed it was too quick, as if it were a question he were constantly pondering.

–What's gone is gone, he said. The memories I lost can't be brought back. They don't exist anymore, so no use dwelling on it.

–I'd want to know, said Yahng Yi. It'd drive me crazy if I couldn't remember what I'd done.

–You're young, said Gabriel. You probably haven't done anything you wouldn't want to remember.

Yahng Yi moved her eyes down toward the tips of her boots, then picked at a lump of dried mud at the crease of the sole and toe. They sat there in silence for a few seconds, and then Gabriel moved his chair closer to her, scooting to the edge of the wood slats, his elbows resting on his knees and hands hanging down between his legs, grabbing each other, fingers long and narrow. The doctored tea had him loose of tongue and he was washed over with some old familiar feeling that made him in the mood for song, as had often happened since his injury, his musical senses heightened and the hearing of simple melodies a salve to his occasional headaches.

–Out of my bondage, sorrow and night, he sang. Jesus, I come, Jesus, I come. Out of my sickness, into thy health, out of my want and into thy wealth, out of my sin and into thyself, Jesus, I come to Thee.

He sang sweetly, and Yahng Yi listened to him and watched the orange embers glowing in the fireplace as the wood logs collapsed upon themselves.

–Out of my shameful failure and loss, he sang. Jesus, I come, Jesus, I come. Into the glorious gain of thy cross, Jesus, I come to Thee.

She made no comment on his singing after he'd finished the last note, and Gabriel took that as its own applause. He smiled and patted her on the knee as he stood up, and then walked toward the Victrola in the corner.

–This thing still work? he asked.

Yahng Yi shrugged her shoulders.

Gabriel knelt down and opened the cabinet and thumbed through the stack of 78s. –This one here calls out to me, he said and held up a disc. I recognize the picture. Glenn Miller. *String of Pearls.*

Gabriel put the 78 on the platter, wound the Victrola and released the brake. The turntable spun and he dropped the tone arm onto the record and the music came out through the bell sounding good and brassy.

–You know how to dance? he asked, smiling and snapping the fingers of his left hand, his left foot tapping. He came to her and lifted her out of the seat and began moving her with the music, not stepping with any kind of pattern, but holding her tense arms and pushing her along as he swayed his hips back and forth. Yahng Yi relaxed and let him lead her and she squealed as he dipped her, and again as he raised up their hands over her head to spin her around. He closed his eyes and pulled her in and the song ended as he dipped her one last time.

–Last dance you'll ever get from me, Patch, she said, trying to hide her amusement.

–One dance is all a man can ask for, he said. I got my wish.

–Then it's my turn for a wish.

–And what's your wish?

–I wanna see under that patch.

Yahng Yi reached up with her right hand. Gabriel grabbed her wrist and turned it away.

–Don't think so, he said.

–I'm gonna see it sooner or later. Might as well get it out of the way.

He thought about it for a moment and then nodded and let go of her wrist. As he reached up to remove the patch, Yahng Yi's Mother appeared in the hallway threshold, holding an old quilt that Gabriel recognized as one of those passed down among generations of Cottages. She went to the Victrola and impatiently anchored the arm.

–Yahng, show Ohpa to the barn, said her mother.

–Sorry, said Gabriel. Forgot you'd gone to bed.

–Go on, Patch, said Yahng Yi, ignoring her mother. Show me.

–No, said Gabriel as he reached up to touch his eye patch, suddenly shameful of his maiming. It's getting late. You heard your mother. Show me the barn.

Yahng Yi pouted as she went to the coat closet to retrieve a flannel overshirt. Gabriel went to Yahng Yi's Mother and took the quilt from her arms and leaned down to kiss her on the head. She looked away as he did so, but did not reject his lips.

–Good night, he whispered.

THE BARN DOORS CLOSED and Gabriel heard it latch from the outside. He hung his satchel over his shoulder and tucked the bedroll and quilt under an arm, then picked up an oil lamp that burned with low yellow light. He walked by the row of animal pens toward the loft ladder. There was rustling in one of the pens, and he peeked over the side. It was the lamb born earlier in the day, lying next to its mother. The ewe's eyes were open and she wagged her tail as they made eye contact. The lamb suckled noisily at its mother's teat, and the ewe blatted softly as Gabriel passed.

Gabriel set the oil lamp down at the base of the ladder and climbed it until he could toss the bedding and his satchel up onto the loft, then climbed back down to retrieve the lamp. He could smell the ewe down there and the lamb, a combination of sweetness in the air from the milk being passed through the newborn and leaking from the ewe's other nipples, and the pungent smell of urine and feces.

As he made up his bed, he hummed the hymn he'd sung to Yahng Yi and took the sweater out of his satchel to bundle for the night. Then he removed the letter from the pages of his Bible and ran his fingers along the seams of the envelope. He thought about what the doctor had told him, how he could still read, just not with his eye. If he were to close that eye and run the fingers of his right hand along the grooves that a pen had made on paper, he would know what those grooves represented—the lines and the loops and the letters, and the letters coming together into words and sentences.

He did not know if he missed reading the Bible. He assumed that he did, as he knew himself to be a man of faith, but there was no visceral longing in him to process the Word from paper. Besides, he could remember most of the important verses, the passages hidden away somewhere in the lockbox of his being, safely stored along with those other things he still inexplicably remembered. Like the smell of his grandfather's cologne.

He had bigger problems than the reading. There was the memory loss, of course, which drove him to near insanity at times, at times so close to seeing so much, then being left with so little. He also could no longer stand for introspection, the right half of his brain creating emotions that he had no recourse to describe, to comprehend, without the language of the left. And then there was the dreaming—the feral dreaming that was so vivid in its projection, but offered no break from reality, simply replaying past events without the tangents and fantasy that accompanied the dreams of an unhindered mind.

But for the most part, he could function normally, even read numbers, since the place where he processed numerical representations resided in the right hemisphere of his brain. He stared at the front side of the envelope, and read the numbers from the mailing and return addresses, something he often did to distract himself from pondering the letter's contents. 112, 59601, 5105 and 64114. *Five Nine Six Zero One*, he said out loud, and then repeated the sequence once more. Every time he spoke the numbers, he saw an old-fashioned stand-alone mailbox framed by a slow creek and some serviceberry bushes, and behind a thin line of trees, a golden meadow with hazy buttes in the distance. It was no place around here.

He stuffed the letter back in his pack, latched the flap tightly, and thought again about the hotel room. Sitting in that hotel room with its water stains on the ceiling and the mildew crawling up and down the walls and tractor trailers humming along the interstate just outside. He remembered writing and crying, and from that he garnered there was something evil in his words. Something he could easily live out the remainder of his days without knowing. But at the same time, whatever those words described had made him into the man he was, and that was something he might want to know after all.

He turned down the oil lamp, filling the barn loft with squares of white where the moonlight shone through the second-story windowpanes. In the darkness he reached up to his face and removed the patch and rubbed the open skin, which was numb where the scar had grown in. And then around the open socket with his fingertips, feeling the puffiness of the sunburn. The swelling had gone down, but it still stung to the touch.

He closed his eye and listened to the swallows rustling in their nests under the eaves, and he drifted away to the image of Yahng Yi's nose browning by the firelight, and his desire to protect her and that which was so alien and pure about her. He wanted to let the weight of her heavy hair lie across his shoulders, his story in her lap while she flipped through the pages, her voice sonorous and those ready lips weaving as she read, restitching the tapestry of his life.

IN THE MIDNIGHT DARKNESS Yahng Yi walked the path that led into the gully, the temperature dropping as she descended the gradual slope and came nearer the creek, its roaring growing louder and drowning out the nocturnal animals foraging in the ground clutter.

Jude Finn was waiting for her on the footbridge, arms resting on the rail and watching the creek pass beneath him, the black Stetson on his head pulled low across his brow as usual, a new green flannel shirt tucked into blue jeans. He kicked at the wooden boards of the bridge with the tip of his right boot as she approached, his chin up to see past the edge of his hat.

–Thought you weren't gonna come, he said.

Yahng Yi walked toward him on the bridge and he grabbed her hand and led her across the water to the neighboring Finn property and then off the path to a little clearing in the forest where there was a blanket laid out on the ground.

–Had things to do, she said.

–Your mother asleep? asked Jude.

–Yeah. Why?

–Just wonderin'.

–Cause you're scared of her, said Yahng Yi.

–Am not, said Jude.

Yahng Yi sat down on the blanket and Jude Finn next to her, old beer on his breath.

–You didn't tell no one about us, did you? she asked as he set his hat behind him and placed his hand on her knee.

He leaned in to kiss her.

–Did you? she asked again, and grabbed his wrist and squeezed it hard. He yelped and some ravens took flight from a tree behind them.

–No I didn't tell no one, he said.

She grabbed him by the chin and turned his face toward her. She had somewhat poor sight at night and he looked handsome through the uncertainty of her vision, his fine flaxen hair hanging down over his forehead and the fire awake within his red-brown eyes.

–You swear? she asked.

–Swear, said Jude and placed his hand on his heart. Why you grillin' me?

–Cause she knows.

–Who?

–Mother.

–Aw, shit.

–Thought you weren't scared of her.

–I ain't.

Yahng Yi lay back with her palms under her head, looking up at the canopy and the dark, star-pocked sky between the boughs. Jude took his boots off and lay down next to her and began kissing her neck. She remained still, letting his lips go up and down her skin until his hot breath flushed her and she turned toward him and they kissed there for a while, his hands groping up and down her back and to her ribs and up toward her underarms, and then moving them back toward him to feel the curve of her small breasts.

He grinned stupidly, undoing his belt with one hand and grabbing at her jeans with the other. She unbuttoned the fly and wormed her way out of the legs while their lips remained together. He reached up to pull down her underpants and then fumbled at his own.

She barely saw him there in the darkness, his hair thickest at the junction high on his legs and spreading up to his belly. He rolled on top of her and she felt him along her right thigh as their pelvic bones butted together. There was wetness on her soft skin where he met her, and then he started breathing all heavy and making grunting noises, his mouth buried in the nook of her neck and his tongue hot in her ear. She felt his muscles going taut along the spine and it hurt a little and then he bit her hard on the earlobe and she sighed and it was over.

He rolled off her, still breathing hard and the scent of him like wild mushrooms. She groped around in the dark and found her underpants and jeans and dressed herself quickly.

Jude reached over to touch her face. She let his hand linger on her chin and put her own on top of it, his skin cold and smooth like river rock.

–Yahng, he said in a whisper and ran his hand through the thickness of her hair. I love you.

Yahng Yi laughed and stood up quickly. She let him look at her for only a moment before sprinting across the bridge and up the incline, Jude Finn calling out her name. She did not slow until she had ascended the gully and reached the plateau where the barn stood. She heard her name once again faintly in a last pathetic cry, the final note lingering in the emptiness between them until it was swallowed by the howl of a coyote.

She looked down the slope into the darkness and listened to the water run, picturing the arroyo that flowed from the mountain and the ripe coulee at the base of the drive that was fed by the creek within the gully. She breathed in the chill, and knelt down and touched the soil, her fingertips brushing through a cool patch of clover just coated with night wetness. She did not belong in this place, she decided. She was merely a graft, like the orphaned lambs who wore the skinned hides of their cousins.

GABRIEL HAD BEEN LYING on his bedroll for an hour, half awake, hearing Yahng Yi's name called out in the night breeze, forcing upon him the image of her face, and those hazel eyes like Emily's. He thought he had lost the urge of sex, but he felt it now, the aching of that unsaintly first lust. He could not control it, as he could not control the lust he'd felt for Emily Cottage in his pubescence.

He sighed. This was not forgiveness, he thought, and when he heard the barn door swing open, he could not help but wish it to be Yahng Yi, and he wished himself to be a boy her age and for her to climb the ladder to his bed and lie beside him until morning. The footsteps came softly and the ladder rungs creaked as the figure ascended the ladder to the platform loft, and Gabriel saw the silhouette of Yahng Yi's Mother, and he was both disappointed and relieved. She said nothing as she crawled along the planks to his side and lay down next to him.

He closed his eye, pretending to be asleep.

–Ohpa, she whispered. I brought you some more healing balm.

Gabriel stirred but said nothing.

–I knew you would come back, she said. We are linked by *palcha*, you and I.

She touched his cheek and he flinched lightly at first, expecting the cold fingers he'd felt earlier in the day, but her hand was warm and he remained silent as she applied the balm. It smelled salty, different from the balm she had given him earlier, and he became groggy from the smell and began seeing colors in the dark where there should have been none. She finished rubbing the medicine into his skin and he felt his pulse from under his scalp. He raised his right hand to skim his cheek, the dead skin feeling ready to be molted away.

THE VILLAGE BURNS, the roaring of the lit thatch roofs sounding like a fleet of trolling tanks. The smoke wafts straight up in the breezeless atmosphere, and the heat of the fire piles onto the heat of the sun and the heat soaked up by the dry ground. There is still light in the air, though the sun is behind mountains, a peaceful pink glowing from the rays still coming up over the ridge. From the corner of his eye he sees another soldier trotting toward him from the brush. The soldier has an unusual face. Short, flat nose. High forehead. Buggy eyes. A few small freckles across the cheekbone. The soldier nods toward the burning village and says they can afford no quarter.

They follow the migration back east toward the battalion post, their normal strides moving them twice as fast as the crowd. Then suddenly the soldier stops and squints his eyes and surveys the crowd, bobbing his head up and down, standing on the tips of his boots. He points a finger at the peasant girl.

The soldier says she is pretty, and jogs off into the sea of refugees, moving through the crowd, a head taller than anyone around him, and then comes up behind the peasant girl and grabs her hand. The girl turns around and smiles wanly.

–Will you save me? she asks. Ohpa. Will you save me?

And then she is gone.

He looks around. There are other soldiers from the battalion milling around, not looking at much of anything. Some of them are sitting along the road, watching the evacuation like they are at the movies, seeing a tribe of migrating Indians in a motion-picture Western. Some of them watch the burning village as the fire dies down and the roofs collapse.

He looks again for the peasant girl, but she is long gone. Instead he spots a woman with a swelling around her torso. She is gripping her belly tightly and swivels her head around as if she is hiding something. A radio maybe. Maybe a bomb. He mounts his rifle on his shoulder and approaches her from behind. The other peasants clear a path for him as he sneaks up behind her. He grabs her by the shoulder and she turns around and he sees the fear in her eyes. She begins to run away from him, clutching her stomach. He sprints after her. He catches her just a few yards away and she tumbles to the ground, hitting the dirt road hard on her side. He lifts his rifle to her head with one hand and with the other pats down her torso, feeling for edges. There is nothing. No bomb. No radio. She is crying, trying to push his hands away. He lifts up her skirt, tearing a hole in the thin fabric as he yanks it up toward her pelvis. He sees the hair between her legs and the smoothness of her swollen belly, and nothing else. He feels the blood run to his own pelvis, feels the hotness transcending the dream. He grabs her by her cuff and helps her to her feet, and she slips out of the frock and now she is naked in the haze. She runs down the road, moving clumsily as she clutches her midsection, still crying. He watches her through the heat and in the distance sees the other soldiers, pumping their fists in the air and cheering.

FOUR

Sunlight came over the eastern ridge as Yahng Yi pitched hay into the bed of the pickup, her breath visible in the chill of early morning. She looked down toward the road and saw the crowd of ewes gathering along the fence, at the feeding spot near the bottom of the drive, and the guard dogs there as well, running through the ewes with their snouts at ground level and making quick random cuts, no doubt chasing voles, and the sheep paying them little heed.

She felt a hollowness as she watched the animals, catching a glimpse of some future time when the valley would hold no trace of her existence. She had never been enamored of this place, never looked upon its vistas with fresh eyes. It was home and it was familiar, the animals the cash crop and she their steward, and the symbiosis of all those things allowing her no room to imagine one without the others.

She had no heavy heart at the thought of leaving, but at the same time this was all she had. All that legacy to be washed away like a weak creek dam, to be unearthed like the roots of heirloom plants turned over by the tiller.

Over the last few days she had seen Ham Finn's cattle loaded into eighteen-wheelers across the gully, off to the slaughterhouses until there were but a few dozen head left. There was only one explanation for such an exodus during this buyer's market. Ham Finn was preparing to leave the land, which meant she and her mother would be leaving the land as well.

She looked upon the small red house on the plateau and wondered if she would miss it, the only home she'd ever known. It had been built by Ham Finn twenty years back as part of the changing of deeds with Emily Cottage. The price of the house had been taken off the selling price of the ranch, and Finn had done his best to keep the building cost low. The frame was a prefab, pieced together by Finn himself with a little aid from some transient Mexicans, whom he'd paid with a single four-year-old dairy cow. The floor plan was simple, a front room that ran from the north wall to just past the front door, and behind that the kitchen.

Jihn had been in Tonkin Bay at the time, and had known nothing about the sale of the ranch to Ham Finn, or that he had been displaced from the large log house that had been home to five generations of Cottages. Emily Cottage had been left with little recourse. Without Jihn to tend the ranch, the flow of money had dried up, and Emily had been unable to keep up with mounting property taxes. The sale of the land left her little after the back taxes were paid—barely enough to feed two mouths and pay the rent on land that had been with her family for more than a century.

While Jihn was away there had been little left to bridge the distance between Emily and Yahng Yi's Mother. Jihn and Emily had grown close over the years, and Emily had placed the weight of her interests on watching him mature. She had come to accept that she would never be a mother herself, and had taken that role with Jihn as best she could, to his true mother's disappointment. But Jihn had come to love Emily as much as he loved his mother, and they became a strange triumvirate, two doting women and an isolated boy. Both women could sense that the boy's happiness would not be complete without each of the other sides of the triangle, and because of that, the house had been kept balanced.

It had worked until Jihn joined the navy, called there by his need to experience something outside the ranch and its imprisoning mountains. Without him as a binder, the two women spoke little to each other, both feeding off each other's depression. Emily dwelled on the wreck that had become her life, her mother and father dead, her land slipped from her fingers, her one love gone, and the only person left in her life a foreigner whom she viewed as both the impetus for all her sadness and a necessary component of her joy.

By the time Jihn had finished his navy enlistment, Yahng Yi's Mother was pregnant with Yahng Yi and the ranch had been sold to Ham Finn. Yahng Yi's Mother and Emily settled into the prefab, and Jihn was forced to move into the bunkhouse with Finn's hands. He spent little time there other than sleeping, having met no friendliness from Uncle Duck and the others who worked the Finn herd back in the late seventies and eighties. In exchange for the cot, Jihn was to keep the bunkhouse and the compound lavatory clean, and he did so, in addition to overseeing the small band of sheep that Emily had kept for herself.

As Jihn grew into adulthood, his relationship with Emily matured as well, and they spent much of their free time together, in the foothills and mountains, wandering, as Emily had done at one time with Gabriel, teaching him the lay of the land. Yahng Yi's Mother spent her time tending the baby, whom Emily had taken little interest in.

But what had worked with three people became tenuous with four, and there was too much jealousy, too much isolation. The breaking point transpired during the spring storm of 1989, as if all the tensions and the opposing fronts had focused upon the valley, taking sides in the seemingly insignificant conflicts within the small red house and meeting in battle at Thalo Valley. The greatest of storms came out of it, and two dead in the aftermath.

As she continued pitching the last of the hay into the bed of the pickup, Yahng Yi thought about the last time she had seen her brother alive, him staring out the window and watching the snow fall upon the valley, upon the land and the animals, the sky uncompromising with its whiteness. Emily in the rocking chair. Rocking back and forth and the passing of time found only in the rhythmic ticking of the mantel clock. Hours elapsing with no change in light or mood.

Him lamenting there at the window, the world outside graveyard quiet, the valley fighting sundown, not letting the light close. All a hazy gray filter, like a faded daguerreotype. She remembered him moving slowly to the door, Auntie pleading with him as he opened the door and set out into the blizzard. She could hear his first footsteps in the shin-deep ground fall, the dry snow cracking under his dense boots. And then Auntie standing, wobbling on weak legs, her eyes taking on the same wideness as his, that of the unright of mind.

A door closed in the near distance, breaking Yahng Yi from the daydream. She realized she was kneeling on the ground with her feet tucked under her backside, her torso swaying softly from front to back. She wiped a touch of moisture away with a clean patch from the back of her hand and as she stood, she saw Gabriel walking toward her, holding a cup of coffee.

–Good morning, he said.

She raised her eyebrows and managed a weak smile, and then walked toward the barn. He followed her. Yahng Yi stopped in front of the paddock where yesterday's dropped lamb slept with its mother. She opened the paddock door.

–You letting her get back to the rest of the band already? Gabriel asked.

Yahng Yi ignored him. The ewe got up on her front legs and stretched them out in front of her. The lamb had been asleep at the nipple and awoke at the movement. It stretched out with its mother, and the ewe walked past Yahng Yi and Gabriel, wagging its tail and the lamb close behind it. Yahng Yi watched them both as they exited the barn and the ewe walked slowly down the incline in the direction of the other ewes milling around the feeding spot. The lamb circled its mother, butting, its mood good with milk and the morning.

–The others look all right? asked Gabriel.

–I put some more hay in there. Plenty of room still. Ain't no rush.

Two more ewes had given birth earlier in the morning, to two pairs of healthy lambs. She had penned them on opposite sides of the barn, and could hear the rustling coming from both sides, the lambs rooting around at the udders, their little bodies twisting in the straw to look for morning milk. Yahng Yi closed the barn doors and Gabriel walked over next to the haystack and began pitching hay into the pickup.

–You sleep okay? she asked.

–I'll live.

–Got a little chilly last night.

–Didn't notice.

–You'll sleep in my room tonight. Mother insists.

–And where will you sleep?

–In Mother's room.

Gabriel nodded his head and resumed stabbing the hay pile. Sweat banded around his forehead and temples and he rested the pitchfork against the truck.

–I really don't mind sleeping in the barn, he said.

Yahng Yi shrugged her shoulders. Gabriel set the pitchfork on the ground and got inside the truck. Yahng Yi watched him drive down to the valley floor and spotted one of the lambs in the distance following its mother around, trying to latch onto a teat. Seeing the lamb follow its mother around made her feel sorry for the grannies, those elder ewes who carried no lambs but still had that motherly wanting when the spring winds blew and the valley filled with the scents of birth. They would sometimes try to steal a fresh lamb from another ewe, so strong was their instinct.

She was about to return to the barn when she heard the truck honking. She jogged a few yards to where she could see the valley floor and saw the truck down there, Gabriel next to it, waving his hand over his head and then toward him. Yahng Yi jogged down the slope, her eyes on Gabriel and the animal next to him, and then the others loitering about, waiting for the hay.

The animal at Gabriel's feet was a ewe, lying on a patch of sagebrush, eyes vacant.

–Is she dead? asked Yahng Yi.

–No. She's breathing.

The ewe's ribcage expanded slowly, and seemed not to want to do even that. Yahng Yi knelt by the ewe and reached her hand inside the vagina. The ewe squirmed but did not try to get up.

–Come hold her down, she said to Gabriel.

Yahng Yi felt inside the ewe and touched the unborn lamb, probing it to gauge its position. The head and legs were facing the right way, but it was cinched in the torso.

–Twisted uterus, she said. You're gonna have to turn the body.

–Which way?

–Try clockwise.

Her hand was tired from being clamped by the ewe's vaginal muscles, but she managed to grab the unborn lamb firmly around the neck along with its forelegs. She nodded to Gabriel, who reached under the ewe and flipped her over. Yahng Yi maintained her grip and felt the lamb loosen as the kink in the uterus came undone. She pulled the lamb out easily after that, cleared the mucous from the lamb's snout and blew some air into it, and then held it up to her cheek. She felt the small breath against her skin and smiled wearily.

–That lamb alive? asked Gabriel.

–She's alive, said Yahng Yi. But I'll need to warm her up inside.

The ewe still lay on the patch of sagebrush, and Yahng Yi knelt down and grabbed a teat and lowered the lamb's snout down to it. She pried open the lamb's jaw with one hand, squirted some milk into its mouth, and pressed on its tongue with her finger to make it swallow. Then she moved the lamb over to the mother's nose to let her smell and taste her offspring, trying to get the ewe to remember their bonding. There was always the chance that the mother would forget. Every lambing season gave rise to orphaned lambs, lambs who came into the world underweight and cold and whom Yahng Yi needed to nurse back to health. After being bathed in warm water, the natural scent that would have bound the lamb to its mother would fade and the mother would not recognize the lamb as her own.

Gabriel pointed at the ewe. –What about her? he asked.

–Let her rest, said Yahng Yi. I think she'll be all right. We'll come pick her up later and put her and the little one in the barn.

Yahng Yi got in the truck with the lamb tucked under her arm. She drove quickly back up to the house, the lamb in her lap covered with an old shirt, a cold dead weight pressing against her abdomen.

HAM FINN WAS WAITING FOR YAHNG YI at the back entrance, and as the truck came up the plateau he cleared a snuff wad from his lower lip, spit out the detritus and wiped his mouth on his shoulder. He stared at the truck as it ascended, waiting to make eye contact with the driver, and as the truck came near, he saw his reflection in the windshield and looked away. His face was amorphous, neither handsome nor ugly, with a pug nose and broad cheekbones. Everything about him was big. Big head and big features and he stood nearly six and a half feet, even after the years had taken off a couple of inches from his stature.

Yahng Yi parked the truck and exited, leaving the door open, the bundle in her arms, and called for Finn to get the door.

–Fine day, ain't it, Yahng, he said, smiling and holding the door open as Yahng Yi rushed by.

–What you got there? he asked. Dead lamb?

–Not dead, said Yahng Yi, grabbing a large mixing bowl from the cabinet and setting it on the counter. She turned the water on and felt the lamb for warmth before holding the bowl under the stream. The lamb squirmed slightly against her chest and she set it gently into the bowl and the water. The lamb kicked upon touching the wetness, sending bits of mucous and blood across Yahng Yi's face.

–Nasty, said Ham.

Yahng Yi cleaned the lamb's soft coat, rubbing it with her hands, and stroked its face along its muzzle. The lamb had stopped struggling, and settled down in the water as if it had returned to the warmth of the womb.

–You been gettin' along all right? asked Ham. Just thought I'd stop by to check.

–Been just fine, Mr. Finn.

–Brought you some duck meat.

–Thank you.

–Your mother up?

–I don't know. Ain't seen her.

Yahng Yi picked the lamb up and held it in the air. The water sloughed from its hide in a thick stream, and the fine hair stayed matted down, the eyes still closed. Yahng Yi brought the lamb to her face and felt that the breathing had steadied as well as the beating of the tiny heart. She set the lamb down in the dish rack to drain while she searched for towels in the kitchen drawers.

Ham sat down at the table, easing his considerable frame upon a chair that had no business bearing him. –I brought you some duck meat, he said.

–I heard you, Mr. Finn. Thank you.

Yahng Yi wrapped the lamb in a large terrycloth towel and held it against her again to keep its temperature constant. She walked back and forth through the kitchen, bouncing the lamb gently, and patting it on the back.

The door swung open and Gabriel came in, stomping his boots on the mat. He looked over at Ham and held out his hand.

–I'm Gabe, he said.

The two of them shook hands, Ham Finn's bearlike paw fully enveloping Gabriel's lean palm and fingers.

–Didn't see you come up, said Gabriel.

–There's a path from our house into the forest and across the gully up to the barn, said Ham.

Gabriel nodded and looked at the large man from his boots to Ham's eyes, noticing a gentleness within them, despite Ham's intimidating size. He reminded Gabriel of his grandfather when his grandfather was straight of spine. The same contradicting eyes, terrible and compassionate, and the same imposing frame that seemed tall in the space between mountains.

–I'll just put this meat in the freezer, said Ham and opened the freezer door and placed the package in with some others.

Gabriel leaned down and gripped his left hand at the wrist, remembering the day his grandfather died. Gabriel had been the one who found him, the body cold and not breathing, and eyes still open, like his grandfather was looking for something—a last look at something he could take with him to wherever he was going next. But instead of catching a glimpse of the valley or the good western ridge or his beloved grandson, his grandfather's last look was at the underside of the kitchen table, and Gabriel had thought that unworthy of such a man, so he'd dragged his hulking grandfather outside and left the body near the bunkhouse, eyes still open and dead, looking up at the clear blue sky while Gabriel wandered off, not to shed a tear until he was sure his grandfather's big eyes had no sight line to him. Once he was within the forest behind the log house, he wailed like the child he was.

Emily had been the first to find him, and they shared no words. She just sat there with him on the fallen trunk of a

Douglas fir, not speaking, but letting him know he was not alone.

–You all right? asked Ham, setting his skillet-sized hand on Gabriel's shoulder. You don't look so good.

–Guess I overexerted myself, said Gabriel. Sometimes I forget how old I am.

–You want some water?

–Just need some air, said Gabriel and went quickly out the door.

Ham went over to the window and pulled the curtain to the side and looked outside. –Kinda strange, he said to Yahng Yi. Don't that eye patch scare you? Like a pirate or somethin'.

–He's too old to be scary, said Yahng Yi.

–He's my age, looks like. Near sixty.

–Like I said. Too old.

Ham walked back over to Yahng Yi and knuckled her softly on the scalp. She ducked away and reached under the damp towels to feel for warmth coming from the lamb's body. It was sleeping, breathing deeper and warmer now, and Yahng Yi unwrapped it from the towels and went to the linen closet for a blanket. Ham took a glass from the cabinet next to the sink and filled it with water. He peered out the window again, but Gabriel was gone.

GABRIEL BREATHED DEEPLY as he walked toward the barn, trying to control his dizziness. *Emily,* he whispered and felt himself collapse, his face pointing up at the sky and his good eye flickering. He remembered an image of himself, as a young man at the edge of town, sitting on the ground among the wild strawberry bushes at the top of a hill. Autumn in the mountains, and the last cutting of the season, the third cutting, when the alfalfa leaves were at their richest, cold weather on its way, medicine for work-lean bodies and burnt skin. Emily sat next to him, her hair long and brown and snaking in the breeze. He stared at the smooth skin of her cheeks and told her he would be leaving her, told her he was enlisting, that it had to be done, and that he couldn't explain it to her because she was a girl. She had cried like he was already dead, and he told her not to worry, that he was in no good danger and nothing could change what they had between them.

THE VILLAGE FIRES HAVE DIED, and he sees some of the 7th digging in on the hillsides. The slopes are steep and there is little cover save for a few trees scattered along the incline. He heads up the hill above the rail tunnel. There are grouse in the hill grass and he scares one from its nest and lifts his rifle toward it, a reflex from pheasant hunting with his grandfather in the prairies east of Harter.

There is a loud pop behind him to the west and a few of the soldiers turn in that direction, and he feels the dry throaty silence of impending chaos, and the muting of the senses that follows, all seen through the low light of dusk and the lingering smoke from the decimated village. Soldiers gather near the culvert that runs alongside the road, some lying on their bellies, as if taking cover from fire. There is air support on its way from the south, and then the silence is broken by the screaming of peasants as a jet fighter streaks by and strafes the road at low altitude, assaulting all ears with displaced air. He takes cover on the ground, hugging the hot earth, his face buried in his shoulder. He rises only when the jet is at a safe distance, his rifle drawn and surveying his position. There are just-shot dead all around him.

A crowd of peasants runs back west toward Yongdong and he sees three fellow soldiers in a concrete culvert, huddled together with helmets pulled low across their eyes. They look young to him, like boys back at the ranch playing cowboys and Indians down by the coulee.

Take cover! They're coming through! Take cover!

The soldiers in the culvert draw their rifles and point them west toward the road and begin squeezing rounds into the crowd, the pops of their rifles muted by another fighter plane approaching and then the casual ripping of its guns through the humid air. The peasants begin running in all directions, the bulk of them headed toward a concrete bridge off the railroad tracks to the east.

He runs to the edge of the tracks and feels the heavy bullets pinging the ground rock. He looks up from under his helmet after the strafing ends and sees the bodies lying there on the ground, unmoving, and a few stray children looking around with big eyes and in disbelief, pleading for someone to help their mothers or their grandfathers or grandmothers off the ground, their clothes dirtying in the mudded road, moist with new sticky blood.

He stands in the middle of the road as the guns cease and hears the faint chirping of crickets. The sunlight has disappeared, and he sees the beginnings of starlight in the dark blue sky, the last light casting a grayness all around, and he looks down at his feet at the glowing white peasant frocks littering the dirt road, some of them still moving, their soft cries blending with the cricket song. He knows within the moment that he will remember the sights of the dust kicked up by the strafing and pieces of white cloth shredded and floating in the turbulence, and the old men and women going down to their hands and knees and then to the ground on their sides, the bundles on their heads falling dumbly to the ground, the whiteness of their flocks blossoming in dark purple, like the late spring sunset over the Spanish Peaks. The sounds layer in his mind, the buzzing of the silence and then the roaring jet engines and the strafing and the crying, coming together in a song that he will forever associate with the hotness of summer.

FIVE

Yahng Yi's Mother stood before the stone shrine at the base of the waterfall, letting the mist collect upon her face. She imagined herself back on the island, standing before the ocean with the cresting waves coming down upon the shoreline, the water broken and airborne and trapped in the strands of her hair, its stickiness clinging to her face.

She knelt down and let the offerings she carried in her skirt fall to the ground—a sack of rice cakes and three unfiltered cigarettes and a bar of chocolate.

–Jihn, do not eat the chocolate all at once this time, she sang. Your belly will ache and we will have heavy snow. Mother, make sure Jihn does not eat the chocolate too quickly.

She positioned the offerings before the shrine, clearing the ground clutter to bare dirt, and then setting the rice cakes in a small pyramid in the center. To the left of the pyramid she placed the chocolate bar for her son. To the right, cigarettes for her mother.

She spoke a quick mantra on behalf of Gabriel, and then unwrapped the chocolate and broke off three squares and ate them. She felt a great heaviness inside her as she imagined the times she'd spent with her mother on the island beach, cooking fish stew at sundown over an open fire, the wind blowing in from the ocean as they laughed together, both of them shirtless and their dark island skin tanning darker as the sun fell to the horizon. And then going to the rocks to look for oysters, and her mother shucking hers and the two of them swallowing the flesh, that briny taste so pure on her tongue and down to her gullet.

Before the missionaries had come, the women of the island wore only *hanbok* skirts in the warm season, their bare backs deep brown from the sun, breasts hanging down as they tended to the gardens or squatted to cook over ground fire. The missionaries had taught them modesty. She remembered the year they'd come, after the war with Japan had ended. She'd been nine and had never seen a white person before, and then they came with their books and their farming tools and their righteousness, and she had gone naked on the beach for the last time.

Then the Buddhist temple had become a church, a great pine cross erected on the newly shingled roof, and before long the missionaries had discovered her mother's shaman rituals.

She had been there when her mother drowned. She had watched the missionaries holding up their Bibles and their crosses, chanting the exorcism rites, pushing her mother out toward the coastline and then into the ocean to purge her, and her mother fighting them and struggling to break the surface as they held her under water. Her mother the *mudang*, the witch they called her.

She thought about her mother's burial site on the island, among the common graves where all the islanders were buried, the site hidden on the side of a small mountain and the path eroded and covered with tall wild grasses. She remembered the smell. That pure smell of a forgotten island, a scent lacking any kind of artifice. No smokestacks, no diesel-burning engines, no synthetic fragrances to hide the odors of the body. Only wild mushroom and pine and the rotting fish entrails and drying seaweed along the coast.

She felt drowsy from the mantra, and keeled to her left side in a nest of pine needles and closed her eyes, hearing the sound of chattering in her head, of men speaking in the slurry tongue of the Westerners. Soldiers milling around in the dusk.

SHE SEES THEIR SHORN HAIR AND FATIGUES, walking in groups of twos and threes, sleeves rolled up and swatting always at the flies and mosquitoes, and cursing. She is wearing dirty hemp pants and a boy's shirt, and her hair cut short and mud smeared all around her face and arms. There is the boisterous laughter of the Americans coming from near the road, and she creeps into a thicket of nettle trees near the base of the foothill behind the village. There she waits for her sisters to come back from the paddy rows.

She hears shuffling in the ground clutter and turns around. A man in uniform is walking toward her quickly, his eyes small and focused. She begins to run, but the man catches her before she can reach the clearing. He brings her to the ground and then slaps her hard across the face before pressing his weight into her chest.

She cannot breathe, cannot scream, while the man rips her loose pants past her hips. She feels his nakedness against her own, and as he reaches between his legs to guide himself, he curses wetly in her ear. She braces herself for the entry pain, and then hears a noise to her left, the sound of running. She sees another soldier jogging toward them, a soldier with deep blue eyes. The man on top of her stands quickly, zipping up his trousers, and hurries out of the thicket.

She pulls her pants up, and the blue-eyed soldier arrives at her side and helps her to her feet. She looks at him, and knows him from a future time, knows they are linked by *palcha*, by fate.

She turns back toward the village and trots away and looks back once as she approaches the edge of the thicket. He is still standing there, his hand up and waving at her, his tall frame dark in the darkness, but the blueness of his eyes still visible. Behind him another figure appears. It is the *mulsin*. The dreamer's elderly mother. She is dressed in *hanbok* pants, and no shirt, her sagging breasts hanging down like tears. She is covered in a film of water, her wrinkled skin like corduroy. She reaches up and cups the swell of the soldier's cheek with her wet right hand.

–Is it love, daughter? she asks.

–Mother, it is love, says the dreamer.

The *mulsin* clicks her tongue and shakes her head and then her body breaks, dropping to the ground in its viscous state, disappearing and leaving the dreamer to end the dream alone.

THE NEAREST FILLING STATION to the Cottage ranch was Rudy's, a small four-pump on the county two-lane, just a few miles west of the Harter city limits and about seven miles southeast of the ranch. The original Rudy had left the gas-pumping trade to join a regional Christian militia that was bunkered among the buttes just east of the Bitterroot Range. Rudy Junior owned and tended the station now, from its 6 AM open to its 6 PM close, six days of the week. After six and on Sundays the back of the house became a makeshift flophouse, a waystation for men of malfeasance, sometimes serviced by the valley whores, including Rudy's half sister, Sweet Crude.

The closing hour was nigh, and Yahng Yi stood in line within the cramped station house, the payment queue three deep and a weak transistor radio providing background music for the periodic exchanging of commerce at the register. She listened to the radio, which was now broadcasting a jingle for an auto dealer just opened off I-90 near Belgrade, and made a mental note of how much money would be left over from the purchase of the fuel. She had filled the tank of the pickup and four five-gallon canisters, nearly thirty-five gallons in all. With so little driving to be done the gas would last until summer, but that knowledge afforded her little comfort. The greenback tucked in her front pocket was the last of their savings and all they would have until shearing season.

A skinny boy with gold-flake freckles stood near the front window, some magazines and empty Coke bottles scattered upon the wide sill behind him. He held a magazine in front of his face though Yahng Yi could tell he was not reading. He was watching her. The top of his head was barely visible, dirty blond hair matted down hard and straight across his narrow skull. Yahng Yi glanced quickly over at him and then shuffled ahead as the line moved, her gaze fixed on the man ahead of her, at the sheen of his crown and the wispy strands of brown hair parted over the scalp and the ring of leftover hair wrapping around the base of his head. There was a dark spot in the swale of his back where the sweat had soaked through the blue shirt, wrinkled and hot from long hours on the highway.

The balding man looked over at the boy at the front window and then turned to look at Yahng Yi. He locked on her face for a moment, and she saw the lust in him, his body chemistry changing to its most atavistic state, dilating his pupils and the blood rushing to his cheeks and lips, and his breathing stifled. She glared at him.

He smiled quickly and turned away and she looked down at the back of his slacks, at the creases along the center of the pant legs and down to the dark brown loafers looking greasy under the white light. The line moved again and she stepped forward and sipped from the bottle of Yoohoo she was holding, a small sip that she swished around before gulping, the heat from her mouth warming the liquid, and her letting the saliva build to add more for her to swallow.

The balding man was at the counter now, and she peered over his shoulder at Rudy Junior, a tall fellow who was once thick from farmwork, but had spent his twenties and much of his thirties driving a tractor trailer. All those days of grinding it out on the road, all those highway bumps and the hours in that vibrating cab had mismolded his body, compacting his organs down along his waist and padding that cargo with sedentary fat, so that he'd taken on the appearance of a pear with legs.

The balding man paid his tab in cash, and she heard Rudy Junior giving directions toward Yellowstone. The balding man made his thanks and walked away from the counter to the exit, glancing one last time at Yahng Yi as he exited. She watched him as he went outside and trotted over to a long blue station wagon, bedrolls and suitcases tied down to the roof rails. She saw the California license plate and the silhouettes of two children in the backseat and the big rounded hair of the wife, the ends curled upward at chin level.

She imagined being inside that station wagon and driving away with that balding man, imagined him abandoning his wife and children and just the two of them heading off into the park and spending the days fishing and camping or whatever it was that Californians did when they vacationed in these parts. And then when the vacation was done, to go back with him to his home in California, away from Montana and away from Harter and the mountains. He would take her home and keep her like a secret. Like a single pearl inside a jewelry box. She knew she had that power over men. Could make them do things they should never do.

The wagon pulled out of the lot and onto the road, heading back toward Harter, the glow of the running lights haloed by the dust kicked up in the darkness. She turned her attention back to the counter and glanced quickly at Rudy Junior.

–Gas, she said. Pump was at forty dollar and thirty-three. And one Yoohoo.

She wedged the cap onto the lip of the bottle so as to make it appear that she hadn't yet opened it, and then set it down on the white Formica counter.

–Yoohoo's on the house, said Rudy Junior.

–Ain't necessary, said Yahng Yi.

–Already done, he said, and began pushing the buttons on the register with fingers stained black at the tips and grease wedged against the cuticles.

–Okay.

–You and your mother gettin' along all right out there? he asked as the register dinged and the till slid out from the base.

Yahng Yi nodded and reached into her pocket for the hundred.

–Ain't seen you in a while, he said.

–Been busy.

–You've gotten bigger.

–So have you.

Rudy Junior laughed and shook his head and Yahng Yi gave him the hundred. He set it under the till and counted out her change and held it out to her. As the currency was traded she felt his stubby index finger brush against the back of her hand, scratchy like a cat's tongue, trying to taste her. She grabbed the bills and coins and slipped them in her jeans pocket without looking at him again. As she made her way to the door, the freckled boy behind the magazine lowered it from his face and spoke in a pitchy pubescent voice.

–Is that the girl from out past Four Corners? he asked.

–That's her, said Rudy Junior.

–Ain't never seen her before, the boy said. She ain't as pretty as they say.

Rudy Junior laughed and Yahng Yi rolled her eyes and stepped outside and walked to her truck, the sun just starting its descent behind the Bridgers. An eighteen-wheeler sped by on the county highway down the road, vibrating the ground as she hoisted the five-gallon canisters from the ground and into the bed of the pickup.

She turned around and saw through the window that the boy had put the magazine down. The two of them made eye contact, and the boy moved quickly to the door. Yahng Yi flipped him her middle finger and then grabbed the last two canisters and tried to lift them up over the sides. The two of them together were too heavy and she set one of them down, spilling gas onto the concrete and filling the air with the easy scent of evaporating petrol.

–Hey you, the boy called out. You need help with that?

Yahng Yi ignored him and lifted the canister over the side, her heart straining from the weight. As she reached for the last one, she felt the cold thin fingers through her shirt around her right biceps, and hot breath at her neck.

–You deaf? he asked.

Yahng Yi twisted her arm away from him, freeing herself from his grip. She saw his freckled face and placed his age at no more than fourteen. The boy grabbed at her shirt and held a handful of cloth that had become untucked from her blue jeans. Yahng Yi chopped at his forearm with her fist, but he was strong for a boy and his hands held firm.

–I'm just tryin' to help, he said.

–Lemme go, you freckle-faced half-wit, she said.

–My name's Hollis, he said, releasing his grip. Just wanted to help you.

–Don't need your help, Hollis the half-wit.

The boy looked away from her briefly, and Yahng Yi lifted one of the last two canisters. He grabbed her arm again, and tried to pull her away from her truck. She looked over at the station window and saw Rudy Junior coming out from behind the counter and toward the front door. As Rudy Junior stood at the door, another truck pulled alongside the gas pumps, the shocks squealing as the right front wheel went across a hole in the dirt. The blond-haired boy released his grip. Yahng Yi moved away from him and reached down to pick up the last canister.

The truck pulled up next to them, and the boy stepped a few yards away from Yahng Yi, his hands in his pockets. Yahng Yi placed the last canister next to the other three already in the bed and recognized the truck as Ham Finn's. She peered into the cab and saw that it was Jude behind the wheel, his black Stetson low on his brow, and sitting next to him, Val Rey, the ranch hand.

Jude exited the truck awkwardly, and Yahng Yi saw his eyes were bloodshot and filled with liquor. His flannel shirt was untucked from his jeans and he had one pant leg tucked into a boot and the other cuffed over it.

–What the hell you doin', said Jude, walking toward Hollis.

–Nothin', Jude, said the boy.

–I seen you grabbin' this here girl. What you call that?

–Come on, Jude. I weren't doin nothin'.

Jude looked over at Yahng Yi. –This boy botherin' you? he asked.

–Leave it be, Jude, she said.

–You like her, Hollis? That why you botherin' her?

Jude grabbed him by the shirt collar. Hollis did not try to move away, and received Jude's words by turning his head and letting Jude's spittle accost his left cheek.

–You think she's pretty, Hollis?

Hollis pushed Jude away and Jude's boot heels caught on the asphalt and he fell backward on his rear. The passenger door of the truck opened and big Val stepped out. The boy's eyes grew big and the blood came up to fill his pale, freckled face. Jude got back to his feet.

–Sorry, Jude, said Hollis. Didn't mean it.

Yahng Yi laughed.

–What you laughin' at? asked Jude, turning his head to Yahng Yi.

–The fact that you're an ass, she said. That's what I'm laughin' at.

Jude chuckled. –She's pretty, ain't she, Hollis, he said. 'Specially when she gets all shitfire like that.

Jude looked over at Val and nodded. Val got back inside the truck.

–Lemme tell you a secret, said Jude and cupped his hand and whispered into Hollis's ear. Hollis giggled and Jude let go of him and slapped him on the back.

–What'd you tell him? asked Yahng Yi and pushed Jude on the shoulder. Jude stumbled backward and nearly fell again.

–Nothin', he said.

–What'd he tell you? she asked Hollis.

Hollis shrugged his shoulders. Yahng Yi went up to Hollis, grabbed his ear and yanked on it until he was down on his knees.

–He said he stuck it to you, said Hollis in a high voice and reached up to remove Yahng Yi's hand.

Yahng Yi went to Jude and began raining blows onto his head and shoulders. Jude stood his ground and held up his forearm to deter her hands, laughing.

–Asshole, she said.

–Ain't no secret we been screwin', said Jude, holding out his arms.

–Gotta last more'n a minute to be screwin', said Yahng Yi.

Hollis laughed. Jude turned to him and backhanded him hard across the face. Hollis tumbled onto his backside and scooted away, a betrayed look on his face.

–What the hell you do that for? he asked, grabbing at his cheek and the trickle of blood running down the corner of his mouth.

–I told you a secret, and you let it out, said Jude. Now git.

Hollis stood up and jogged back to the entrance of the station house, looking back once at Yahng Yi as he reached the door.

–Such an ass, she said.

–That's the Arnold boy, said Jude. Ain't got a whole lot of sense.

–Was talkin' about you.

Jude chuckled and reached into his shirt pocket and removed a small steel flask and uncapped it.

–We gonna get together later tonight? he asked, taking a generous swallow from the flask.

Yahng Yi got in her truck and stared out through the windshield toward the shadows of the mountains, black under a bluish night sky. She turned away as Jude reached his right hand into the cab and rubbed her cheek.

–Don't know yet, she said.

He slid his right hand down her face and to the back of her neck and squeezed it lightly and then began working it into the base of her head where the hair began. He moved his fingers through the thickness, and she let him, the truth being that she did enjoy his touch.

–Been thinkin' about you all day, he said.

–Yeah? she asked, eyes closed.

–Yeah. My balls done swole up like melons.

She pushed his hand away. –That why you're here?

–What's that supposed to mean?

–Don't play dumb. I know what goes on around here after close.

–What? said Jude, holding his hands to his heart. Came to get some windshield fluid. Don't know what you're talkin' about.

–Goddammit, Jude.

–I swear.

Yahng Yi shook her head, started the engine quickly and shifted into gear.

–I'll see you in about an hour then, said Jude and backed away, slapping the side panel lightly with his open palm as the truck passed him. Yahng Yi looked in the rearview mirror as she pulled away from the lot, and watched Jude shuffling back toward his truck. She wished for him to turn his head to see her off, but he did not. Instead it was tall Val Rey who was staring at her.

VAL WATCHED YAHNG YI'S TRUCK until it curled around a bend and disappeared. Only fifteen, he still did not understand what it meant to love, but he was learning, and had been admiring Yahng Yi from afar since he'd arrived at the Finn compound. He had heard Jude speak about her and knew what she and Jude did in the gully and in the bunkhouse when the hands were away, and it had made him jealous.

It was a different world here in Thalo Valley from what he'd known. So unlike his mother's dying house, unlike the foster homes and the reservation. There was something secure about this place, about the wideness of it. It was sturdy, like Ham Finn, like himself. But only Yahng Yi made him feel like he was meant to live in the valley.

On the reservation he had stayed with the doctor who ran the clinic—Yumi, his father's cousin's firstborn, and a half-breed like himself. He missed her at times, missed her femaleness. At that young age, he admired her like he admired Ham Finn, and he had thought of becoming a doctor, like her, to know what she knew about the body, about what lay beneath the skin, what things hid deep within the flesh. So many layers to be peeled away of muscle and fat and tissue, where secrets could be concealed. Things are rarely as they seem, Yumi had once told him. *The body is full of tricks*, she'd said. *It can fool you, like a fish faking its death before flipping itself back into the water.*

It was always interesting at the clinic. Always people coming and going and some kind of drama. He remembered the day Denny Bird came to the clinic and Yumi cut out a small piece of shrapnel from his hand, left there from the war in Vietnam. It was a curious thing, to watch as a man had his flesh incised, and at the time Val wondered only about the pain. It had not occurred to him what relief there must have been, what a symbolic gesture it was for Denny to have that piece of himself excised after so many years. But he understood it now. Because he understood he had his own artifacts that he harbored within his body, things that needed to be excised as well.

SIX

In the waning light of a cloud-covered dusk, Yahng Yi's Mother set some platters and wine cups on mats upon a flat spot just beyond the front entrance of the house. She was wearing her shaman garb, a homemade red silk robe that she had sewn in the days after Gabriel had left, when she had taken up the ancient religion of her mother, the *mansin*, remembering the rituals she had witnessed from her childhood, when she had served as her mother's assistant.

She had her hair pulled back tightly into a bun and her face made up, complexion whitened with powder, her lips red and full, and a deep blue eye shadow. The platters held red bean rice cakes, sesame seed cookies, bowls of steamed rice, and various smoked fishes and dried meats that Ham Finn had given her over the winter.

She took a bowl full of millet and tossed pinches of grain around the front door, then went back inside and through the rooms, tossing millet through all the doorways. The men watched her—Ham Finn and Jude and Gabriel. They were all sitting in the front room, holding tall glasses of the homemade rice wine that they had been drinking for the past hour, and all three with silly grins on their faces.

–What the hell's she doin'? asked Jude.

Ham shot him a reprobate glance.

Jude rolled his eyes. –Where the hell's Yahng? he asked.

–Haven't seen her, said Gabriel.

–This is borin' as shit, said Jude. You got cards around here?

Yahng Yi's Mother shook her head, carrying a plate of rice cakes. As she passed the men, Jude stood up and tried to pick one of the cakes. Yahng Yi's Mother slapped his hand, and then Ham cuffed him on the back of the head.

–Shit, said Jude.

Ham cuffed him again.

–You play cards, old man? Jude asked Gabriel, rubbing his crown.

Gabriel shook his head.

–You play the machines then? asked Jude.

–Not regularly, said Gabriel, and imagined himself sitting at a bar stool not long ago in the past, maybe two years ago, not in Thalo Valley, but maybe Bozeman, maybe Billings, and he remembered the darkness of the bar, both in lighting and mood, and all the desperate souls in there, hoping their lives could be affirmed in playing games of chance, hoping that the grace of God would shine luck upon them and they would maybe hit for a few hundred. He remembered doing the same thing in that dark place, in his heart praying that the numbers would come up on the electronic keno machine, at first running just seven numbers at a time, and using the numbers most familiar to him, like his age and birth date, and some other numbers he remembered as significant, if not why. Those numbers never did hit, and after a while he would play random numbers in fives, but those numbers never came up either.

–Real men play cards, said Jude.

–Playin' a machine, least you know what you're up against, said Ham. Can't say that when you're playing against another man. Money's money anyway. Don't matter if you're playin' the machines or Texas hold'm. Quicker getting it playin' the machines.

–Quicker nothin', said Jude.

Yahng Yi's Mother came back inside and pointed at the front door. –You must be outside when the gods awaken, she said.

Ham opened the door and grabbed Jude by the shirt-sleeve and pushed him outside. Jude's momentum carried him several yards from the house to where the incline began and his feet tried to catch up with his body, but failed, and he tumbled face-first, arms flailing.

–Strong wine, said Ham as he and Gabriel stepped outside. Ain't had wine like this since they blew up my uncle's distillery back in Casper.

Gabriel grinned and nodded. –Mr. Cottage used to make some good stuff, I remember, he said. Barley wine. Emily and I used to get in it and some nights if I had enough I swear I could see through time.

Ham laughed.

–You know whatever happened to them? The Cottages? asked Gabriel.

–Ain't sure, said Ham. I know they left for California sometime in the early sixties. Back then they raised Rambouillet. Market couldn't hold because people stopped eating so much mutton. That's when Emily took over. Her and Yahng's mother and Jihn. Started raisin' Shetlands. Just for the wool.

Gabriel nodded, remembering those days with his grandfather and how at times the valley seemed so overrun with the Cottages' Rambouillet. He would look down upon them from higher on the mountain and watch the dull white pods ruminating at their leisure.

–I assume they're dead, continued Ham. When I bought the land, Emily held the title. Weren't no other name on the deed. You were close with them?

–They were like family, said Gabriel.

–Shame about what happened to them. All the Cottages. Used to be the biggest name in Thalo Valley goin' back more'n a hundred years.

Ham shook his head. –Hard to pass land down to your kin in this country, he said. Gotta sell off chunks at a time just to keep your taxes square. It's getting to be the only people that can afford land ain't usin' it for nothing more than looking.

Ham went to help Jude to his feet. He hoisted his grandson up and then smacked him all around the back and legs to coax the dust off him, and then brought him back to the front of the house. Jude sat down and stared at the front door, his back to the darkening valley.

–I haven't visited Emily's burial site yet, said Gabriel. You know where it's at?

–Emily and Yahng's brother were cremated. Yahng's mother spread the ashes on the mountain.

Gabriel turned and looked up at the mountain.

–Let me ask you something, he said.

–Shoot.

–I don't figure you'd know the answer to this question, but it's something that's been bothering me. Why was Emily out there with him in that blizzard?

–Don't know.

–I'm guessing the boy went to dig out the animals, said Gabriel. But why was Emily out there too? Yahng told me Emily didn't have any part in the ranch work, so why was she out there?

–Never thought about it, said Ham, shrugging off Gabriel's curiosity. Gabriel tried to gauge whether Ham was hiding anything, but could gain no insight, the wine having snookered his judgment and Ham's expression a permanent droop now as the alcohol relaxed all the muscles in his face and his eyes squinty and swollen.

While the drunk men stared off into the gray horizon, Yahng Yi came outside quietly, her face made up like her mother's. Jude saw her first, then the elders looked where he was looking. All three had loosened jaws from seeing her, her makeup accentuating the Oriental bones she inherited from her mother, the long neck and shapely nose of her white father. She looked uncomfortable, dressed in a blue silk robe patterned like her mother's, and holding a large homemade drum—lambskin stretched taut over a hollowed-out section of tree trunk.

Her mother followed behind her, walking regally in slow strides.

–The Yi family holds a *kut* today, she said. Gods. Ancestors. Join us and feast. Be entertained.

Yahng Yi began beating the drum steadily, and her mother started to sing, her voice strong and sweet even though the notes she sang were twangy. The melody reminded both Ham and Gabriel of the folk songs they'd heard in the Korean War, the traveling songs of the peasant refugees.

I sing for the yongsan in this house.
The ghosts of unlucky dead.
And sangmun, spirits unclean.
And kamang, the dead far from home.

Yahng Yi's Mother went to one of the food platters, picked up a handful of rice cakes and threw them down the incline. Then she emptied a wine cup on the ground and turned to Yahng Yi and relaxed her face for a moment before tensing it again, her brow furrowed and lips tight as she embodied the spirit of the *Taegam.*

–I am the *Taegam*, she sang in an authoritative voice. You, girl. You call this offering? Where is the rest of the wine? These cakes are dried on the outside. This jerky is too salty. The fish are puny.

–I am truly sorry, said Yahng Yi with a touch of sarcasm. I promise you more wine later if you will help purge our weary traveler of bad influence.

–And better food? asked Yahng Yi's Mother.

–Yes, said Yahng Yi. Better food.

Yahng Yi's Mother took one of the smoked brown trout that was part of the offering platter, picking it up with her toes and tossing it in the air. The fish landed with its decapitated body pointing toward the valley.

–The Official is satisfied, she said. We may return to the house.

Yahng Yi's Mother and Yahng Yi went back inside the house. Gabriel looked over and saw that Jude was passed out. Ham went over to him and patted him on the cheek.

–Wake up, boy! he yelled.

Jude stirred, but did not open his eyes.

–Boy can't hold his liquor, said Ham and slapped Gabriel on the back. Gabriel fell forward from the heaviness of the blow, falling on his face, and with Ham's momentum unchecked by Gabriel's light frame, Ham fell to the ground as well. They lay there side by side on their backs, looking up at the emerging moon.

–Nice night, said Ham.

–Sure is, said Gabriel.

They got to their knees and stumbled to the front door, tumbling inside. Yahng Yi's Mother was already into her song and did not waver at the interruption, continuing the ritual as Yahng Yi beat the drum.

The Yi family's most devoted mansin was Yi Ch'ong,
Born to a mudang and her worthless husband.
Her beloved mother cast into the sea,
Where she became mulsin, water god.

Ham and Gabriel watched Yahng Yi's Mother as she danced gracefully around the front room, her figure so lithe, so lovely in line, hypnotizing them with her movements. She danced to the fireplace and turned her back to them. Yahng Yi halted the drum. Gabriel stared at Yahng Yi, and she reminded him of the peasant girls walking the evacuation road, how they had looked both so alien and inviting. How he had imagined what it would be like to kiss their thin lips, and the smooth brown skin that looked the color and taste of caramel. And what the flesh would feel like, that thin, bony flesh, what it would feel like in his hands and under him. The thoughts shamed him, and he shook his head and reached up and felt his eye patch, to remind him he was no longer a boy, and then he looked back at Yahng Yi's Mother, who had turned around and begun singing again.

The kunung defeated the emperor's guards,
With a halberd fashioned by the fire god.
When he was wounded,
Yi Ch'ong rolled him in an empty cart.
To the secret camp of his brethren,
Where he was nursed back to health.

As Yahng Yi's Mother drew out the last note, the front door opened and Jude stumbled inside. He looked at

Ham and Gabriel, wobbled a bit, and then saw Yahng Yi. He walked toward her.

–This sucks, he said. Let's get outta here.

–Show some respect, boy, said Ham and stood up. He grabbed Jude's arm and brought him down to the floor, and then wrapped Jude up in a headlock.

–Continue, said Ham as Jude tried to pry himself free. Yahng Yi's Mother nodded and resumed her performance.

> Yi Ch'ong waited for him in the mountains,
> Singing the muga, holding the healing kut.
> When he was well, he brought her back to the Dream Cloud
>   Temple,
> And then to Yi Mountain and the land of many grains.
> They lived there happily,
> Growing fat for ten thousand years.

Jude finally freed himself from Ham's headlock, and before Ham could bring him down again Jude reached Yahng Yi and snatched the drum away from her, and then began beating on it and singing his own tune.

–I fell into a burnin' ring of fire, he sang. Went down, down, down and the flames grew higher . . .

–Boy, sit down! yelled Ham.

Jude kept singing, and Ham caught up with his grandson and open-handed him on the back of his head. Jude dropped the drum and went down on one knee, dazed from the blow. Ham picked him up and carried him out the front door.

Yahng Yi looked over at Gabriel. Gabriel shrugged his shoulders and looked at Yahng Yi's Mother, who was standing in the corner, straight-faced.

Ham Finn returned and sat back down on the floor next to Gabriel. –Continue, he said. Jude won't bother you no more.

–It is done, said Yahng Yi's Mother, letting her hair down and walking out of the front room and into the kitchen.

Ham nodded and stood up. He and Gabriel walked to the door together. They shook hands, and then Ham turned around and waved at Yahng Yi before stepping outside.

–Make sure that boy don't swallow his tongue, said Yahng Yi as Ham exited.

Gabriel watched her as she shut the door and latched it, and then as she turned to him, their gazes fixed upon each other, Gabriel staring into her with his drunk eye and seeing her from the inside out, seeing her mother at that age, the straight, black hair and brown skin and the feline eyes, upturned at the outer corners and the lips painted wine red and eyelids the color of sapphire. Looking like her mother, like her mother's outer layer, the locust shell left clinging to the branch of a maple tree, and Yahng Yi springing from the molt.

IT WAS STILL SHY OF THE MIDNIGHT HOUR, and Gabriel was awake and alert, the sugars in the wine staving off any notions of sleep. Yahng Yi's Mother set a plate of rice cakes in front of him and he took one of the doughy bricks, which were covered in broken, sweet red beans, and ate it, nodding his head as if to signal his satisfaction, but in his heart believing it to be bland.

Yahng Yi's Mother watched him eat, staring at him as he chewed his food, and he smiled at her, his good eye creasing shut and a crow's foot appearing at the outside edge, making him look wise.

–Ohpa, she said. It has been good for me to have you here. I feel like a girl again.

100

–Been good for me too, he said. Good to be home like this.

He ate quickly and when the plate was half empty he drank from a cup of fresh tea, looking around the kitchen, as he had done so frequently over the last week, somewhat melancholy with drink and the knowledge that Emily had once sat in the chair he sat in now, once walked the floorboards his feet rested on.

–Do you miss her still? asked Yahng Yi's Mother, sensing his nostalgia.

–Yes, he answered. I suppose I do.

–Did you miss me as well?

–Of course I did.

–I thought of you often.

–I thought about you too, he said and stared at her, his vision loose and making her features blur slightly, smoothing out her years so she looked as he remembered forty years ago, a scared peasant girl, and then the memory of the two of them standing on the tarmac at the army post in Pusan, waiting to board a cargo plane home. He felt the heat and humidity, the moving of that thick air like the weight of dense smoke. He remembered arguing with one of the MPs about her, about whether she would be allowed to fly with him. She had stood meekly by his side, unaffected by the noise of the turbines or the coming and going of vehicles with gun mounts, her shapeless round face with no wrinkling, no folding, no emotion, as if she were already dead or in open-eyed slumber. They had boarded the plane together, he remembered, and he remembered that it was through the trading of favors, as often happened in the army.

–Thought by now you would have left this place, he said, and drank fully from his teacup, wishing he had some whiskey left, or something harder that would give him a better burn than the thin rice wine.

–If I had left, then how would you have found me again? asked Yahng Yi's Mother.

He smiled. –You stayed here all this time for me?

–Yes.

The warmth of the hot tea caused some moisture to collect along the strap of his patch and he reached up to clear it. Yahng Yi's Mother was still staring at him and it made him nervous, something in the way she stared, her angled eyes looking too focused and serpentine, looking singular and making him wonder what she saw when she looked at him like that, looking almost like hate, and at the same time like an unbearable love.

–I'm sorry, Ohpa, she said, seeing his uneasiness and looking down at her lap. I cannot help myself.

–Something on your mind? he asked.

–No. Just thinking how it has always been my wish for you to return.

–Now why would you want to go and wish that? I could think of a million better things to wish for.

–Not I. They were my happiest days, when we were here together.

She stood up, hurt that he did not overtly share her enthusiasm. She went to the sink and set her hands gently upon the basin and closed her eyes. The spout was dribbling water and she reached out and let the drops fall upon her open palm. Gabriel watched her at the sink, the outline of her form unfocused, like two identical images superimposed and just slightly off kilter. He named it just a hallucination brought on by too much drink. It did not occur to him that having just one eye, he had no binary focus.

–You hardly speak to me since you have returned, she said, her back to him.

–Guess I've forgotten how to talk to you, he said, not wanting to tell her that he did not remember her as she remembered him. He realized they must have been close at one time. Maybe even lovers. But he did not remember their love to any degree.

–It was never about words, she said.

He looked at the back of her head and the ink-black hair that he remembered would shine blue in full moonlight and he realized he must have walked with her in the night. He looked at her shoulders, imagining them unrobed, and realized that he must have seen her naked more than once. He could picture the porcelain skin of her back and how the ridge of her spine bowed to the left. But he could not remember loving her.

He could only remember loving Emily, and when he was inside this house, it was Emily he smelled, the comforting scent of her trapped somewhere in the fibers of the upholstery and bed linens, her essence lingering in the wood grains, in the dust collected beneath the bottom edge of the toe molding and in the ancient untouched cobwebs that eluded the spring cleanings. Parts of her in there, her skin, her hair. He could sense that, could smell that. Her scent like wildflowers, seraphic and hale.

–She always blamed me for your leaving, said Yahng Yi's Mother.

–Emily?

–Yes. She blamed me. She always hated me.

–That doesn't sound like her.

–You were wrong to leave me with her.

Yahng Yi's Mother turned around and glared at him, and it was the first time he could remember that she had looked him in the eye for more than a moment. She stared into him, as if trying to pry him open for some acceptable excuse, some fantastic story that would affirm his undying devotion for her, something that would explain why he would betray her.

–Why, Ohpa? she asked, finally looking away when he did not. Why did you leave me like that?

–I don't know, he said, the events surrounding his departure fogged. He could only remember himself walking away from the ranch on that dirt road under the cover of darkness, and he searched for its emotional trunking. Was it anger? Did he leave in anger?

–Do not say that you do not know, Ohpa. You hurt me by saying that.

She looked him in the eye again, but softer this time, trying to see him as she had seen him forty years ago. –Do you not remember our love? she asked.

He hesitated before saying no, wanting to find that love, as pretty as she looked with her face made up like that.

–No, he said. I don't remember.

She collapsed to the floor onto her side, her left shoulder against the cabinets under the sink, and her thin body wrapped in silk looking so fragile against the sturdiness of the wood. Gabriel knelt down beside her and placed his hand on her hip.

–You were my world, she said through the sobbing. My whole world. How could you not remember?

–There's a lot of things I don't remember, he said.

She looked up at him and smeared the tears away with her wrist, careful to work around the borders of her eye makeup. –I don't understand, she said.

–I was shot, he said and pointed at his skull.

She reached up and touched him where he pointed, at the right edge of the ocular cavity, at that strong bone that was partially covered by the eye patch. She noticed the raised skin of the small crescent scar.

–It makes it hard for me to remember some things, he said. Some years I don't remember at all.

–You do not remember your love for me, she said softly.

–The only feelings I can really remember are from when I was younger. From before the war.

–When you loved Emily?

Gabriel nodded. –I suppose, he said.

–You do not remember your heart changing?

He shook his head slowly, waiting for some part of him to hold him back, some part of him other than his brain, some other place touched by that historical blood that had flowed through him in those years.

–The nights we spent together? she asked.

–Only that we may have done so.

He watched as her lips trembled, starting with the lower as a weak quivering, and then moving to the upper and then the soft air coming through as she tried to hold in her crying. He moved his body next to hers, and then lifted his left arm to invite her into him, and she moved her head there, her right shoulder at his ribcage and her head where the chest met arm. He stroked her hair, his fingers sliding through the coarse fibers until she closed her eyes and her breathing slowed to normal.

They listened to the stillness of the night and she looked up at him, the water still lingering over her smallish eyes and making her look childlike, and for a moment he was taken back to the time she spoke of, and there was a cinder in him somewhere, growing larger as they stared, and he leaned in to kiss her. She did not resist, but her lips on his were like a stranger's, a new taste familiar only from the memory of kissing other women.

They kissed again, and she pressed harder this time, receiving what was owed to her, a reward for her diligence.

But he was not there. She pushed away from him, leaving him with mouth agape and eye still closed and a thin trickle of saliva at the left corner of his mouth, the moisture milky with rice film, glistening like molten pearl.

–You will sleep in Yahng's room, she said and smiled briefly as she wiped away the saliva from his mouth. She held on to his hand as she stood up and let him look upon her for a few seconds before releasing his grip. She could feel his eye on her back as she turned. There was something missing in the air between them, and as she walked the long walk away from him, she swore to herself that she would make it all new again, take them back to their war's beginning, back before the last good-byes.

SEVEN

He hunkers down next to a thick scrub oak on a narrow ledge twenty yards up the hill from the concrete rail tunnel. The hillsides are steep and barren save for the grass and scrub brush and a few scattered trees. He sits next to another soldier, saying nothing, both of them looking down the road toward the west and the Yongdong front. The other soldier sits Indian-style with an M-1 in his lap, both his knees bouncing up and down like wings. There is movement all around them, and the soft whispers of men amidst the crickets and squawking magpies.

There is enough moonlight that he can see the road and a few white bodies walking it, the sounds of the ox-carts barely audible, and the low groaning of stray cattle roaming along the ditches in search of water. Then a rumbling in the distance, heading toward them from the west.

–Tanks, says the other soldier.

A convoy approaches, the low guttural growl of diesel engines, and then voices growing louder all around them.

–Jesus Christ. They're coming.

He sees the machines traveling the road at a quick pace, and the white bodies running away from them, some heading up the mountain. Shots ring out and he stands up and aims toward the valley and watches as muzzle fire flashes all around him in the darkness and then white bodies fall to the ground on the road. The sound of M-1 fire popping and then the sinister rattling of the .30-calibers kicking up the dirt in the road into small wispy columns and the tracers lighting the path of the bullets with lines of white fire.

There is yelling from up the hill and the sounds of rustling grass and falling bodies and then men running past him down the mountain.

–They broke through! screams the other soldier and follows the crowd down the hillside. Dozens of men appear to the left and right, panic in their eyes and in their gaits, some of them without their rifles. He walks down the hill with his rifle readied, the blur of bodies surreal through all the darkness.

He reaches the base of the hill and a narrow path that runs parallel to the rail tracks. He jogs briskly, a few soldiers visible on the path in front of him, lit occasionally by stray tracers from the .30-cals, the sound of mortar shells exploding down the road near the regiment post. He can hear the groaning of wounded peasants seeking shelter in the ditches and the abandoned foxholes dug in along the rail line.

There is heavy fire still coming from spots above him on the hill and he leaves the path and settles into a shallow streambed, dry from the heat and dust and the long-forgotten rains. He looks over toward the road and sees the bodies. White bodies all stained dark and the dust of the strafed earth lingering just above the road like thin fog. There is a headless torso several yards away from him and he sees its flattened skull, severed and crushed by the weight of some heavy machine.

He rests in the streambed while the gunfire wanes, and he removes his canteen and drinks from it silently. The dust has settled and the stars shine bright in the cloudless night sky, reminding him of when he and Emily would lie on the hillside below the house with the sheep sleeping down on the valley floor and the stars up there and vibrating and the two of them holding hands and just watching. Just watching the stars.

The crickets begin their chirping again and there is a gentle breeze rolling across the tall grasses. Beyond the rustling, he hears the faint groaning of the wounded on the road. He covers his ears and looks skyward with wet eyes, imagining himself up there in the heavens and soaring above it all, above the scrubby hills and paddy rows and the rail tracks and the dead in the road, above the peninsula and the Pacific wide and dark in the night, flying over that ocean and coming stateside to the California coast and then to the mountains and the girl he'd left within them. He imagines her undressing in the piney hills as the moon shines through the boughs, lighting her body with pale moonlight.

GABRIEL AWOKE ON THE COUCH SUDDENLY, at first trying to remember the dream and then trying to forget. He swung his legs off the couch and hunched down, running his hands through his hair, his neck sticky from dried night sweat. The mantel clock timed the silence as he sat there, rubbing his skin and the scratchy stubble over his cheeks like nettle rash. He wrapped his arms around himself and rubbed his shoulders to goad the circulation. He was cold, though the midmorning sun had already shown in full.

He heard the back door open and footsteps coming through the kitchen. Yahng Yi appeared in the threshold and scowled at him.

–You ain't doin' much good for someone who calls himself a do-gooder, she said.

–Tired, said Gabriel. What time is it?

–Near nine. Had a couple births already this mornin'.

–You should have woken me.

–I tried. You weren't havin' it, Patch. Thought you was dead.

Gabriel palmed his face and rubbed it vigorously. –Haven't slept this much since I was a kid, he said.

–It's Mother. She's cursed you.

Gabriel grunted. –Is she up? he asked.

–She's up, said Yahng Yi. But she ain't here.

–Where is she?

–Maybe up in the mountains. Maybe the Finns'.

–Why would she be at the Finns'?

–Gotta pay the rent, snapped Yahng Yi and went back into the kitchen. Gabriel watched her stepping lightly on the hardwood, the hollow clucking of her boot soles vibrating the boards under his feet. He felt around near the end of the couch and retrieved his own boots, slipping them on as he heard Yahng Yi go out through the back door. Gabriel followed her outside, walking quickly to keep up with her as she made her way to the barn. The cold hit him and he stopped and wrapped his arms around himself. He was about to call something out to her, maybe tell her that he was going over to the Finns', maybe ask her if she wanted to eat breakfast with him. But he stopped and shook himself as the shock of the cold wore down, and felt a trace of emptiness as he watched Yahng Yi disappear into the barn to check on the newborns.

He turned back to the house, his footsteps printed in the ground frost, and went inside and sat down at the kitchen table for a few seconds before standing up again and going to the window to look outside. He watched Yahng Yi come out of the barn and drive the truck over to the hay pile. She exited the truck and went to the pile and began pitching the last of the hay into the bed. He watched her for a few moments and then went back outside, the cold hitting him again.

–I'll be back, he called out. I'm going over to the Finn compound. See if your mother's there.

She ignored him and he felt sad, and from his sadness came guilt for letting himself be enamored of her. He walked past the barn and then into the forest, walking briskly to keep his blood running. The slope was mild going down into the gully and he felt the air growing colder as he approached the creek. It was running fast and he crossed the wooden footbridge, the planks covered with patches of ice where the mist had frozen, and he slipped twice before reaching the other side, both times barely grabbing the handrail in time to keep his feet.

A clump of thorny bushes lined the path to his right going back up the slope, and he noticed a clearing beyond them and something glimmering in the low light coming through the pines. He walked from the path through the brambles and came upon a fire pit covered with black ash. The glimmering object was a beer can and he picked it up and smelled it, the scent of yeast still in there. He tossed the beer can back to the ground and rejoined the path a ways up the slope.

He saw through the final line of trees where the sky met ground with the mountain peaks just visible, then came out of the gully to the clear-cut foothill, which was separated from the forest by a cattleguard that ran the length of the gully down to the road. There were patches of wild rose, burgundy and yellow, and meadow grass on the forest side of the fence where the animals had not grazed. But on the other side of the fence the ground was patchy with dirt and grass nibbled down to the ground. The path continued along the mound up to the hewn-log house on top of the rise, the gabled roof looking down upon the valley.

The house rested on a plateau with its back facing the mountain and the tree line starting farther up the slope. Gabriel made out a stack of firewood just behind the house and Ham Finn there, huge even in the distance, going back and forth from the wood pile to the house. A large horse stood near the wood pile, looking bored.

Gabriel began walking the path toward the house, and Ham spotted him as he was carrying an armload of wood. He waved and Gabriel waved back and kept walking. Ham set the wood down, untied the halter from his horse's post and mounted up. Gabriel kept his eye on the valley, the land looking the same as from the other side of the gully, but not as pretty. Near the valley floor there was a compound surrounded by cross-fenced holding pens with cattle in them and spring calves, and a few riders milling around and some standing. Open-air stables stood where the floor met the rise of the foothill and there were some horses in there. A couple of large, shake-roof log barns were visible past the cattle pens, and a log bunkhouse with a tin roof next to the barns and a tall silver granary jutting out from the flatland near the compound outskirts.

Ham neared him on horseback, and Gabriel kept along the path to meet him. The mare came to Gabriel and circled him quickly and Gabriel nodded his head up at Ham, and then reached out and scratched Ham's mare on its crop.

–Saddlebred? he asked.

Ham nodded. –Five-gaited, he said. Trained for the show ring, but she seems to get along out here on the ranch. Cuts good and I need a tall mount.

–Eighteen hands?

–Nineteen.

–Big saddlebred.

Ham reached down and Gabriel shook his hand. –If you came lookin' for Yahng or her mother, they ain't here, he said.

–That's fine, said Gabriel. Just thought I'd come by and take a look around. If that's all right.

Ham laughed. –Didn't mean to be rude, he said. Of course you're welcome to look around. I forgot you've got some history here. Why don't you come inside and visit for a spell. Ain't had my coffee yet.

Ham dismounted the mare, not losing much height doing so, and led the horse back up the path. Gabriel walked next to him, Ham's strides long and fast and Gabriel almost trotting to keep up. Ham pointed down at the compound.

–Used to be a baler, he said. Contract baler. Then I bought a parcel of land north of here and baled hay after that. Money's in cattle, though.

Gabriel kept silent as Ham talked, his body warming with the quick pace and the sun fully exposed from beyond the ridge, coloring the land, the browns of the worn earth made starker by the sunlight.

–Been balin' hay most of my life, Ham continued. We hayed grass back on our old farm down near Casper. I didn't even know what alfalfa was back then.

He chuckled weakly, almost gurgling, and wiped at his leathered chin. –In those years we used horse-drawn swathers, he said. I remember a cousin of mine, Don Gunderson, lost a leg one year when my uncle was tryin' out a

113

new bronc on the mower. Didn't know it was still gun-shy. Somebody fired off a round from the other side of the hill and the bronc just took off. Damn thing mowed down twenty yards of grass and one of Donnie's legs before it cut a short turn and broke off the harness.

Gabriel shook his head somberly as they reached the end of the house. He noticed the large woodpile, the logs cut neatly in quarters and a chopping block nearby with a sledgehammer leaning against it and an iron wedge on the ground.

–Poor kid, he said.

–Poor kid nothin', said Ham. His old man, my uncle, felt so bad about the whole thing he gave Donnie everything he owned. Donnie's livin' well, last I heard. Down in California. Sold off his daddy's land and equipment and bought a condo in Santa Barbara.

Ham tied the mare back to the post near the woodpile and walked toward the back of the house, motioning Gabriel to follow. Gabriel smelled the wood smoke coming out of the chimney and saw on the other side of the house a cement garage. Two newer-model pickups and a dark blue Cadillac were parked in front of it, on an asphalt driveway that led all the way down to the road.

–Don't know if Yahng's mother told you, but I'm thinking about sellin' the ranch, said Ham as they entered through the back door.

–That right? asked Gabriel, picturing the dearth of good grazing land left on the property.

–Ain't no one to take care of it when I'm gone. Only kin I got now is Jude, and he's got about as much sense as an elk in heat. Most of my hands are too busy drinking, or thinkin' about drinking, or gettin' sober after drinking. They're getting on in years too. Except for Val. Good kid, but the others tell me he's soft in the head. Some nights Val don't sleep at all. Just sits on his cot and stares out the window.

–The big kid?

Ham nodded. –His dad ran off before he was born and his mom's dead, he said. I took him in a few years ago. Biggest twelve-year-old I ever saw.

The back entrance led into a small foyer with a marble floor and a high ceiling covered with molded plaster shaped into stalactites. There was a picture window facing the mountain and a few houseplants below it. Gabriel confirmed the layout of the house within his memory as the two of them walked through the foyer and under an arched doorway into a living room. Ham waited for Gabriel to walk in front of him and placed his hand on Gabriel's shoulder as he passed.

On the walls of the living room were mounted trophy heads, elk and mulies and pronghorn and a giant moose head high near the exposed rafters, the antlers several feet wide. Most of the furniture was dark wood and the walls were paneled in mahogany. In the far corner stood a seven-foot black bear on its hind legs, stuffed and posed, jaws open.

–Bagged that moose in Canada five years ago, said Ham, pointing up. Bear came out of Bear Canyon. Shit, must have been ten years ago. Like to add a grizzly one of these days. Got one in mind.

–Can't kill a grizzly, can you? asked Gabriel.

–If she's killin' my animals I can.

–There's one been eating from round here?

–Lost a few animals already this year. Hired a tracker but he ain't had any luck. Rangers say she must have wandered here from the park. If I ever see her, she's gonna end up in this here room, that's for sure. I'd be careful if

I was you. She'll be makin' her way toward the gully. If she gets into them sheep down there . . .

Ham shook his head and whistled. Gabriel nodded and they walked through the living area and into a dining room where a large oak hutch in the corner displayed decorative table settings and a few porcelain miniatures. Gabriel peered through the glass as they walked by.

–Wife used to collect that shit, said Ham in a whisper. I keep it around. You know. She's been dead a long time. Nice to have somethin' to remind me of her.

They went into the kitchen and Ham prepared the coffee. The house was as Gabriel remembered it save the furniture and wall mountings. There were a few pictures above the fireplace on the mantel and he went to look at them. An old black-and-white of a young Ham and his bride, a Scandinavian-looking woman with lush blond hair and angular cheekbones. Next to it a studio photograph of a young man in army uniform. And then a picture of a baby dressed in Sunday best.

Ham came into the hearth room and handed Gabriel a mug of coffee. –That there's baby Jude, he said. Next to him's my boy Nathan. Dead in Vietnam. Silver Star.

–Sorry to hear that.

–Don't be. Died for his country. Ain't nothin' nobler. You been in the service?

–7th Cavalry.

–The Garryowens, said Ham. I knew a few Garryowens in my day.

Gabriel smiled and nodded. –You? he asked.

–24th Infantry.

–Knew a lotta guys in the 24th.

–You were there in Korea too, then, said Ham, clearing his throat. He went quickly to the mantel and picked up the old black-and-white and stared at it.

–Caroline, he said and shook his head. –Now her dyin'
. . . weren't no reason for that.

–Accident? asked Gabriel.

–Cancer. Nasty one. She fought, though. It was good
havin' little Jude around. Think it kept her going. Probably a few more months than she should of. I been grateful
to Jude for that. Always will be.

–What about Jude's mother?

–Nathan's girl? She weren't never in the picture. You
know the type. More concerned with havin' fun than any
kind of responsibility. Jude still sees her in the summers,
but we all thought he was better off here on the ranch.

Ham gave the picture one last look before setting it
down. –What about you, he said. You been married?

Gabriel paused and his eye moved to the high right corner of the socket, and then he squinted for a moment and
his eyelid fluttered. –Never, he said.

–No kids?

–None.

–No women in your life? asked Ham as he sat down on
a large stuffed chair.

Gabriel shook his head and took a seat in an old
wooden rocking chair next to it. –Just you and Jude live
here? he asked.

–Right now, yeah, said Ham. Ranch hands got a
bunkhouse down near the pens.

–How many hands you got?

–Down to four, including Jude. Like I said, I been
thinkin' about selling it.

–And what about the Cottages' old place?

–I'd have to sell it too.

–You wouldn't consider deeding it to Yahng and her
mother?

–I've thought about it.

–She hasn't paid enough in rent over the years to just let her have it?

Ham reached around to his back pocket and brought out a can of snuff. He packed the can twice on his thigh and then opened it and pinched out a large wad and put it inside his bottom lip.

–Truth is, she ain't never paid rent, he said and offered the can to Gabriel.

Gabriel waved it away and sat up in the rocking chair. –Come on now, he said. I don't believe that.

–Ain't never had enough sheep to get a positive cash flow. All the money that comes out of that ranch goes into utilities and supplies.

–And you just let them stay this whole time for nothing?

–Weren't for nothin', said Ham and stood up. Gabriel watched him pace back and forth in front of the hearth.

–Something wrong?

–Excuse me for a second, said Ham and left the room. Gabriel stood up and went to the door and watched as Ham walked down the hallway. When Ham was out of sight, he turned his attention to the bookshelves that lined the walls of the study. There was a wet bar across the room and he went to it casually, eyeing a bottle of small-batch bourbon. He opened the bottle and smelled it and took a short swig straight from the bottle. Then he went to the gun cabinet and looked in at the mounted firearms. A couple of expensive pump-action shotguns and a .45 and two nickel-plated 9-millimeters. And a single .22 Colt Huntsman with an ivory handle.

He stared at the Colt and reached up with his fingers and touched the cabinet glass, able to imagine the weight of the gun in his hand, able to feel the curve of the grip and the tension of the trigger. He could feel the dense metal pressed against his temple, and how it was cold and the mouth of the barrel small like the tip of a finger. Such a small thing. Such an easy thing.

Ham came back into the room, and Gabriel turned away from the gun cabinet. Ham was holding a large black Bible in his right hand. –Thought you might want this, he said. It's the Cottage family Bible. Was left here when we moved in. I tried to give it back to Emily, but she didn't want it. It's got the whole family line in there.

Gabriel looked at the black leather binding and thought about the Sunday evenings of his teenage years, when Mrs. Cottage would read verses from that same Bible in this same hearth room by lantern light, boring him and Emily to tears. They would wait impatiently for her mother to finish, counting down the syllables until they could go outside and walk the remaining night.

–I appreciate the offer, said Gabriel. But why don't you go ahead and keep it, in case one of their relatives gets ahold of you looking for it. Easier to find you than me.

–Suit yourself, said Ham, setting the Bible on the mantel. So, Jude tells me you're a preacher?

–I'm no preacher, said Gabriel. I spread the Word, yes, but I'm not ordained.

Ham began brushing the dust off the mantel with his palms, lifting his chin up to the ceiling and appearing to grind his jaw. –I was raised a Methodist, he said. But I ain't been to service in some time.

–Sounds like you feel it may be time again.

–You could say that, said Ham and hung his heavy chin back down, still grinding his teeth.

–Something bothering you? asked Gabriel. You can tell me. I won't judge you.

Ham wiped his greasy forehead on the meat of his right arm. –There was a girl I knew over in Tokyo. Girl I met during my service.

–Yeah?

Ham started rolling his big right hand in a circular motion as if to goad his tongue.

–You know how it was over there, he said. You were there.

–Go on, Ham, said Gabriel, furrowing his brow. Say what you have to say. Told you I wouldn't judge you.

–Well, Yahng's mother reminded me of her.

–Reminded you of a girl back in Tokyo?

Ham nodded.

–So? asked Gabriel.

–So I just wanted you to say a little prayer for me.

–Got to know what to pray for, Ham.

–Just pray for my forgiveness.

Ham walked over and laid his hands on Gabriel's shoulders and squeezed firmly. Gabriel shook off the hands, stood up and looked at the large man. They peered into each other's eyes. The sun had risen well above the ridge and light came in through the window at an angle and Gabriel saw the dust floating in the air.

–Did you do something to her? he asked, stepping forward into Ham's space and disregarding his instinct that it was not a good idea to grapple a man of that size. He did not care. What he did was not of his own volition, but some reflex that compelled him to protect that same peasant girl he'd protected before.

–It ain't what you think, said Ham, holding his hands up to block Gabriel's advance. I didn't force her do nothin'. It was an arrangement.

–What kind of arrangement?

–Remember what I told you about how they never paid me rent, said Ham, and turned away and went back to his safe place near the hearth.

Gabriel took in the words and felt a slight twitching in his left arm, the same twitching he'd felt at the roadhouse, his first night back in Thalo Valley. He looked down and saw the hand opening and closing though he was not directing it to do so, the muscles moving on their own in response to the emotion that was taking place in the right half of his brain.

–Emily too? he asked.

–No, said Ham. Just Yahng's mother. And in all fairness, I wanted it to be more than just business. Always wanted it to be just like any other meeting between man and woman. But I know that weren't the case. What she did was out of duty. And I think a part of me always knew that. Being lonely, I didn't care at the time. Now I know it was the wrong thing. Shoulda never let it happen.

–And Yahng? asked Gabriel. She your daughter then?

Ham nodded in confirmation and Gabriel felt the left half of his body begin to tingle, as if that half were being overloaded. It made him dizzy, having no outlet for his emotional right brain to disperse its storming, and he made his way to the door, his left leg stepping strongly and the left hand still fisting.

THEY WENT OUT THE SAME WAY THEY CAME IN, out the back door to where Ham's horse was still tied to its post, still looking bored. Ham spit a huge mess of brown saliva upon the ground and then smiled at Gabriel, the top of the chaw visible halfway up his bottom row of teeth. Gabriel smiled back, but halfheartedly. The dizziness had stopped, replaced by confusion as the emotions began to take shape. There was jealousy in there, something he could not remember feeling. Jealousy that Ham had been with a woman whom he had loved and who loved him still. Jealousy that Ham had fathered Yahng Yi. Not him.

–I'll ride back with you, said Ham. Looks like the boy's comin' up.

Gabriel looked down the hill and saw Jude riding a black quarter horse, heading their way. He stared at the boy and for a moment saw himself there, a young boy riding a horse all cocky up the rise, and the memory calmed him. Ham whistled and raised his hand over his head and motioned for Jude to come toward him. Jude kept the same pace coming up the path, his face pale and blank and the black Stetson low on his head as usual.

Ham grabbed the horse's bridle as it came within arm's length and the stallion jerked his head away and reared back. Jude leaned into it and the stallion came down face-to-face with Gabriel, its eyes blue and looking weak, the blaze upon its head bright white against the dark coat.

–We're takin' this here, said Ham and grabbed the reins.

–Don't worry about it, said Gabe. I'll walk.

–Save a little boot leather, said Ham. Ain't costing you nothin' to ride.

Jude dismounted and went toward the back door, walking unsteadily, his legs still rubbery from the previous night's wine. Ham offered the reins to Gabriel and then went to unhitch his own horse.

Ham spit another wad on the ground and wiped his mouth on his shirtsleeve.

–You can handle a stallion, can't you? he asked.

–This a stud horse? asked Gabriel.

–Will be.

–Got weak eyes. Blue eyes.

–Don't need good eyes to run fast, said Ham and laughed and reached over and slapped the stallion on the crop and the horse headed in a flat-out gallop toward the gully, nearly leaving Gabriel behind.

Gabriel centered himself on the saddle and hunched down and gripped the reins tightly. He let the horse run and heard the wind whipping by him and the thumping of the hooves and a whistling in the spaces around his eye patch. He looked behind him and saw Ham's saddlebred following in a high, disciplined stride, chasing him, like when he and Emily used to run the Cottage horses up and down the banks of the Madison.

Gabriel prodded the horse until the last moment he could before approaching the gully forest and then slowed the stallion and let Ham catch up. The two of them rode several yards in silence toward the beginning break of the tree line. They rode an easy pace, the clopping of the horses muted in the dirt path.

–You won't tell Yahng, will you? asked Ham. I promised her mother not to tell anyone.

–She wouldn't believe it anyway. She hasn't exactly taken a liking to me.

Ham chuckled. –Tell you what, he said. Why don't you take a couple of these horses and take her ridin' up in the mountains. Perfect day for a ride.

–Can't. Last ewes could be dropping.

–I'll send Jude and Val over to watch the grounds. You ain't got but a couple left. Just take her ridin'. It'll get you on her good side. I promise.

They approached the tree line and Gabriel reined in the stallion. Ham circled around and stopped next to Gabriel. They faced each other, their horses' snouts within touching distance. Ham reached over and began stroking the stallion's withers.

Gabriel stared at Ham's blunt face and felt that feeling again, that jealousy, and his left hand began its twitching again. He looked away into the forest and used his right hand to subdue the left. –Maybe we'll go for a ride after all, he said.

–Atta boy. I'll send over a couple quarter horses. Don't worry about the band. My boys've all done sheep before.

Gabriel dismounted the stallion. He handed the reins to Ham and Ham let them go and waved his hand out, sending the stallion back to the valley floor. Ham headed back toward the house and Gabriel watched him for a few yards and then turned toward the gully, removing his eye patch as he absconded into the forest. It was getting warmer and he wiped the moisture from his empty right socket on his shirtsleeve and walked down the incline to the footbridge.

He headed up the creek until he saw a rock big enough to hold him. Then he stepped on the rock and squatted down and closed his eye and dipped his right hand into the water, recalling one of the experiments they'd done at the hospital, when they'd given him the same object to hold in each hand and asked him to describe it, to see how one half of the brain classified things as opposed to the other.

As the water flowed through his right hand, he let the words come to him. Wet. Cold. Creek. Then he removed the right and dried it on his pant leg and dipped in the left. The words were always different with the left, that hand wired to the sentimental half of his brain.

Thirst. Blessing. Forgiveness.

He removed his left hand from the creek and squatted there, listening to the running water hiss like the white noise of a lost radio, then reached down with both hands, palms cupped, and brought some water to his face. He drank a bit and splashed the rest over the empty socket, the cold good on those spots around the edge where the patch bit in and the scar ran, the new nerves inside there weak so they felt only hot and cold and pressure. No pain there. Not on that dead skin.

YAHNG YI SAT UPON THE SLOPE in front of the house, daydreaming and looking up as some low white clouds, swirling and amorphous, drifted into the vista. She remembered when she was much younger, when she and Jihn and her mother drove down to the Tetons one summer, the only time she'd been out of the state. They'd hiked to the top of a ridge, and below them a low thunderstorm had rolled in and blanketed the valley, a churning sea of grayish smoke and mist. The lightning streaked across the cloud cover below them, followed by the shaking of pebbles under their feet. And meanwhile they all stood dry under the blue sky and sun, a world away, the difference between heaven and earth.

She looked over toward the gully as Gabriel came out from the trees. She did not watch him as he walked over to where she was sitting. He sat down next to her and then leaned back on his elbows and turned his face up to the sky.

–Daydreaming? he asked.

–No, she answered. Where's Mother?

–Wasn't over there.

Yahng Yi raked her fingers across a clover patch, the leaflets cool on her fingertips.

–Kind of strange being in that house after all those years, said Gabriel and dug into the earth with his fingernail, moving the grass roots away and feeling the graininess of the sod. He came upon a small shard of broken glass, and held it up to the light. The glass was grimed but it still refracted the sunlight, looking like quartz. He threw the shard high into the air and the swirling breeze pushed it to the north as it flew.

–You were right, he said. Finn's land is hurting pretty bad. Hardly any grazing left. He says he's thinking about selling it.

–I've heard.

–What would you do if he sells?

–Don't know. Can't afford to buy the land off him.

–Would you stay here if you could?

–Don't know that neither.

–He should give it to you. You and your mother.

–Why would he do that? He don't owe us nothin'. Besides, Mother says any money he gets is goin' right to the bank. Ole boy's near bankrupt. That's why he wants to sell.

–That right? asked Gabriel. He didn't mention that.

–Of course he wouldn't. He's a man. Wouldn't say nothin' to let you think otherwise.

Gabriel pushed himself up into a squatting position and began running his knuckles along the ground. He closed his eye and let a short breeze come across his face, breathing it deep as its momentum wound down.

–Sounds like you don't have much fondness for him, he said.

–Sure, Patch. You could say that.

–That why you've been a bear toward me? Because I remind you of him?

–You're talkin' senile again, Patch. You and him are a world different.

–So you're fond of me after all.

Yahng Yi made a face at him and began combing the clover again. –I ain't scared of leavin' this place, she said. I'd leave in a heartbeat.

–I don't believe that. This is your home. Hard to leave home.

Yahng Yi lay back, her hair splayed out and a few tendrils brushed into a patch of grass nibbled down to stubs where one of the birthing ewes had taken a meal before dropping. She stared at the sky, and the clouds still rolling by, white and downy as they moved across the valley to the south, like the migrating birds and the elk leaving before the beginning of the winter storms.

They lay together in silence for a few moments, and then Yahng Yi looked over at him and saw him watching the sky as well and some kind of melancholy about him.

–You got a lot of sadness today, she said, her voice soft and the words unsure, probing, like toes testing the temperature of water.

Gabriel looked over at her. –Wouldn't call it sadness, he said.

–Then what would you call it?

–Unhappiness, maybe.

–What's the difference?

Gabriel shrugged his shoulders.

–Well what are you unhappy about? she asked.

–There's always something to be unhappy about, I guess.

–Oh, she said, looking away, believing her first foray into an earnest connection with him had failed. There was a pause, and in the interim she tried to think no more about it, somewhat relieved that he had no deeper answer, but at the same time unable to shake the feeling that he had some secret to behold to her, some sad secret that would make her own secrets worth telling.

He broke the silence, and in doing so made her relieved that he did not change subjects. –What about you? he asked. What do you get sad about?

–Don't know. Sometimes I just get sad. You think there's somethin' wrong with me?

–No. That's part of being human. We are made of our pain. It's how God made us.

–You believe that?

–I do. It's the way God is. He makes it hard on us sometimes, to let us know this life's not to be held on to. He's just letting us get used to the whole pattern of things, needing to wound us before He heals us. Taking stuff away and then giving it back to us, only better. Like the fact that we must die in order to live forever.

Yahng Yi watched a cloud pass above them, moving slower than the others and on a different plane. A viscous, swirling cloud that appeared at first to have appendages, twisting arms and legs, like an unearthed root. She remembered how she and Jihn would watch the clouds in the spring. The two of them on their backs like she and Gabriel were now. Not saying much, but the little they said poignant. He would tell her his hopes for the future, how he wanted so much for her and for their mother. How he had been heartbroken to see their mother being ridiculed, how he himself had been ridiculed by the valley men, by the valley women. He had never been eloquent, or as smart as Yahng Yi, but she understood him. She understood that this place was a different kind of place. It was singular. Single-minded. Like a lovely old woman who had lived her years the same way every day. A beautiful artifact.

She had made him promise to take them away. She had told him that the world was filled with places, and people belonged in some places and some they didn't, and they did not belong in this place. Just the three of them. No more sheep. No more Auntie. It had made her happy to think about such things, the three of them together always and everywhere. All around the world searching for that place that existed only for them. Those were happy times, dreaming in those times. Lying on the grass and watching the clouds, like she was now, and just dreaming.

She looked over at Gabriel, at his profile, the patch over his left eye invisible. She looked at his eye, at the crow's foot at the corner, and how it turned downward there, looking sad at one glance and hopeful at another, and sympathetic as well, as if all the concerns in Thalo Valley had collected there on the edge of his eye, and sagged it like a tree limb weighted with snow.

–Do you hate me? she asked him.

–No, said Gabriel without hesitation. But I will say that sometimes you aren't good company.

–I wasn't always like that, she said.

–I know, he said. We are never as good company as we were as children.

Gabriel reached over and patted her lightly on the hand. They stared up at the clouds together and in silence until they heard an animal walking up the rise. Gabriel sat up and spotted the ewe coming toward them, halfway up the incline already. Yahng Yi sat up as well and brushed the grass out of her hair and off her shirt.

All but two of the pregnant ewes had given birth already. Of the eight births, six had been twins, and two singles. Yahng Yi had let the orphan rejoin the band and could see it in the distance. She turned her attention back to the ewe, which had angled off toward the barn. As she stood up and followed it, she saw that the membrane had ruptured, the birth sac protruding. The ewe hung its head low to the ground and sidestepped suddenly, as if to catch its balance. Gabriel jogged up behind her.

–Something isn't right, he said. She doesn't look good.

–Check her out, said Yahng Yi. I'm gonna go down and get the orphan.

Yahng Yi ran over to the truck and peeled out in the gravel, sending chunks of rock flying into the air, nearly hitting the ewe. She sped down the slope to the end of the drive. The sheep scattered slowly as she made her way into their midst. The little orphan was not hard to find. It was still trying to steal a quick snack from a mother ewe, the top of its head stained brown with feces from sneaking in behind.

Yahng Yi stepped down from the truck and scooped the orphan in her arms and drove back up the incline. She hoped the pregnant ewe would give birth to a single. If there were twins or triplets, the orphan would remain motherless, three lambs being too much for one ewe. She parked the truck near the barn and got out with the lamb cradled in her arm.

Gabriel was kneeling by the side of the ewe, a puddle of blood near his feet. –Dead in the womb, he said.

Yahng Yi walked up to them and looked down at the ground and saw the dead lamb, the eyes closed, the limbs twisted out of their natural position.

–I had to break its legs to get it out, said Gabriel, his arm covered in a coat of rotten brown fluid.

Yahng Yi handed the orphan to Gabriel, and Gabriel rubbed his soiled arm on the orphan's wool. Yahng Yi took the dead lamb from the ground, pulled up her jeans leg to get her boot knife, and began to skin the carcass, cutting it around its neck and limb sockets, and then down its underbelly. She peeled off the hide and draped the heavy mess onto the orphan.

–How's the mother? she asked.

–Seems okay, said Gabriel.

Yahng Yi took the squirming orphan, bulkier with its double hide, and let it suckle a few times from the ewe's teat. The ewe was lying on her side, eyes open, and Yahng Yi could see the faint movement of her breathing. Yahng Yi pulled the orphan's mouth off the teat with her fingers and placed the lamb near the ewe's snout. The ewe smelled the scent of her own milk on the lamb's mouth, and tried to clean some of the birthing mucous from the lamb's face.

–Should we pen them up? asked Gabriel.

–Yeah, said Yahng Yi, standing up with the lamb in her arms. Can you handle that ewe on your own?

Gabriel nodded.

–You sure? she asked.

–Go on, said Gabriel. She's just a baby. I got her.

Yahng Yi picked up the lamb and headed to the barn. Gabriel squatted down facing the ewe's underbelly, and tried to slide his arms underneath it. The ewe blatted noisily and jerked its hind legs. Gabriel fell to his backside and looked back to see if Yahng Yi had seen him, but she was already in the barn. He went to the ewe again and knelt down on one knee next to the ewe's head and stroked the side of her face and pressed his thumb along her cheekbone. The ewe closed her eyes and steadied her breathing. This time he braced himself on his knees and lowered his chest into its side and slid his arms between the ewe's ribs and the ground, up his biceps and then to his shoulders. He lifted her up, planting one foot then the next, trying to keep as much pressure as he could off her uterus.

Yahng Yi was waiting for him, holding the paddock door open with one hand and the lamb in the other. Gabriel got down on one knee and lowered the ewe onto the ground. The ewe kicked at him weakly as he released his grip. Yahng Yi held the lamb in front of the ewe's snout, letting her sniff the dead hide, and then laid the lamb down near the udder. The lamb began suckling and the ewe rested her head on the ground and closed her eyes.

–You think she'll take? Gabriel asked.

–Hope so, said Yahng Yi and closed up the paddock. The two of them went behind the barn into the thicket of trees where the meltwater brook flowed. They squatted down before the stream and rinsed the slime from their hands and arms, the stink of natal blood and tissue-rot heavy as it dissolved into the running water.

Gabriel wrung the soiled water from his arms and dried them on his pants. Yahng Yi shook her hands, and then began clapping them together to get the blood flowing back into the constricted vessels. They walked out of the tree cover and over to the birthing spot. Yahng Yi picked up the skinned lamb by the hind legs.

–What are you going to do with that? asked Gabriel.

–Bury it. Ain't no sense startin' a dead lamb pile now.

–Bury it deep then.

Yahng Yi went behind the barn and tossed the lamb onto a patch of dirt. Gabriel waited there for her as she went into the barn to get a shovel and pickax. She handed him the shovel and he stamped the blade into the ground. Yahng Yi stood behind him holding the pickax, upwind from the dead lamb.

–What happened to the garden over there? asked Gabriel. He pointed a few yards in front of him at a square patch of tilled earth in the open land between the barn and the house.

–Ain't planted nothin' since Auntie died.

–That's too bad. Looks like some nice soil in there.

–Dead animals buried all around there, said Yahng Yi.

Gabriel stopped shoveling and wiped his brow on his arm. Yahng Yi got to her feet and dusted off her backside. She stepped behind Gabriel and looked into the hole. Gabriel thrust the tip of the shovel into the ground and it caught, the steel head vibrating up the wood handle to his hands. He knelt down in front of the hole and picked out a small rock.

Yahng Yi raised her chin and looked at him through the bottoms of her eyes. Next to the rock was a sliver of white showing through the ground. Gabriel mined around it with his fingers and revealed a patch of bones.

He looked over at Yahng Yi and saw that she had her head turned over her shoulder, staring behind her into the forest. He moved his hand around the hole and pulled out a small appendage bone and blew on it to clear the dirt and held it up to his eye. He rolled it around in his fingers and then slipped it into his pocket and then stood up.

–Probably a chicken bone, said Yahng Yi. Bunch of dead chickens round here. Mother used'm for death scapegoats. Anytime one of us was real sick, she'd buy a chicken and rub it all over us and then go out and bury it alive.

–Why?

–To trick death.

Yahng Yi picked up the skinned lamb and dropped it in the hole. Gabriel covered the burial ground with a mound of dirt and matted it down with the shovel blade and then stomped on it with his boots. He stood there, catching his breath, his hands on the end of the shovel handle and his chin resting on top of his hands.

–I worry about your mother, he said. Seems like she takes the witchy stuff too far.

–She's always been like that, said Yahng Yi. Always talkin' in her sleep. Chanting mantras and whatnot. She has real bad nightmares sometimes. Wakes up screaming bloody murder and scares me shitless.

–Haven't noticed.

–Well she hasn't done it since you been here. Don't know if it's because you're here, or because she just don't have the dreams no more.

–What's she got such bad nightmares about?

–Don't know. She don't talk about things like that.

–Sometimes I hear her getting up and going outside in the middle of the night.

–She goes up the mountain after midnight to pray to the mountain god sometimes. There's a shrine up next to the waterfall that feeds the gully creek. She built it after Jihn died. You ain't seen it yet?

–No.

–She used to take me up there. Made me carry the stew pot so she could cook rice for him and Grandmother. Always gave me the creeps. Anyway, it ain't that far away. You wanna see?

Yahng Yi brushed the hair away from her cheeks, and Gabriel looked at her face dead-on, hypnotized by her prettiness and taken back to when he was her age. She let him look, her just standing there, face lit up in the sun. He imagined being a boy and burning, and the girls in the summertime and their sundresses pressing hard from the front, hard around their hips, so he could make out the swell of their breasts as their hair whipped all around in the wind. Them tossing their heads to brush away the locks from their face, and him staring from afar at the flatness between their legs, and the good pain and the good burning that comes from seeing that flatness, the burning that could be felt fully only by a boy.

He looked away and shook his head and from the corner of his eye he saw two men on horseback ascending the driveway. It was Jude Finn and Val, on quarter horses. Gabriel watched the horses amble slowly up the drive, the two boys both wearing Stetsons low across the brow, Jude's black and Val's tan, and both of them wearing dark canvas shirts and blue jeans.

Jude picked up the pace of his horse and approached Gabriel and Yahng Yi, and Gabriel saw how Yahng Yi looked at him, with some amusement and a semblance of condescension. Jude circled them and then stopped the horse in between.

–Granddaddy said to bring these horses by, he said as he dismounted. Said you'd wanna go ridin'.

–Tell your granddad we appreciate it, said Gabriel. But we've got work to do here.

–Come on, Patch, said Yahng Yi, her words toward Gabriel but her eyes on Jude and her look mischievous. Let's go. I ain't been ridin' in so long.

–What about the band? asked Gabriel. Got one ewe yet to drop.

–Jude here knows plenty about ewes. Ain't that right, Jude? Real fond of'm. I seen it with my own two eyes when he thought weren't no one around.

Jude scowled at her, and Gabriel walked over to her and grabbed her lightly on the arm and guided her toward one of the mounts. He looked over at the ranch hand, Val, and saw that the big boy was staring off into nothingness, and Gabriel knew that he was trying his hardest not to look at Yahng Yi.

Yahng Yi gripped the saddlehorn of the horse Jude had been riding and stepped up and swung her leg over the saddle.

–Come on, Patch, she said. We'll go up to the waterfall. Mount up.

Gabriel nodded. –Got one left in the drop band, he said to Jude as he mounted up. Tell your granddad we'll bring these horses back in the afternoon.

Jude tipped his hat and Gabriel guided the horse toward Yahng Yi, who was already headed toward an opening in the forest behind the barn. As he caught up with her he looked back and saw Jude still watching them ride away and Val finally able to look at Yahng Yi now that her back was turned.

–Jude Finn your boyfriend? asked Gabriel when they were out of earshot.

–No.

–That's good.

–You jealous, Patch?

–No.

–Well what do you care if he's my boyfriend or not, then?

Gabriel thought about what Ham had told him earlier in the day, the fact that Yahng Yi and Jude were blood relations, that he was her nephew. But he would not tell her that, being a man of his word. –Just something about him, he said. Don't trust him much.

–Don't start with me, Patch. I'll live my life the way I see fit.

–I'm sorry, said Gabriel. Didn't mean nothing by it. Just the way he looks at you. Seems pretty worked up.

–It happens.

–The other one looks it too.

–Who? Val?

–Yeah.

–There somethin' about Val you don't trust neither? asked Yahng Yi.

–No, he said, remembering the roadhouse lot and Val helping him escape from the whore and the big brothers. He seems all right.

–They're peas in a pod, Patch. Can't like one and dislike the other.

–I don't believe they're alike, said Gabriel.

–You trying to matchmake us or somethin', Patch? Why you dropping crumbs in my ear about Val Rey?

–I'm not, said Gabriel. But if I was, I think the two of you'd be all right.

–Jude says he's a half-wit.

–I don't believe that.

–Well, he don't talk.

–Plenty of reasons not to talk. Doesn't mean you're dumb.

Yahng Yi shrugged.

–Anyway, said Gabriel. Some people belong together and some people don't. You always find out sooner or later.

As he spoke the words, an image flashed before him— an old house with a tin roof, low buttes in the backdrop and tall grasses and an old goat tied to a tether. He saw a gray cat and a rickety porch swing, and then the face of a woman. A white woman. Pretty. Kind. Similar to Emily, but not Emily. He could not remember the place or time, but it was not like his other lost memories. There was no foreboding, no suggestion of guilt. It was good, this place, this woman, this time. All of it was good.

While he was caught in the memory, Yahng Yi clicked her heels to get her horse trotting through the underbrush until they reached a worn spot in the forest and a deer run leading out from it. Gabriel shook off the image of the strange woman and followed. There were some bear prints in the mud where a stream had broken through from a creek and sent water down toward the valley across the worn earth where the animals ran. Some cloud cover rolled in as they followed the run along the girth of the mountain, and then headed straight up the mountainside at an incline through a narrow column unclaimed by the trees, and then into an open patch on the slope that was covered with bitterroot blossoms. They crossed that open field and reentered the forest and stopped near a fallen tree stump, looking back across the field. Gabriel tucked his chin into his chest and let down the reins as they stared across the opening and the prettiness of the meadow.

–Used to come up here a lot when I was young, he said and remembered his grandfather kneeling among the new firs, looking out across the mountain meadow, patches of tall wild grasses, and a buck elk standing halfway up from the stalks. He could smell the bitterroot blossoms, and he thought about how he and Emily would spend summer nights in the clearing, staring up past the canopy to the open sky.

He dismounted and strolled into the clearing and knelt down and touched the cool earth and picked a blossom from the ground.

–Bitterroot, he said as he walked back to the horses.

He reached up and gave Yahng Yi the flower and she took it and sniffed it and then tucked the tiny blossom into her hair. The air began to warm and they continued up the mountain through the pines, Gabriel leading this time. They ascended the slope and the fallen needles that covered the forest floor, the faint noise of the waterfall now audible in the distance.

Yahng Yi pointed to the south and Gabriel nodded and they rode toward the crashing sound, along another path to where the waterfall came down from high up on the mountain ledge, spilling over the rocks and onto more water below.

Gabriel looked up at the falls and felt the force of displaced air against his skin, the wet wind blowing hard. The water falling. Carving the brown rock on both sides. White and angry near the top and then coming down, millions of drops together, down to the waiting pool below where it became whole and peaceful as it moved away from the falls.

They dismounted and led their horses to the edge of the pool. Yahng Yi pointed to a pile of stones and a bound twig effigy of a kneeling figure in front of a rock face adjacent to the waterfall. There were a couple of empty platters set in front of the stone pile and some droppings several feet away to the right.

–She leaves the food there and the animals come and eat it, said Yahng Yi above the ambient noise of the crashing water.

Gabriel felt the hairs on his neck stand in attention as he stared down at the wooden effigy. –That supposed to be your brother? he asked.

–No, said Yahng Yi. That's a Buddha.

–I see what you mean about it being creepy.

–Told you. Something evil goin' on up here.

–Wouldn't call it evil, said Gabriel. Bad, but not evil.

–Well what the hell's the difference?

–Evil's evil through and through. Bad's sometimes just a good person's mistake.

Gabriel reached down and picked up the wooden Buddha.

–What you gonna do? asked Yahng Yi.

–Your mother needs help, and this thing isn't helping her.

Gabriel broke off the head and the limbs of the wooden Buddha and tossed the pieces into the water, watching as they became caught in the vortex and went under for a moment until resurfacing where the water continued on into the gully.

–Shouldn't of done that, said Yahng Yi.

–I'm bound by a covenant. Part of that covenant's to break the hold of false idols.

–She's gonna be pissed.

–She's not herself. She's possessed by something un-
godly.

–Then she's gonna be really pissed.

Gabriel picked up the empty platters and tossed them
deep into the woods and then swept with the side of his
boot some pine needles onto the bare spot where the
shrine was built.

–Your brother deserves to be remembered properly, he
said. Emily too. Your mother ought to let them rest in
peace.

Yahng Yi nodded, staring into the forest. –They was
lovers, you know, she said.

–No, said Gabriel, looking over at her quickly. I don't
believe that.

–That's why she killed them.

–Come on, now.

–It's true, Patch. That's why Mother killed them.

–No, said Gabriel, shaking his head. They weren't lovers
and your mother didn't kill nobody. A quick snow isn't
anyone's fault.

–Was her fault they was out there to begin with, said
Yahng Yi.

Gabriel looked over at her.

–I remember that night, she continued. She gave them
something that made them act funny. Two of them just
kept starin' off into nothing. Then Jihn went off into the
storm and Auntie followed him. Never came back.

–Thought they went out to dig the sheep from smothering, he said.

–Nope. They just took off.

–You sure? Maybe you don't remember right.

–Something like that you always remember right, she
said and then mounted her horse and rode quickly away

from the falls, onto a wider path that led across the mountain and angled upward toward the ridge. Gabriel followed her, and they rode silently until the sound of crashing water was no longer audible and the moisture layering their skin had dissipated in a breeze. They exited the forested section of the mountain into a clear-cut gentle rise, wildflowers all around them, the cloud cover gone and the sun come out, clearing their bodies and minds of the reach of the waterfall.

EIGHT

Ham Finn spent the afternoon driving around the mountains on the old logging switchbacks, staring down into the valley and thinking about what his life had become. Since Gabriel had arrived at the Cottage ranch, he'd been wading through sleepless nights and unsettled days, Gabriel's presence reminding him of his sins, in war and in love.

He'd returned to the town limits of Harter just before suppertime and parked his truck in front of the abandoned depot just east of Main Street. He pulled his hat down over his eyes and drifted off in a light slumber, thinking of Caroline, his dead wife and the one person in the world who had made his life redemptive. It was hard for him to remember how she looked before the cancer. In his dreams it was usually the sick Caroline, the shell.

But not this time. Not this dream. He willed himself to dream of her not with eyes jutting out from the sockets or the old summer dresses hanging over her like burial shrouds, the flowered prints perverse over those sharpened bones. He dreamed her as she was when she was lovely, with lush blond hair the thickness of baled hay and the blood in her lips not yet thinned. Her skin tanned in the sun, dark and dulcet like sugarcane.

He hunched down in the truck cab and dreamed her young and lovely, and the two of them picking wild berries all through the foothills outside Casper, her with the baskets and him running off just far enough so that he would still see her over his shoulder. They chased each other across the hills and he would have kept running with her forever, would have lived inside the dream forever, if he could.

There was a hollow metal thud and he awoke and saw a small raven picking at the butterfly carcasses that had collected on the truck's windshield. He exited the truck as the raven flew away, and he watched it take off into the oak trees across the train tracks.

On the other side of the tracks was a field of prairie grass and then a neighborhood of abandoned Victorian houses that had been overrun by oaks. There hadn't been rich folk in the town since the last century. Most of the townspeople lived in the small bungalows behind Main or in the trailer park a mile down the road. The city hall was at the end of the row of buildings on Main, the hall itself crumbling, the stone facade in need of repair, a monument to the town's erosion.

There were school kids playing in the field behind the depot, throwing rocks at the back wood wall, all the windows having already been stoned to the frames years before. Ham stuck his fingers in his mouth and whistled as he came around the side of the depot into the field. The field had become a makeshift dump and the ground was littered with junk, old appliances and box springs.

The kids came running over to him, about a dozen of them, mostly boys and one small girl, their ages as young as five and as old as fourteen. The schoolhouse in Harter had been shut down since before World War II and the state had mandated a bus to ship the school-age kids the twenty miles into Bozeman.

–You all have fun in school today? Ham asked, the kids collecting around him in a semicircle.

–Bus never came, said one of the older boys.

Ham nodded and reached into his deep pockets for the hard cream candies he always carried around. He passed them out, one for each of the kids, and then told them to behave themselves. They nodded and ran off into the junk piles. Ham wiped his brow on his shirtsleeve, popped a candy into his mouth and walked down Main Street.

He crossed the only intersection in town and turned left into the doorway of the old diner. He opened the door, the bells ringing upon his entrance, and nodded at the old men who sipped coffee near the front window. He sat down on a stool at the counter and pulled out his handkerchief and dabbed at his forehead.

–Takin' the day off, Ham? asked the waitress as she came up to where he was sitting and wiped down the counter with a worn rag. She had a weathered, freckled face and graying brown hair curled tightly in a home perm.

–Hi, Trudy, he said. Gimme the chicken-fried steak.

Ham bit down on the hard candy and crunched it around his mouth as Trudy went to the order window, where the diner's old fry cook was poking his head out from the kitchen.

–You been stayin' outta trouble, Cort? Ham called out.

The fry cook, Cortney Clyde, stuck his hand out the window and showed Ham the middle finger. Ham laughed and shook his head. –You're gonna get it, you ole coot, he said.

Trudy came back over to him and Ham watched her wide hips move back and forth, the apron cinched tight around her waist and her breasts hanging down nearly to the ties. He shifted in his seat and then held his hands out to receive the cup of coffee she held out to him.

–How's that old man of yours? he asked.

–Don't know, said Trudy. Ain't seen him in a few days.

Ham smiled and winked at her and she nodded. Ham went around to the doorway leading into the kitchen. Trudy untied her apron and they went out the back door together. Cortney Clyde chuckled as they passed him, his eyes down at Ham's steak frying in a cast-iron skillet.

Ham and Trudy went outside behind the trash dumpster and Ham unbuckled his pants and pulled them down around his ankles, his belt limp among the bunching of his trousers and the leather tip flailing a patch of decaying lettuce on the ground. Trudy pulled her underpants down to her knees and hiked up her skirt. Ham grabbed her hips and swiveled her around so her back was to his front. She braced herself against the dumpster and then groaned a little, trying to stifle her noises, mindful of the houses within earshot.

Ham gripped her hard as he moved, his big belly shifting up and down with the rhythm, and he closed his eyes and imagined Yahng Yi's Mother, and then Trudy reached back and grabbed his hand and brought it forward to support her breasts. He resisted.

–Somethin' wrong? she asked.

Ham ignored her, clenching her waist as he finished, then moved away from her quickly and pulled up his pants. Trudy smoothed out her skirt and then went back

145

into the diner. Ham matted his hair down and waited a few moments before going back in as well.

Cortney Clyde was sitting on the prep counter, smoking a cigarette, when Ham came in.

–That was fast, he said to Ham. Food ain't even cold.

–You know I don't let nothin' get in the way of a hot meal, Cort.

Ham went back into the diner and sidled up to his plate at the counter. As he took his first bite of steak, the diner door opened, clanging the cheap brass bell. Yahng Yi's Mother entered to the hard stares of the patrons and employees both, and she sat down at the stool next to Ham. She had her hair pulled into a tight bun and a dark shawl across her shoulders falling down to her thighs.

–Evenin', said Ham without looking at her.

Trudy looked at Yahng Yi's Mother and pointed at the coffeepot. Yahng Yi's Mother shook her head, watching Ham eat, the big man working the plate like it was his last, rendering the meat in his mouth like a grinder.

–What do you want, Mr. Finn? she asked.

–Wanted to let you know my plans, said Ham with his mouth full.

–And what are they?

Ham grunted, mopping up the gravy from his plate with a biscuit. –Why don't you order some food, he said.

–I am busy, Mr. Finn, she said. Say what you need to say.

Ham mopped up the last of his gravy with a biscuit nub and then pushed his plate away. –I want you to come with me, he said. You and Yahng.

–Come where?

–California.

–What would we do in California?

–Live.

–No, she said.

146

–Why not?

–For one thing, I do not want your grandson to live with my daughter.

–All right, said Ham. He's gettin' old enough. He can get out on his own.

Yahng Yi's Mother did not respond.

–What else? he asked.

She remained silent.

–What else? he asked again.

–No, she said, looking down at the floor. I will not go.

–You gotta come with me, said Ham. I'm leavin' for good. Might never see you again.

–Then you will never see me again.

Ham nodded and wiped his mouth with his fingertips. –Be off my land by Monday then, he said. I'm goin' to California this weekend. When I get back, I'll expect you to be gone.

He removed his wallet and took out a twenty and tossed it casually on the counter. As he turned from her, he did not let his hard face waver, though in his mind he was seething.

GABRIEL AND YAHNG YI RODE ALL DAY, lazily following an elk herd that was wandering among the foothills on the lee side of the mountain, until they reached the west bank of the Madison. The river ran fast, swollen with meltwater, and the sun had descended past the low western ridge, casting a shadow upon the river and a blue tint to the river rocks along the banks and the high cliffs upstream. Gabriel had forded the river first at a thirty-yard crossing and waited as Yahng Yi's mare moved toward him at an angle with the current, watching her lean back in the saddle to put tension to the reins.

–You all right? Gabriel called out above the roar of whitewater.

–She don't like the water much, said Yahng Yi.

–Give her a kick. We've got to head back. It's getting late.

Yahng Yi squeezed her legs together, and the mare whinnied, jerking its head to the side. The horse fought the bit for a moment, flaring out its nostrils and curling its lips, and then Yahng Yi kicked her heels again. The mare reared high in the air, lifting its forelegs out of the river. Yahng Yi leaned forward to keep her balance, her arms spread out and still holding a rein in each hand.

–Try again, Gabriel called out.

–I don't want to fall, Patch. I can't swim good. Especially in this fast water.

–Don't worry. If you fall, I'll get you.

Yahng Yi reached down just below the mare's neck and combed her fingers through a lock of its hair at the withers and then tugged hard to her right. The mare's head pivoted toward Gabriel.

Gabriel whistled and the mare sidestepped toward him. Yahng Yi kicked and pulled again with her right arm, and the mare jumped in that direction, lifting them both nearly out of the water. As it landed on its forelegs it lost its footing, sending its head splashing into the river. Yahng Yi tumbled over the mare's neck, reaching back for the saddlehorn but unable to grip it flush. She rolled over and hit the water on her back, and Gabriel saw the current pick her up and carry her downstream. Her head bobbed up and into the river, hair plastered across her face. The mare had regained its balance without the extra weight and leaped toward the riverbank and up onto the short mud slope, snorting and shaking the moisture from its coat.

Gabriel moved by reflex, getting his horse galloping downstream along the bank. Up ahead was the steel rail bridge that spanned the river, just ten yards above the water level. Yahng Yi's head moved in the current steadily toward it. He reached the bridge and dismounted, removing a thirty-foot riata secured to the back of the saddle. He ran alongside the rail ties down the tracks and lined himself up with Yahng Yi's approaching body. On the other side of the bridge he saw the whitewater and the bigger rocks poking out from the foam just a hundred yards away.

He dropped the riata over the guardrail, but the end still hung too high above the water. Yahng Yi's head came closer, moving faster now as the river narrowed under the bridge. Gabriel got down on his stomach and threaded the rope through the crossbars of the guardrail, reaching his hand and the rope down toward the river, stretching as far as he could. He peeked over the edge and saw Yahng Yi's head a few yards upstream.

Yahng Yi reached up feebly as she passed under the bridge, but couldn't take the rope. Gabriel got back to his feet and ran back across the railroad ties to the riverbank, watching as her head picked up speed toward the whitewater and the rocks.

He jumped off the bridge a few yards from where the steel girders met the ground, landing awkwardly on the embankment. His boot soles couldn't keep their footing as he slid down the dirt slope on his backside, bracing himself with his open palms. His feet hit a small ledge halfway down and he rolled onto his side, tumbling down the embankment the rest of the way in a barrel roll before landing on the small rock flats that lined the riverbank. He looked toward the whitewater, but did not see Yahng Yi.

Then he heard her voice slightly upstream.

–Save me! she cried. Save me, oh please. Patch, save me!

Gabriel turned his head toward the voice. Yahng Yi was standing in the river, the water barely to her waist. She laughed, her black hair all wet and in tangles down the sides of her face, her white shirt clinging to her torso and the sleeves hanging heavy upon her arms.

Gabriel shook his head. –I thought you were gonna hit those rocks, he said.

–Nah, said Yahng Yi. I knew the river petered out a bit around here. Gets wider past the bridge and narrows back up near the rocks.

–Why didn't you say something then? Old man like myself can't take too much excitement, you know.

–I'm sorry, Patch. You was actin' such a hero, I didn't want to spoil your fun. Didn't know you was gonna be so graceful coming down.

Gabriel waded out into the river to meet her. The river was shallow, but still ran fast, and his boot soles slipped on the slick rocks. He lost his footing and had to lower himself into the water and lean into the current to regain his balance.

–Just wait there, old man, said Yahng Yi, laughing. I'll come to you.

Gabriel stopped and waited as she moved slowly toward him. She looked so pretty under the waning light of the dusk, her face rose-colored through the copper, the blood run up from her struggle and settling within her cheeks to warm it from the coldness of the river water. She came to him and jumped into his arms.

–My hero, she said and pressed her weight onto his shoulders so that he slipped and his head went under water. His feet flailed at the ground, trying to gain footing on the rocks, and he felt himself moving downstream. He struggled below the surface, kicking wildly until he was able to clear his head from the water's plane.

Yahng Yi was already near the bank when he resurfaced, and he squatted down to regain his balance and then followed her, stepping sideways. The two of them reached the rocks that lined the earthen embankment and hiked back up the river until they found a slope not too steep to climb. Yahng Yi dug her boots into the loam and scaled the embankment, grabbing clumps of grass for support. Gabriel leveraged her up by her backside when she got high enough, then ambled up the embankment and over the side next to her.

They led the horses away from the river, and Gabriel tied the horses' halters to a low branch near a clearing where a lodgepole pine had fallen. Yahng Yi sat down on the fallen trunk and wrung the water from her hair. She smiled at him, and Gabriel looked into her eyes and felt the ritual burning coming up from his stomach. His eyes moved downward along her moistened neck and to the wet white shirt that clung to her chest.

–We should mount up and head back, he said, looking away. It'll be getting dark soon.

–Ride back in these wet clothes? said Yahng Yi. We'll both catch cold. Maybe we should dry off awhile. You can build a fire.

–Your mother will worry.

–In a few minutes. We need to warm up first. You can build a fire, can't you, Patch?

–Just for a few minutes, then we go, said Gabriel and went to his gelding. He removed from under the saddle the blanket that was used for padding, and then reached into a saddlebag and fished around in it until he found a book of matches.

–Blanket's dry, he said, and tossed it to Yahng Yi, and then went into the trees to collect some kindling. The ground clutter was ripe with dry broken twigs, and he bundled some into his arms and then reached down to grab a handful of browned pine needles.

When he returned, he saw Yahng Yi huddling under the picnic blanket, sitting on the fallen tree trunk, her shirt and blue jeans laid out next to her, dense with river water. He swept the ground clutter with his boots until there was a bare spot in the dirt, and then clumped the pine needles on the ground and leaned a few twigs against the mound.

–You cold? he asked.

Yahng Yi nodded, and he heard the chattering of her delicate teeth. He lit a match and held it to the pine needles, inhaling the pleasant scent of the sulfur match as the fire took. Then he placed some twigs around the growing flame.

–I'll gather some deadwood, he said and saw her dark legs glistening in the low firelight as she raised the blanket to knee level.

–What about you? she asked. Ain't you cold in those wet clothes?

–No.

–It's gettin' colder, Patch. You're gonna need to dry off too. Why don't you come in here and we'll share body heat.

–Don't think that's a good idea.

–Man your age shouldn't be tempting death. You'll be asking for it in them wet clothes.

Gabriel chuckled weakly. –Don't worry about me, he said. Cold never bothered me.

Yahng Yi opened up the blanket, exposing her small white bra and underwear to the low firelight, and Gabriel could see the little dark circles behind the cups and the darkness down below her waistline as well. He turned away from her and went quickly to the woods to gather the wood.

When he returned he did not look at her and went straight to the fire, stacking the thicker logs crosswise and leaning against each other. Then he dragged a large dead branch from near the fallen pine tree and set it down near the fire so that a few of the smaller limbs stuck out toward the flames. He retrieved Yahng Yi's shirt and pants from the trunk and spread them out on the limbs. He sat down on the fallen tree with his hands in his lap, a yard from where Yahng Yi was sitting. From the corner of his eye he could see that she hung the blanket over her shoulders, with her front side open to the fire. He sensed her wet body slick and glowing in the firelight, her legs crossed and the top one bouncing and the thin bra still damp and clinging to her breasts, the nipples hard and visible under the wet cloth.

–Fire feels good, he said in a breaking voice.

–You're shiverin', said Yahng Yi.

–I'm not.

–You are, said Yahng Yi and turned to face him. You're gonna catch pneumonia if you don't get out of them clothes. Quit tryin' to act so tough and huddle with me. We need to share body heat.

–It's all right, said Gabriel and stood up and squatted down in front of the fire. See. I'm already dry.

–I ain't flirtin' with you, Patch. Quit acting all nervous. Shit, you're worse than a little boy.

Yahng Yi closed the blanket over her body and gripped the folds tightly around her chest, then kicked at Gabriel's legs, and Gabriel jumped away, stumbling on some branches on the ground. His momentum carried him toward the fire, and he turned around to regain his balance and leaped over the flames to the other side, his feet scarcely missing the embers creeping under the stacked logs.

Yahng Yi laughed and smiled at him, and Gabriel smiled back and stared at her face. The blood was still up there, keeping her rosy-cheeked and innocent, even though she had already exposed her beautiful parts to him in their wetness.

–You ain't so tough, she said. Can't even walk straight.

Gabriel went to check her clothes for dryness and then sat back on the fallen tree, closer to her this time. He stared straight ahead at the fire, though he felt Yahng Yi looking at his right side. They sat in silence for a moment, both watching the fire, and both sensing something unnatural in its burning, as if the fire itself watched them with measuring eyes. Yahng Yi sighed.

–What is it? asked Gabriel.

–You've grown on me, Patch, she said. Like moss.

Gabriel laughed. –Moss, huh? Guess there's worse things.

–I been thinking, she said abruptly.

–Thinking about what?

–Thinking about leavin' it all. Just running off and keeping running until I find myself in a place I think I ought to be.

Gabriel nodded. –This place doesn't seem to suit you much, he said. I've been sure of that since I first saw you.

–It's home, though, said Yahng Yi. Like you said. Hard to leave home.

She stood up and let the blanket fall to the ground. Her undergarments were drier now, but the bright light of the fire allowed visibility through the thin fabric. Gabriel stared at the ground in front of her.

–We should get going, he said and gathered her clothes.

–Okay, Patch, but not home.

Gabriel looked up. She took the damp clothes from him and began to dress herself.

–Back up the mountain, she said.

–Huh?

–Back up the mountain.

154

–It's dark, said Gabriel. We've got to stick to the road.

–I ain't talkin' about going back to the ranch.

–Well where are you talking about going then?

–Anywhere else, I guess.

Gabriel looked at her face and saw the first tears take shape around her lovely dark eyes. She wrapped the blanket tightly around her and sat down on the ground in front of the fire, her face gone expressionless and those first tears meandering down to her jawbone without her reacting to their falling.

–Don't care if you come with me or not, Patch, she said. Just leave me a horse.

–I didn't say I wouldn't come with you.

–Then let's go. Let's leave this place. Never come back.

–Can't do that, said Gabriel. Can't just leave your mother.

–Stay with her then, she said, tightening the hold of her crossed arms. I don't care.

–Well what are you gonna do?

–I told you. Get away from all this madness. I'm sick of the mountains and the rivers and the lambs. Sick of Mother. I don't belong here, you said so yourself. I ain't gonna be like Auntie, born and dead on the same fifty acres.

Gabriel sat down next to her so that he faced her profile. The fire cast half of his face in its light, the other dark half shadowed even darker by the coming night. –Just wait a spell, he said. See what happens with the ranch. Then you can move on if you still think you ought to.

–Don't you wanna come with me, Patch? she asked and then looked at his round good eye and the oldness of his cheeks where the wrinkles had burrowed in, and the gray hairs matted down across his forehead.

–No, said Gabriel. Wouldn't be right.

–We'll wander around like the old times. Like we did today. Traveling around on horseback, eatin' from the land. Sleeping under stars.

–Can't just leave your mother, said Gabriel.

–Yes, we can, said Yahng Yi, nodding her head for each time he shook his, until Gabriel was nodding too, his eye gone in hers and some kind of bodily fullness taking hold of him, making him whole like he was in the days before he went to war, when he understood the nature of want and the gifting that comes from the love between sexes. The gifting he once shared with Emily, the one whose memory he had betrayed by lusting for this girl, this girl who was so much like Emily in soul and wit, and who made him both guilty and content, enough so that the fever of the fire and the chill of the river water and the softness of earth and the glow of the heavens had him falling. Falling out of himself and into another.

THE DAWN HAS BEGUN and he hears the morning song of the magpies. He awakens to the sight of hundreds of bodies strewn along the road, all dressed in white and all unmoving, a few heads of cattle milling around the dead. And then the thundering of jet fighters echoes in the distance. He begins jogging down the side of the road back toward Chu Gok Ri, his head down and searching for any disturbed earth for the presence of mines, and trying also not to look at the carnage all around him.

The red sun rises to the east, and begins coloring the ravaged valley. There are bodies everywhere, their white frocks flooded with old blood and various limbs and dark skins of all sizes. There is no enemy in there and he knows it. The dead are the same refugees he'd seen three days ago in an open-air railcar as they'd made the twenty-hour train ride northwest from Pohang to the Yongdong front.

He jogs dutifully, like a good soldier, like a soldier who knows his duty and knows that in the course of that duty he will see things that he will regret seeing. Still he jogs. Back toward the regiment post.

The sound of the morning birds stops with the distant cracking of gunfire. He runs faster. The gunfire grows louder, and soon he is there, behind the line of his fellow soldiers, their guns drawn toward the twin tunnels of the rail bridge at No Gun Ri. In the darkness within the tunnel arcs, he sees the mass of white, the refugees there huddled together, screaming at the steady popping of guns and the sparking of bullets pinging the girders and concrete. He hears an officer yelling at him to engage, and he goes to the ground, his rifle drawn toward the tunnel.

Then the bullets stop, and the sun goes no higher in the east. All is still as he looks down the line of his gun barrel, the defenseless peasants in his sight. It is not the end of the dream, and he knows it, but he cannot make the dream move on.

AN HOUR LATER, YAHNG YI ARRIVED back at the ranch in darkness, leading Gabriel's horse by its halter and Gabriel huddled down in the saddle with the blanket over his shoulders. She was cold, the wetness from the river still caught in the fuller parts of her hair, and she clenched her jaw down hard to keep from shivering. She looked behind her as they ascended the driveway up to the barn and saw that Gabriel was looking pale and blue of lip in the moonlight.

She rode to the barn doors and opened them, and then led her horse and Gabriel's inside. It was dark and the low ambient light afforded her only visibility of shapes. She heard the lambs rustling a bit and saw a body on the ground lying on a thin layer of straw, and the glimmer of a liquor bottle at its side. It was Jude, sleeping.

She shook Gabriel on the knee. –Patch, she said. Wake up. We're home.

Gabriel stirred and let out a boyish whine, and Yahng Yi helped him down from the saddle. She led him out of the barn, shutting the door to keep the horses in, and then over to the house, an arm around his waist and feeling through the blanket the dampness of his clothes and his body the same chilliness as the air.

–Umma! she called out as she entered the house. Umma, you home?

There was no answer and she set Gabriel down on the floor next to the fireplace.

–Mother! she called out again and went to the hallway to check the bedrooms. The house was empty, so she took the quilts from Gabriel's bed and returned to the fireplace and stacked some logs on the grate and started a fire.

As the kindling burned, she removed his damp clothing down to his undershirt and underpants and then draped the quilts over him. He was lying on his back and she slapped him gently on the face but he did not stir.

Some color returned to his face from her slapping and the warmth of the growing fire, but his eye remained closed. She examined his face and the grooves within it, and the leather patch strapped around his head. She fingered it, running the tip along the band and then around the patch itself. She had yet to see beneath it, but though she was tempted, she did not look.

She stood up and left him there, returning outside without changing her own wet clothing. She went to the barn and walked up to Jude's prostrate body and toed him along the head.

–Wake up, boy! she yelled.

Jude shot up awake and alert, his eyes wide, and he backed away in the darkness until he heard giggling.

–Damn, he said and scowled at Yahng Yi and then reached over and opened the whiskey bottle and took a pull.

–That ewe drop? she asked.

Jude shook his head.

–Where's Val?

He shrugged his shoulders.

–You just been sittin' in here drinking whiskey all day?

–Cold out there. Got windy.

–Why didn't you go inside the house then?

–Your mother don't like me. You know that.

–I knew you were scared of her.

–I ain't, he said, looking away.

–You should be. She's got it in for you.

–She's a old lady. I ain't scared of no old lady.

–You're a liar.

He took another pull from the bottle.

–And a drunk, she said.

–And you're a bitch, he said.

She kicked the bottle out of his hand as he brought it to his mouth, and it coasted along the ground, splattering. –Get your horses and get out of here, she said.

–Bitch, he said and stood up and locked eyes with her, and then went over and picked up his whiskey bottle. He took the horses' halters and led them out of the barn, walking clumsily and raising the bottle every fifth step.

Yahng Yi followed him outside and watched him walk toward the gully until he disappeared into the forest, then she went back around the barn and began the hike up to her mother's mountain shrine.

GABRIEL STARED MINDLESSLY into the fire. He had taken ill and now thought of nothing more than the flickering of the flame and how it danced lightly from the draft come through the window. He watched it like a child, watching the randomness of the fire's tip, and how it moved so quickly, like an angry spirit tethered at the base.

The sickness had locked itself in his blood, swelling his brain and making him focus only on the movement and the lighting of the flame, which looked to be building upon itself in volume, the outer layer casting a prismed halo and then the halo itself with a haze around it as well.

Around the flame, as the outer halo faded into the darkness of the room, he saw a phosphorescent lattice that filled the empty air within the room, making him feel trapped as if within a heavy fog.

Then one of the logs cracked, sending an ember into his lap, and he lost focus of the flame to smother the ember, breaking away from his hypnosis, and becoming aware again of the real, of the blanket around his shoulders and the way he sat hunched over with crossed legs, and the dampness of his hair and the dryness of his mouth, and the heat on his feet, which were bare and exposed to the fire.

He focused on that for a moment, the sweating of his toes, and then lifted his hand up to his face and saw the streak of motion from where his hand had moved before him, the tracer, like the tracers lighting up the .30-cals on that hillside near Chu Gok Ri. And he tried to find that memory of war, tried to hold on to it long enough to engage a timeline from which he could garner present time and place.

Was it a week ago that he beached with the 7th at Osan? Was it a month ago that he left Emily at the ranch, left her waving feebly and twittering her shoulders as she cried? Was it autumn? Was her skin darkened by the summer sun? Was it spring? Did she hide the bitterroots in her hair? Was he just a boy? Barely eighteen and ready for nights on the Ginza? Was he a man? Come home from war with the peasant girl at his side?

He stood up and looked at a framed picture on the fireplace mantel. A picture of the peasant's daughter. He looked at his reflection in the frame glass, saw the patch around his face. He stared at that patch, his most prominent feature, the patch that signified his maiming but hid its details and allowed him the satisfaction that his disfigurement could be seen only in another's mind, only in the imagination.

It had happened after the war. He knew that now, and he knew the patch to be the most shameful of his features, and at the same time the most precious. Precious because it distracted him from the real devastation and the scarring on his body in places always covered with cloth. He stared at the patch and then looked at the face around it, and the face came clearer, and he saw that the creases in his skin were not a trick of lighting and shadow, but wrinkles, and he saw the hairline of his forehead showing thin and starting to gray.

Was he old? In the days just before his death? The days he dreamed of even as a child, growing old on the ranch like his grandfather. Dying on the ranch like his grandfather. He dropped the picture and it fell slowly to the ground, falling and breaking, and breaking further yet.

He stared at the broken shards, the hundreds, the thousands of broken fragments on the ground, the fragments that showed him his face just a second before and now reflected the weak light of the fire in the darkness like inverted starlight just after dusk or the dawn thereafter. Like the stars he would watch upon the mountainside, watching with the one he loved.

The one he loved.

As he stared at the broken shards, he thought of her. Was it her? The one he saved in the nettle trees? Or was it the other? The one he lay with among the primrose?

–Forgive me, he whispered. For love is of God, and every one that loveth is born of God, and knoweth God, and it is love that is my sin.

He breathed deeply some good deep breaths and opened his eye and became aware again of time and place, his head still cloudy and his blood running hot so that he could feel its pulsing from within like a well-rained river trying to free itself from bondage. But he had placed himself in the house and remembered again how it was he came to be here.

He remembered sitting with Yahng Yi in the forest, and he remembered his guilt. It was a guilt he should have felt within the moment, but being too enamored of her and defenseless and outside himself that he could find no fault in their exchange of words and his lusting for her.

Then a voice.

–Gabe.

He heard her, and stirred, and though the voice was in a whisper he recognized it quickly, a voice whose timbre he had not heard in four decades. He sat up and saw her standing before him, and she was young and lovely, her skin tanned dark from the summer work, and wearing the white nightgown that he remembered from their child-hood days, and her hair golden and braided in the back and wearing a flower garland around her crown, as she would have worn on their wedding day.

–Emily, he said and felt his throat gurgling with river water.

–Missed you, Gabe, she said.

–I'm dreaming, he said, and lay back down and rubbed his fingers against his throbbing head.

–Not dreaming, Gabe. Just seeing something different. Something that's always been around. You just haven't been tuned right to see it.

–Don't understand, Em. My head hurts pretty fierce.

Emily laughed and it eased him, that laugh, and her young pink lips still full when parted.

–Don't think too hard, Gabe. You weren't ever too keen on thinking hard.

Gabriel laughed as well and stood up slowly and reached for her. She reached back and their hands met and he expected his to go through hers like through a cloud, but she held it and he felt her holding it, felt its fullness, and he began weeping and laughing in tandem.

–Come on, Gabe, she said, and then the arm of the Victrola dropped and the music came. Let's dance. Like old times.

–Feeling weak, Em. Don't know if I'm up for it.

She took his half-naked body into hers and he strengthened at her touch, feeling his bones grow stiffer and muscles taut and ready, and they danced around the perimeter of the room, Gabriel's arm on her back and their ribs together on one side and Gabriel watching her as they danced together, easily at first. Then he reached up to touch her face and saw his wrinkled, mottled skin against her cheek so white and pure, and he went soft, killing the easiness between them and also the idea that they were alive together, like the old times, when they danced all the time, even without music, the two of them hearing the rhythms in their heads and always in time, always together.

The song ended and Gabriel went to the Victrola and anchored the arm. Emily sat down in front of the fire, the skirt of her nightgown bunched up and piled onto her lap. She looked out the window and then removed the flower garland from her head and began playing with it, unweaving the stems and picking the petals off the blooms and letting them drop to the floor next to her bare feet.

–I listened to that song every night after you left for the army, she said. I never told you that.

Gabriel sat down next to her. –There's plenty of things I never got to tell you either, Em, he said.

–Like what?

–Never got to tell you I'm sorry.

–Hush, Gabe. Sorry for what?

–Sorry for ruining things.

She laughed. –Don't be sorry, Gabe. I wasn't ever angry with you. You had to bring that girl home after what you did. She didn't have anyplace else to go. I didn't mind looking after her. She was like a sister.

–I don't remember.

She sighed. –You came back with so much sadness, she said. So much guilt.

–Guilt over what, Em?

–Sorry, Gabe. If you don't remember it, I can't make you remember. But you know it's there. One day you'll have to face it.

–I can't remember, Em. The bullet.

–Bullet, nothing, Gabe. You don't remember because you don't want to remember. You can't kill a memory like that. A memory like that lives forever.

–Then tell me, Em.

–Still stubborn as a mule, she said and removed the pins from her hair and let her long brown locks fall down across her shoulders, shaking her head to let the weight of her tresses straighten out the tangles. She set her hands in her lap and began playing with the lace fringes of her nightgown.

–You looked so handsome in your uniform, she said. I remember the day you came home. How handsome you looked.

–Shoot, Em. That uniform never did fit right.

–Gabe, she said and stood up and went to the window and drew the curtain back. Do you still love me?

–Yes.

Emily turned around and came back to him. She stood there and then let the gown fall over her shoulders to the ground, and she was naked in front of the fire, her whole body darkly tanned, even those areas that should not have seen sun. Gabriel looked away, suddenly conscious of his own bareness, his chest and back showing off the shrapnel scars, pink and raised and wormy.

Emily walked to him. –It's okay, she said. Let me see. You never did let me see.

Gabriel nodded and removed his underpants and Emily saw the grooves in his flesh, all around him and spreading outward like simple sun rays. She laughed girlishly. Gabriel pulled up his underpants and stood back up.

–Lie down, Gabriel, said Emily. Stop acting like a baby.

Gabriel lay down on the quilts in front of the fireplace and Emily down with him. They wrapped their arms around each other and Emily began kissing his head and then his face and his neck, and then placed his hand over her cold breast. Gabriel gripped it hard and began kissing her again and she sighed and moved her knee between his legs and he began to breathe heavily, kissing her all around the neck and then reaching behind to her backside and kneading her and letting his fingers move along the cleft of her to the hair sticking out between the folds.

–Do I feel like her? she asked, giggling.

–What, Em?

–Do I feel like her? The one who takes my place in your dreams.

–No, Em. I don't know what you're talking about.

–I see things now, Gabe. You can't hide anything from me.

She pushed him away from her and stood up and walked to the door, her naked body growing pale as it escaped the reach of the low firelight. Gabriel watched her walking in the darkness and her skin glowing as it turned to whiteness and she looked back at him as she entered the moonlight coming through from the window.

–She's just a girl, Gabe, she said.

–What about you, Em? asked Gabriel as he stood quickly. I heard about you and her brother. Grown woman like yourself, laying down with a boy half your age, a boy that was family.

She laughed. –You haven't changed a bit, Gabe, she said. Always believe everything you hear. Always so trusting.

She smiled at him thoughtfully, so beautiful, the light of the half moon coming through the window, covering her face with squares of framed white light. Her mouth open barely and the sound of her breaths sibilant like a mother shushing her child.

–I never laid with that boy, Gabe, she said. You know me better than that.

–Well why would she tell me you did?

She shrugged her shoulders and her whiteness began to fade as the drowsiness came back and his good eye began eclipsing.

–I forgive you, Gabe, she said.

–Forgive me for what?

–For bringing Yahng's mother back here. For falling in love with her like you did. I see now why you did it. Why you had to do it. It's just the type of man you are. And it's why I loved you and love you still. You're just one of those men. Too good for his own good.

He shook his head. –I never loved her, he said. That's a lie. You were the only one. I only loved you.

She laughed.

–What's funny? he asked.

–How old are you now?

He paused.

–How many years do you remember? she asked.

He didn't answer.

–You still want to believe that you lived your whole life in the valley. That everything you ever wanted or needed was here. And that just isn't true.

–I don't remember, Em. You gotta tell me.

–You can remember, Gabe. You just don't want to.

–No.

–I can't say I'm not pleased, though, that I'm the one you want to remember the most.

She waved at him. It was the same wave he knew from his dreams, the wave she granted him when he left for the army, when he walked away from her along the valley floor, along the dirt road that led to the county highway and away from the ranch and the wildflowers and the slow meltwater stream and the one thing that he should have always kept close to him, then and forever.

NINE

Val Rey sat on the chopping block next to the rear entrance of the log house, the inside of the house all dark,
and the darkness comforting. He heard some muttering
to his left and saw Jude approaching the house from the
Cottage side, skulking like a drunk. Jude laughed abruptly
at nothing in particular and raised his arm to tip back a
bottle. It took him several minutes to walk the last dozen
yards, and he was surprised in the darkness by Val sitting
in front of the house.

–What the hell you doin', Val? he asked.

–Waitin' for you.

–Why didn't you go inside?

–Nobody was home.

–Shit, man. Door ain't locked.

Jude stumbled past him to the back door and they
walked through the foyer and into the living room. Val sat
down on Ham's custom oversized chair, and picked up a
hunting magazine from the reading table and began leaf-
ing through the pages.

–You pretendin' you can read? asked Jude as he collapsed to the couch.

Val set the magazine back on the table. Jude stood above him and handed Val the whiskey bottle.

–Drink up, dumdum, he said.

Val took the bottle and raised it to his pursed lips and pretended to swig it.

–Granddad really gonna sell the place? he asked.

Jude nodded and snatched the bottle back.

–What's he gonna do with the money? asked Val.

–How the hell should I know?

–You gonna see any of it?

–Doubt it.

–He said anythin' about me and the rest of the hands?

–Said you was S.O.L. Shit outta luck.

Jude laughed and fell upon the couch. Val stared at him until Jude looked over. Their eyes met and Val did not look away.

–Shit, Val, said Jude. You know I'm joking. I'm sure Granddad'll make sure you're taken care of.

Val reached into his pocket and pulled out a plastic bag filled with dried psilocybin mushrooms. He pinched a handful and ate them and tossed the bag to Jude and Jude ate some as well.

–Horace says he's gonna send the Engbretson brothers after me if he don't get his money before next Sunday, said Jude.

–Horace from the Cat's Paw?

–You know any other Horaces I owe money to, dumdum?

–Guess not.

–You got my back, don't you, Val?

Val nodded. –Engbretson brothers is after that drifter too, he said.

–Yeah? asked Jude, sitting up. What for?

–Couple weeks ago when we was at the Filler I saw that drifter come runnin' outside holding this pack, and then Sweet Crude and the Engbretsons come chasing him.

–Well what's he got?

–Don't know for sure. He was holding that pack pretty tight when I seen him runnin' and I heard one of the Engbretsons ask Sweet Crude if they was gonna get paid and Sweet Crude told him not unless they got that pack from him.

–Shit, said Jude, leaning forward and his right knee bouncing. It's probably money in that pack. Remember when Cortney Clyde found two grand in that dead drifter's sleepin' bag a few years back?

Val nodded.

–Let's go get it, then, said Jude.

–What?

–Let's go get it.

–Go over there and take it from him? asked Val.

–Of course, dumdum. He ain't gonna just hand it over.

–Don't know, Jude. Somethin' about him I don't like.

–Shit, Val. He ain't but an old man with one eye.

–I ain't scared of him. Just makes me nervous.

–Why?

–He's bad luck. Don't like bein' around bad luck.

Jude furrowed his brow and nodded with blank eyes, the mushrooms already working him, leeching him of his senses. Then he laughed and took a cigarette lighter out of his pocket and flamed it and began moving it slowly in front of his face, amused by the line of light left in its path.

–I'll get him myself then, he said, removing a cigarette from his breast pocket and lighting it. Gonna get him and gut him. Slit him from his sack to his neck. Then I'm gonna get her, too. Gonna get her good.

–Gonna get who?

–You know who. Gonna get her and give it to her.

–Give what to her?

–*It*, numbnuts, said Jude and paused, holding a draw in his lungs. Where'd you get them mushrooms, anyway? he asked as he exhaled.

–Same place I always get'm, said Val, staring into the glowing cherry of Jude's cigarette and its ember prisming and casting a halo around the tip.

–Where's that? asked Jude.

–Cowpies.

–No kiddin'?

–Yeah.

–You pick'm straight off the pies?

–Yeah.

–You wash'm first?

Val shook his head.

–You didn't wash'm? asked Jude.

–No.

–There's still shit on'm?

–Guess so. Little bit probably.

–You're an idiot, Val. You know that? You fuckin' dumdum. We're gonna get sick now. Gonna get scrapie and shit.

–Cows don't get scrapie.

–Well we're gonna get somethin'. Eatin' shit ain't good for you.

–We ain't gonna get sick. I eat these mushrooms all the time. Ain't never got sick.

–Maybe you're used to it. I ain't.

–You eat them mushrooms all the time too, Jude.

–What?

–Same mushrooms we always eat.

–Oh.

Jude laughed suddenly and went to the floor and lay down on his stomach and scratched himself behind the ear. Then he got to all fours and crawled over to the stuffed bear and curled up at its feet. Val saw Jude's head turn into Coyote's head, and he watched Coyote smoking and scratching his balls and then Coyote clear his throat and spit out a snot wad onto the hardwood.

Val whistled. –Coyote, he said, grinning, the hallucination filling out and warming him and making him feel strong and beloved.

–What? said Jude, looking up at Val.

–You wanna hear a Coyote story, Coyote? asked Val.

–Whatever, said Jude and scratched at his balls again.

–One night Coyote raided a chicken coop. Got himself seven chickens. Big, juicy chickens. So he's runnin' off with these chickens and gets pretty tired. He decides to rest and buries the chickens in the ground up to their necks and builds a cooking fire. By this time, he's spent. Don't got the energy to cook no more, so he tells his asshole to watch the chickens while he takes a nap. To make sure no one comes by and steals'm. While he's sleeping, Badger comes by and sees the chickens and he sees Coyote's asleep. Badger eats all seven chickens and goes on his way. Coyote wakes up, sees his chickens eaten, and gets mad. Gets mad at his asshole for not keeping watch of the chickens. So, Coyote takes a stick from the fire and sticks it right in his own asshole.

Jude started laughing and then coughing, and then his laughing slowed a little and he looked up at the ceiling, puzzled.

–Shit, Val, he said. That ain't funny. That's the goddamned dumbest joke I ever heard. Don't even make sense.

–Ain't a joke. It's an old Indian story.

–Then it's the dumbest story I ever heard.

–That's cause you don't understand it.

–There ain't even a punch line.

–Ain't supposed to be one.

–You should say at the end somethin' like, *he stuck a hot poker in his asshole and burned the shit out of himself.* Now that'd be some funny shit.

–It ain't a joke, said Val.

–Cause it ain't funny.

–It ain't a joke cause it ain't a joke.

Jude shook his head and put his cigarette out on the floor, and then stood up and walked toward the hallway bathroom. Val watched him walking away, thinking about how he used to admire Jude. How he had wanted so badly to be his brother, to be a part of the Finn family. He had idolized Jude, and had always done whatever it was that Jude wanted, even if it meant putting himself at great risk for no other reason than to help Jude quench his appetite for all things worldly.

Jude, the trickster. The coyote. Creature of appetite. He had no reason to trust him. No reason to love him. But he did. Trusted him like his own blood brother. Loved him like his own blood brother.

–Let's hit it, dumdum, said Jude as he came out of the bathroom.

–Hit what?

–I'm going over. You comin' with?

–I don't think so, Jude. You don't wanna mess with that man. Bad luck.

–You're a pussy.

–That don't change my mind.

–All right, but if I find that money over there, I ain't sharin' none.

–That's fine.

–Gonna take that money and get me three whores and a bottle of whiskey and a bag of weed and a new sweater.

–Okay, Jude.

Jude stood there motionless for a second, and their eyes met, and for a moment Val was shown Jude's loneliness. Bleak like winter.

Jude looked away. –There's food in the fridge if you get hungry, he said. But don't come looking for me if I don't come home. I'm gonna be out all night tappin' whores.

–Sure, Jude.

Jude walked slowly to the foyer and stopped for a moment, looking at nothing in particular. He laughed stupidly and shook his head as he sprinted to the back door, and then he was off into the darkness, not closing the door behind him.

TEN

At the base of White Horse Mountain she rests. She squats beneath a short acacia, waiting for her sisters to return with water-filled gourds. All around her are displaced villagers seeking shade from the heat or cooking the midday meal. Hundreds of refugees trying to make sense of what is happening to them and to their homeland. She sees the Americans among the hills, some talking on radios, some looking toward the sky with binoculars. When the song of the cicadas is drowned out by the distant hum of jet planes, the Americans disappear.

And then the bombing begins. Thundering blows shake the ground and send fountains of earth and flesh toward the heavens. She screams for her sisters and runs toward the culvert. Around her, villagers scatter in a panic as the bombs and missiles rain down upon them, and she maneuvers around the dead and the dismembered, entrails of cattle and people mixing together in the carnage.

The planes disappear, but the explosions continue from artillery units embedded in the hills. She sees bodies without heads and disemboweled babies and newly orphaned children screaming and crying for their mothers to rise from the blood-soaked ground. She runs as the dirt and cloth fall upon her, runs past men and cows on fire. She runs until she sees her eldest sister, her Un-nee, kneeling and wailing near some brambles, oblivious to the bullets popping the ground all around her. Her Un-nee is kneeling before the wounded body of her other sister, Hyuhna, whose back is still smoking where a piece of shrapnel has burned into her.

The bullets and mortar shells continue to fly as they carry Hyuhna away, following a group of villagers back to the culvert to hide below the tunnels of the rail bridge near No Gun Ri. By the time they reach the tunnels, Hyuhna is dead.

Within the tall tunnels, parents call for their lost children. Children cry for their dead parents. Soon the tunnels are packed with villagers seeking refuge from the shelling and gunfire. She and her Un-nee hold hands and try to keep silent, unable to mourn their dead sister, whose body lies just outside the tunnel, where people have stacked the dead into barricades.

Three hundred of them packed into the tunnels, many dead or dying. When dusk comes the gunfire thickens again, M-1s and .30-calibers and the burning tracers, swarming upon them, and the dead becoming more in number than the living.

She and her sister keep their hands tightly together, their backs pressed against the interior wall of the tunnel and hunched down among the crowd. They cry and huddle closely as the bodies keep falling around them, bullets riddling both the living and already dead, ricocheting here and there off the concrete and finding even those who are hidden well.

It is one of those ricocheted bullets that enters her Un-nee's heart. Her Un-nee squeezes her hand one last time before going limp. She begins to wail and pulls her dead sister's body close, hugging it tightly in a final embrace. And then she walks out of the tunnel into the line of fire, nothing left for her anymore. An elderly woman tries to grab her, but she shrugs away her grasp and walks out into the ruddy light of dusk. The bullets fly around her and she sees some tracers to her left and right, and she turns around once, looking back toward the tunnel to wish her sisters a good afterlife. She walks as the ground behind her blows into the air, and keeps walking toward the guns, toward the muzzle fire, waiting for the one that will send her far away.

But it does not come. She is brought down from behind. She looks up and sees the face of the same blue-eyed soldier who saved her from rape in the nettle trees. He covers her as the ground is pocked around them with flying dirt. She tries to break free, screaming her sisters' names, then her mother's.

The dream comes to a halt. No more bullets flying. No crying, no screaming. Nothing.

And then her mother's ghost standing in the tall grass in front of her. It is her mother from the early days of her childhood, still with dark black hair and eyes made kind by ocean water and sun. She is sympathetic, as if preparing to soothe the child's first heartbreak.

The dreamer climbs from under her soldier. He remains in the same pose, hunched over, his body there to shield her. She runs her fingers along his face. The man who would have died to save a stranger.

Her mother kneels down next to her and tries to pull her away from him. The dreamer resists. She looks up at

177

her mother, and then her mother takes on the other form, that of the water god, the moisture layering the skin that grows wrinkled with aging. The *mulsin* squats and waves her hand, and the bodies in the rail tunnel disappear, and the other Americans disappear, and all is quiet, and it is just the two of them in the tall grass, squatting side by side and her soldier before them.

–Why do you love this man? asks the *mulsin*.

–Because it is *palcha*, she says. Can you not see it? We are bound by fate. He saved me.

–He saved you from what? He saved you from your homeland? Your own ancestors? He brought you here to this land where you are unwanted, separated by an ocean from your proper place.

–It is *palcha*. Only two lovers bound by fate could die for each other before loving each other.

–He loved you only out of guilt. And now that he does not remember that guilt, he loves you no more. It is shameful, daughter, what you are trying to do with this man.

–It is *palcha*, said Yahng Yi's Mother as she came out of the dream. You cannot bend *palcha*.

She wept there on a bed of pine needles in front of the rebuilt shrine, until she saw a shadow moving toward her from below.

–Umma, said the approaching figure.

Yahng Yi's Mother stood quickly to meet her daughter. She grabbed Yahng Yi by the wrist and forced her to the ground in front of the shrine.

–Beg forgiveness! she yelled.

–For what? asked Yahng Yi, trying to squirm away, but her mother was too strong.

–You have angered your ancestors, said her mother. And they punish me for it. Not you! They punish me!

–Ain't in need of forgiveness. Didn't do nothin'.

Yahng Yi's Mother pinned her daughter to the ground and reached across for a platter of rice cake that was sitting next to a pile of river stones.

–You will eat the *chesu* and beg forgiveness, she said.

Yahng Yi struggled as her mother tried to force the rice cake into her mouth. She pursed her lips tight and felt her mother's fingers trying to open her mouth to receive the offering. Her mother succeeded and Yahng Yi felt the semisweet rice cake on her tongue. She relaxed her struggling and accepted the food and her mother relaxed as well.

–Umma, said Yahng Yi as she chewed the sticky rice cake. Gabe is sick. He fell in the river.

Yahng Yi's Mother released her grip and rolled off of her daughter. She held out her hand so that Yahng Yi could spit out the half-eaten rice cake into her palm. –I am sorry, Yahng, she said, throwing the chewed cake into the trees.

–Gabe is sick, Umma, said Yahng Yi, standing up and brushing the dust off from her arms. Did you hear me? Gabe is sick.

Her mother just stood there, mouth open and eyes unfocused. Yahng Yi saw that her mother was not right of mind, that she had ingested one of the visionary teas, as she often did when she went to the mountain shrine in the night.

–Gabe is sick, said Yahng Yi one last time before heading down the dark path back to the house, jogging during the stretches where the path was not strewn with loose rock or fallen limbs. She slowed her pace thirty yards down the mountain to listen for her mother, and heard some twigs breaking not far behind.

THERE WAS AN ERRATIC POUNDING at the front door and Gabriel woke suddenly in a mature sweat, lying in his undershorts on the quilts in front of the weak fire. He heard some rustling in the chokecherry bushes outside the windows, and then a muted voice come through the glass panes.

–I know you're in there, called out the slurry voice. I can see the smoke comin' up from the chimney.

The rustling moved back toward the door and the knocking resumed, harder this time. Gabriel backed himself against the wall and sat there with his knees up, listening, his body racked with the river fever and head distant from his still-fresh vision of Emily.

He heard grumbling coming from outside and then movement away from the house. He stood up and crawled to the front windows and peeked behind the curtain, his good eye just past the edge of the sill. He saw nobody and moved slowly away from the window and lay back down on the quilts. The fire had dwindled and was smoldering now, some minor crackling as the wood turned to coals.

The back door opened, swinging hard, the inside knob butting against a wall, and footsteps coming through the kitchen. He rose to his knees and gathered up his damp clothes as Jude appeared in the threshold.

–Why didn't you answer the door? asked Jude, staring at Gabriel, bleary-eyed and teetering.

–Must've dozed off, said Gabriel as he dressed himself.

Jude went off into the hallway and Gabriel heard him stumbling around, banging into walls and opening the doors to the bedrooms.

–What the hell you doing lyin' around in your drawers? asked Jude as he returned to the front room.

–Fell in the river, said Gabriel.

–Where is it? asked Jude.

–What?

–You know what.

–No, son. I don't.

Jude stared hard at him and Gabriel became dizzy and looked away.

–You scared of me or somethin'? asked Jude.

–No. Just feeling ill.

–You're scared. I can see it in your eye.

Jude walked to him precariously, and Gabriel backed away.

–You're drunk, said Gabriel.

–So?

–So, you're full of courage you don't normally have.

Jude laughed. –Don't need extra courage to beat on an old man.

–Go home, said Gabriel.

–I'll be taking that money from you one way or the other, old man. Better off tellin' me now.

–What money?

–The money you got in that bag of yours. I ain't stupid. It's gotta be here somewhere.

Gabriel laughed. Jude's face softened suddenly and he tilted his head. –Lemme see under that patch, he said. Lift it up. I wanna see what you got under there.

Jude reached for Gabriel's head, and Gabriel flinched back and raised his arm to push Jude's hand away, the effort making him weak and bringing him to his knees. Jude lost his balance as well and fell to the ground next to him. Gabriel put his hands down on the floor and breathed deeply to keep his bearings.

–I'm just curious, that's all, said Jude, lying on his side and making no effort yet to get up. Maybe ain't nothin' wrong with your eye and you just wear that thing because you think it makes you look tough.

Jude got to his hands and knees and crawled around Gabriel and overtook him from behind, grabbing the crook of Gabriel's elbow and wrapping his other arm around Gabriel's neck. Gabriel struggled for a moment, and Jude squeezed harder until Gabriel went limp. Then Jude reached up and stripped the eye patch from Gabriel's head and pushed him down to his stomach. Jude took his hat off and tossed it onto a chair, his eyes swollen almost to closing and the redness dark where there should have been white.

–Where can I get me one of these? he asked, sitting with his legs crossed as he strapped on Gabriel's patch.

Gabriel reached for it feebly, and Jude slapped his hand away as if rebuking a child. The muscles around Gabriel's eyeless socket went lax, enabling Jude to see fully the scarring and skin grown over where Gabriel's eye should have sat.

–Shit, you weren't fibbin', said Jude and removed the patch and tossed it in front of the fireplace. He knelt down in front of Gabriel and grabbed Gabriel's shirt with one hand and reached up with the other toward the socket. Lemme touch that scar, he said.

Gabriel twisted free and tried to crawl away, but Jude tackled him, and rolled Gabriel onto his back and then sat on his abdomen.

–You ain't got nothin' in there at all, said Jude, peering into Gabriel's face. Just a hole.

–Let me up, said Gabriel, his head already full of blood and Jude's weight on his torso making the pressure higher. Can't breathe.

Jude reached down quickly to touch Gabriel's scar. –Feels like leather, he said and began probing the emptiness with his index finger. Gabriel winced at the touching and reached up with his free hand and grabbed Jude's wrist. He tried to move it away, but Jude was too strong and he was too weak, and Jude's finger went all around inside the cavity where the unnatural skin had grown in.

As they struggled on the floor, the back door opened and there were light footsteps coming toward the front room. Yahng Yi appeared and saw Jude there sitting on top of Gabriel and Gabriel looking up at her and helpless. She rushed at Jude and Jude stood up and received her, shifting her weight downward to the ground.

He pinned her down and slapped her hard across the face. Gabriel rose weakly to his knees and tried to aid her, but as he grabbed for Jude's arm, Jude turned around and punched him square in the nose. Gabriel fell backward, his eye watering and blinded.

–Bitch, said Jude and gripped Yahng Yi's shirt at the shoulders and lifted her torso a few inches above the ground and then slammed her down to the floor.

Yahng Yi yelped softly, but did not cry. She began bucking her hips to get Jude off her, but could not move him.

–I swear to God, Jude, if you don't get off me, I'm gonna kill you, she said.

–Tell me where he's hidin' the money, and I'll let you up.

–What money?

–You gonna play that game too?

Jude raised his hand to slap her again just as Yahng Yi's Mother entered the front room. She was carrying a carving knife in her right hand and it hung down at her side, the wide blade reflecting the firelight. Jude looked over at her and their eyes locked briefly before Jude shifted his weight off Yahng Yi. He rose slowly to his feet. Yahng Yi's Mother did not move.

Jude laughed nervously and took two steps backward. –What're you gonna do with that knife?

–It is for the healing *kut*, said Yahng Yi's Mother. Will you be joining us again?

Jude snorted and looked over at Yahng Yi and then at Gabriel. –You're crazy, he said.

He continued backing up until he touched the front door and then reached behind him and turned the knob. –You're all crazy, he said. I should kill the whole lotta you. Burn this place down.

Yahng Yi's Mother raised her eyebrows at him, and Jude opened the door and exited, slamming it shut as he left. Yahng Yi crawled over to where Gabriel was lying and shook him.

–Patch, you all right? she asked.

–Yeah, said Gabriel, self-conscious and reaching up to cover his bare eye.

–Don't worry about that none, said Yahng Yi. It ain't bad.

Gabriel nodded and removed his hand. Yahng Yi placed her face on his cheek, near where the cicatrix began, and felt his hot skin still throbbing. –You're burning up, she said. Umma, feel him.

Yahng Yi's Mother kneeled down, still holding the knife, and touched Gabriel's forehead and then began stroking his cheek. –*Mulsin,* she said under her breath. Why do you try to drown my love? Take back the bad spirits you enslave in the water.

Gabriel took her wrist and moved it away. Yahng Yi's Mother stood up quickly, gripping the knife tightly enough that her tendons emerged from beneath her skin, and she heard her dead mother's voice as she sliced at the air with the knife. Gabriel was saying something, something about Jihn and Emily and the digging of sheep and her lies, but she did not understand him, could not hear him through the haze of the hallucinatory tea and the false voice of her mother.

She finished the ritual and sat down in a reading chair, running the point of the knife through the wisps of her black hair. She felt a chill spread over her scalp as she saw a spirit moving around her, circling her twice before disappearing. Then she looked over at Gabriel and her daughter on the floor, and watched as they stared back at her, taunting her, reminding her of her loneliness, and she did feel alone, alone and unloved, as she had always felt, alone since the day she left the island forty years ago.

Better to be trapped and loved than free and alone, daughter. I always told you. Why do you think I stayed on that wretched island with that wretched man for so long?

–I see your tricks, Mother. You place feelings in him. You make him angry with me.

Stupid, daughter. You have played this game too long. Look at him. Look at the way he looks at you. He is disgusted. Do a final kut *and return.*

–What about Yahng Yi? She will be alone.

Let Yahng Yi live her earthbound days in freedom. She is a good girl. Give her that at least. She is not of god-stock anyway. Let her live without this madness.

Yahng Yi's Mother stared at her daughter. She saw how Yahng Yi looked at her, partly with contempt and partly with pity, and she felt an emptiness within her, knowing that she had not treated her daughter fairly. She had forced Yahng Yi into this life on the ranch, away from the wideness of the world and away from those things that could have brought her happiness. It was always about herself. Always about *her* pain and *her* injustices. Never her daughter's, as it should have been.

She dropped the knife to the floor and walked quickly to her bedroom. Gabriel and Yahng Yi looked at each other, exchanging no words, and then Gabriel stood and went to the hallway and inside the dark room where Yahng Yi's Mother was sitting on the bed staring out the window. He sat down next to her.

–Who were you speaking to? he asked softly.

She did not answer.

–I worry about you, he said.

–What do you care? You have no love for me anymore.

–That's not true.

–I was a fool to hold on for so long, she said. You were just a boy back then. I was just a girl. The love between children is like paper in wind. I made it into something else. And wasted my life in doing so.

Gabriel shook his head. –No, he said.

The tea had run its course and now left her with the postvision melancholy. Her eyes glassed over as she thought of all the years she had spent praying to the ancestors, making those visionary teas, chanting the mantras. It was all for nothing, she decided. It was all in her head. All birthed in a child's imagination, a child's weak rendering of the world. An illusion. There was no such thing as eternal love. No such thing as *palcha*, no such thing as fate. Her mother was no god. She was simply dead, as dead as her sisters, as dead as her son.

–I may as well join them, she said. There is nothing left for me anymore.

–Join who? asked Gabriel.

–The dead.

Gabriel reached for her face and touched her there softly, and she laid her cheek upon his shoulder.

–A life is not wasted until the last day is lived, he said. And besides, you must be strong for your daughter. You are all she has.

–She hates me.

–She doesn't hate you.

–She thinks it is my fault that her brother is dead.

Gabriel grew rigid, remembering what Yahng Yi had told him up in the mountains earlier in the day. –Is it? he asked, his eye tightly on her face, reading it for deception.

She smiled. –Is that what she told you?

–Is it true? he asked and stood up.

–No, she said, reaching up and taking his arm to bring him back next to her.

–Then tell me what happened, said Gabriel.

–It was Yahng, she answered.

ELEVEN

Thick cloud cover had blown in and the valley was gray and the flora rippled steadily in the strong wind. The dogs were barking on the valley floor, and Yahng Yi heard them clearly from within the barn. She checked the paddocks one last time to make sure the lambs were feeding and then headed outside. As she closed the barn doors she noticed the first sparse flakes of a nascent snowfall. The dogs began barking again, and she went to the truck and drove down the incline to where the band was grazing.

The dogs were waiting for her as she exited the cab. They led her to a spot several yards away from the band, on the other side of the arroyo. The last pregnant ewe was there, one of the two-year-olds that Yahng Yi was fond of. The ewe responded to the sound of her voice, and walked to Yahng Yi slowly, her tail between her legs. She had a blank look in her eyes, and Yahng Yi gently pushed her to the ground and examined her womb from the outside. The uterus was contracting, but the birth membrane had yet to rupture. As Yahng Yi rolled her sleeve up, the dogs took off, heading back toward the house. She looked up and saw them as they circled the figure descending the slope toward her. It was Gabriel.

Yahng Yi shuttled around behind the ewe's hind quarters and reached her hand past the ewe's vulva and into the vagina. She moved her fingers around the ewe's cavity and felt that the cervix had not dilated. –Shit, she muttered.

Gabriel neared her as she removed her arm and shook off the loose fluid. –What are you doin' out of bed? she asked him.

–Feel fine, said Gabriel.

–Thought you was gonna leave us last night.

Gabriel smiled. –It'll take more than just a river chill to send me home, he said and squatted down next to her. Need some help?

–Go get the .22 off the rifle rack, she said, pointing at the truck, her brown arm oily from the ewe's natal juices.

–Why?

–Why do you think?

–You aren't going to call the vet?

–Can't afford a vet.

Gabriel nodded and jogged over to the truck and took down the .22 and brought it over, gripping it tightly with the barrel angled toward the sky. He remembered the last time he'd held a rifle, four decades ago on a dark Korean hillside.

–Somethin' wrong? asked Yahng Yi.

Gabriel looked down at the dying ewe and shook his head. –It's a shame, he said. Would of liked to end the season on a good note.

–Come on, Patch, said Yahng Yi and held out her hand. Gimme the gun. She's in pain.

Gabriel hesitated. –No, he said. I'll do it.

Yahng Yi stood up next to him and laid her hand on his shoulder. Gabriel looked at her and at the ewe on the ground a few yards in front of him, and quickly pointed the rifle at the ewe's skull and gripped the trigger. He held it there for a moment, shaking, and then pulled up.

Yahng Yi snatched the rifle from his hands and took aim and fired. The shot was true, entering the ewe's head just in front of the ear. A few tufts of hide and some bone shards popped up as the bullet entered the skull and the blood drained fast from the gaping hole. The ewe's dorsal eye remained open, a black pearl with the gray sky reflected within it, and the snow began to collect upon the fibers of its short wool. The dogs barked as the echo of the gunshot rolled across the valley. Yahng Yi whistled loudly and pointed toward the rest of the herd and the dogs looked at her briefly and then took off.

She stared at the dead ewe for a moment, the smoke from the barrel wafting among the falling snowflakes, which were growing in size and speed, her hair already dampened and the valley floor dusted and cold and looking ready to take on the full weight of the storm.

–Had to be done, said Gabriel, holding out his hand.

She nodded and handed Gabriel the rifle and then knelt down by the ewe. The head had emptied and the blood pooled at her feet. She reached inside her boot for her knife and with the other hand felt around the ewe's abdomen for the fundus. She held her hand at that spot and then made a shallow incision and ran it down the belly. The blood washed over her fingers, and she reached her hand into the cavity and felt the lamb within. She grabbed the lamb tightly around the underside and pulled it out through the ewe's open underbelly.

It appeared dead and she turned its head upside down and stuck her fingers in the mouth to try to open an air passage. There was breath, and she knelt by the ewe's eviscerated body and cut open the udder and held the little lamb under the flow of colostrum.

–Wait here, she said when the udder had emptied. I'll be back with the truck to pick up that ewe.

Gabriel nodded and brushed the loose snow from his hair and shoulders. Yahng Yi cradled the lamb against her chest, and jogged over to her truck. Gabriel watched as she drove up toward the house, the rear wheels fishtailing a bit when she accelerated, and then the truck disappeared into the snowfall just thirty yards away.

The snow was falling too quickly, he thought. Too thoroughly. He wiped the sides of his bloodied boots in a patch of snow-covered sagebrush, and then heard the truck door slam shut in the distance. Though he could not see the house through the snow, he could imagine Yahng Yi running to the back door, her black hair bouncing and her lithe arms cinched around the bundled lamb, looking so pretty running like that. So pretty with that dark skin and dark hair and the whiteness all around her. And he imagined her not with any kind of lust, but the same way a father imagines his daughter, seeing her in her most idyllic moments, always the prettiness of her. Always her perfection.

THE TRUE EDGE OF THE STORM CAME IN as Gabriel hauled the dead ewe off the bed of the truck, the wind picking up and swirling all through the valley and up the mountain, moving the body of airborne snow around in a steady rhythm of intermittent aggression. He pulled the ewe's hind legs and dragged it over behind the barn where he'd buried the dead lamb, and then grabbed the shovel and began digging just a few yards away from the other mound, an inch of snow already collected on the ground. Yahng Yi stood near him, holding the new lamb in her arms in a swaddling of old blankets and the snowflakes holding shape in her mess of cold wet hair and clinging there even as the wind blew.

–Lamb came just in time, she said.

–You keeping it? asked Gabriel.

–Maybe I'll keep it around the house. Can't graft it.

–It'll become a house sheep.

–I guess.

–You ever had a house sheep before?

–Once.

–It get along all right?

–Not really. She walked around the dinner table at night in circles. Then she'd start blattin' at the door. We'd let her out and she'd stare off into nothing for a while and then come back to the house and start blattin' to be let back in.

–It's not in their nature to live a life like that, away from their own. She live long?

–No.

Gabriel nodded and then stopped digging and went over to the side of the barn and sat down under the eaves to rest, his back against the wall and his knees up. He watched Yahng Yi rocking the lamb in her arms, looking out toward the forest. Yahng Yi turned around and then came over to Gabriel and stood above him.

–You all right, Patch? You want me to finish up?

–Just need to catch my breath. That's all.

Gabriel shifted his weight and let his hands down to his sides. He felt a rock at his fingers and picked it up and tossed it over at the dead ewe. Yahng Yi sat down next to him and leaned against his shoulder to share in his warmth.

–You cold? he asked.

–Little bit.

–You better get that head of yours dry.

–I'm fine, she said. Got warmed up inside tending the lamb. Besides, I like it out here. It's pretty.

–Pretty, sure. But I got a bad feeling about it.

–It'll be fine, Patch.

–I forgot how quick the weather moves around here.

The two of them stared straight ahead as the snow came down harder before them, collecting on the ground and among the curls of the dead ewe's fleece.

–You're awfully somber today, Patch, said Yahng Yi. You sure you're feelin' okay? Something you wanna tell me?

–No. You?

–No, but there's somethin' I wanna ask you.

–What's that?

Yahng Yi stroked the dead ewe's neck. –What was Jude talkin' about last night? About that money?

–He was drunk.

–Come on, Patch. He wouldn't just make somethin' like that up. And I ain't in the mood for no guessing game. You know we need money here, Patch. I'm gonna be pissed if you got money and ain't sharing. We coulda called a vet and saved that ewe.

Gabriel shook his head. –There's no money, he said.

–Well why would he think that then? asked Yahng Yi.

–Probably because of something a whore named Sweet Crude told him.

–And why would she?

–Don't know, said Gabriel. Guess it's just something people do. Believe what they want to believe sometimes. She saw my bag and just assumed there was money in there because it was money she wanted.

Yahng Yi nodded slowly in agreement, somewhat disappointed that there would be no windfall as she had dreamed about the night before, dreaming herself in the settings of those stories her brother told, of the south of Spain, and the beaches of the Mediterranean and the olive-skinned beauties who were always harassed by the men.

–I better get that hole dug, said Gabriel and stood up and walked toward the hole. He picked up the shovel and began digging again.

Yahng Yi followed him, remaining close as he dug, watching him under the falling snow, watching the leanness of his limbs, striations in his muscles visible in all their tautness. His hair coming down in all directions and the soulful good eye, good and blue, and the empty socket and the scarring on the other side. True beauty and its contrary both on the same face, the good face, kind and gentle even with the hurt crying out from that dead skin and emptiness. He turned his head toward her and smiled, and she opened her lips and felt her own fullness as their eyes met, and then his smile disappeared, as if he'd just remembered something terrible.

He turned away and started digging again, and she saw in his profile that his brow was furrowed and his mouth tight from an inner tension.

–What is it, Patch? she asked.

–Nothing, he said.

–No, she said. Something's botherin' you. Tell me.

–Later, he said.

–You got a grievance with me? she asked nervously, squeezing the lamb tighter and moving some ground fall around with her boot toe.

Gabriel knelt down and pushed the carcass into the hole, then looked up at her.

–You might say that, he said.

–What for, Patch? Was it because of those things I said last night? About runnin' off and leaving Mother behind?

–No. I'm not mad about that. That's just how people feel sometimes about people. Sometimes we hate them. Even the ones we love.

–Well, what is it then, Patch?

Gabriel hung his head down, still squatting, and began folding his hands and rubbing the mud off them, and moving the skin around, its elasticity having deteriorated and the skin itself feeling as if it could be peeled off should he find the right starting place. He was still not completely comfortable with his age, the lost years from his memory giving him little reference for the passing of time, the breaking down of the body, the gaining of wisdom.

–Those things you told me up on the mountain, he said. They weren't true.

–What things?

–You said Emily and your brother were lovers.

Yahng Yi looked away.

–And you said your mother poisoned them and that's why they went off into the storm.

She slumped her shoulders suddenly, her body seeming to collapse inward, as if the weight of her guilt had finally ground those thin bones to dust. Her lip began trembling and a small tear fell to the ground in the whirling of snowflakes as the wind pressed into her and sent the snow behind her into drifts along the barn wall.

–I know you didn't mean it, said Gabriel. I know you didn't mean for anybody to die.

She squeezed the lamb and ran to the house. Gabriel watched her until she disappeared, and then picked up the shovel and finished burying the ewe, the loose dirt mixing with the snow and the snow grown brown and filthy, making the burial dirt seem even sadder than it already was. He patted down the mound and tossed the shovel away and went back to the house. He came inside the kitchen and then walked to the front room, where Yahng Yi was sitting next to the window with the lamb against her chest, watching the snow come down and not turning her head.

Gabriel took a seat next to her and they sat in silence. The dogs were just outside the front of the house, and Yahng Yi watched them chasing each other in the powder, kicking up the snow as they sprinted, and then heading down the incline toward the valley and disappearing into the thickness of the snowfall. She watched the flakes come down in tides, her body wrapped in a blanket, the orphan lamb in her lap sleeping. She held the lamb at her chest, letting it nuzzle in there as it stirred. It rooted around within the folds of her shirt and began nibbling at the point of the breast, sending a shock through her like the touching of scar tissue. She pulled it away and it squirmed in her arms until she squeezed it and rocked it and let her body heat trick it into thinking it was back in the womb. The lamb resumed its sleeping and she watched through the window as the snow fell from the sky in silence, downy silence.

–I won't say anything more about it, said Gabriel without looking at her. She did not respond, and he stood up and began pacing around the room and then sighed and squatted down in front of the hearth and stared into the empty fireplace, the dead black coals of the used pine logs resting upon the grate.

Yahng Yi had been ready for a fight, and now that she knew there would be none, she began her crying, a hard cry that was due for some time. She let it come forth from her derelict insides, washing through those places she had not wanted to touch.

–I'm sorry, she said, sobbing. I didn't know.

–It was an accident, said Gabriel, his voice weak and un-affirming and sounding almost childlike. He picked up a poker and began moving the coals around inside the fire-place, breaking them into dust.

–I feel sick, she said and retched a little.

Gabriel stood up and went to the window, reaching down and touching Yahng Yi's shoulder as he came near her, touching her lightly and with no fervor, like the brushing touch of a ghost. He peered out the window and saw there was almost a half foot of snow already on the ground and the flakes still coming down steady like clock-work and making him feel antsy, knowing there was some-thing he needed to attend to.

–No matter how much I say I'm sorry, it don't change nothin', said Yahng Yi. I just keep telling myself, *it ain't your fault. It ain't your fault.* But it was my fault. I can't ever forget that. I knew what I was doing. I knew where Mother hid that special tea up on the top shelf in the pantry, and I knew it was gonna make Jihn and Auntie sick. Nobody forced me to do it. The only thing I didn't know was that they'd run off into the storm. I just wanted to make them sick awhile. Like I seen Mother get sick when she drank it up at the shrine. It was an accident, Patch. Like you said. But they died all the same.

–I know.

–But that don't change the fact that they're dead be-cause of me.

–You've got to move on, Yahng, said Gabriel, his voice still with no inflection or emotion. You can't blame your-self forever. God forgives.

–You don't know what it's like, Patch, she said, the cry-ing coming harder so that the lamb came awake and hopped down from her lap to the floor and went toward the hearth and lay back down where the dogs usually lay.

Yahng Yi took the blanket and buried her face in it, muting the sobs as best she could.

Gabriel began fumbling with his eye patch, moving it around and running his finger under the strap and looking as if he had something to say, but saying nothing. Yahng Yi caught a glimpse of him through the blanket, and slowed her crying enough to watch him. He looked beaten, his posture slouched and the muscles in his face tensed up, his color pale like the dying. At first she thought it was the sickness, the river fever coming back and draining him of his strength. But it was too quick, the way the life had left him, and she knew that he was thinking upon his own guilt, upon his own dark secrets.

–What is it, Patch? she asked, her crying finished and her own sins forgotten for the moment and all her attention on him.

He continued to adjust the eye patch, and she imagined him without it, his face naked as she had seen him the night before. She imagined the scar that ran along his temple, the perverted skin like plastic, shiny in the low light of the fire and the eyelid open and the flesh between the folds where there should have been the matching blue iris. How it had seemed so much a part of him and natural, and in a way beautiful.

–I have something to show you, he said in a monotone, and then turned quickly and headed to the kitchen and out the back door.

Yahng Yi left the lamb there sleeping before the hearth and followed him outside, the blanket still around her shoulders. She matched his path in the snow with her steps, her small footprints in the holes of his, and she saw how the lips of the holes were slanted forward, and how the loose powder had been tossed backward onto the unbroken snow behind the prints. He had been running. All the way from the house to the barn. She thought that odd, and picked up her own pace, her heart racing and the blanket dragging behind her and smoothing out their tracks.

As she entered the barn, Gabriel was descending from the loft ladder with his satchel slung over his right shoulder. The light through the windows was low and colorless, calming and reminding her of the times she spent during summer showers in the barn with her brother, warm in there and outside the skies good and gray. The two of them just sitting there in piles of loose straw. Sometimes talking. Sometimes just listening to the sounds of the rain. She could be like that with Gabriel. She could be that easy with him because she knew he wanted nothing from her, needed nothing from her.

Gabriel hopped down to the ground from the third-to-last rung and walked quickly to her. There was rustling in the pens as he passed, as if the lambs and mothers sensed his urgency. There would be a defining moment for him in this barn, on this plateau, as if past and future had been swept up with the storm and been compacted upon this time and place, insulated from all else by the pressure of the falling snow, the valley sealed off like the dark corridors of his memory. All the noises of the animals muted by the ground fall and the water's run slowed to near nothing. The folds in the mountains shrouded and the pines like dead nerve endings, their branches sunken by the wet snow collecting within their needles.

He took the satchel and dumped the contents onto the floor, and then knelt beside the pile.

–I've had this for a long time, he said, picking up his Bible and bobbing it up and down to feel the comforting weight of it. I remember I used to read from it night and day. It's funny, though. Now that I can't read anymore, I don't miss it. For some reason I don't miss reading it at all.

–You didn't run up here to show me a Bible, did you? asked Yahng Yi, dropping the blanket from her shoulders and kneeling down in front of the pile.

–No, said Gabriel and set the Bible back down and moved the clutter around until he found the letter. It was stained with browned blood, the sturdiness of its paper stock long compromised, the shape of it flimsy and the edges dulled. He took the envelope and then held it with both hands in front of him, pulling on the edges and stretching it, as if smoothing out the wrinkles in its skin.

–What is it? asked Yahng Yi.

–A letter.

–No shit, Patch. Who's it a letter to?

–Don't know, said Gabriel. I remember writing it. But I don't remember who it's written to. Don't remember what it's about.

–Well lemme see it, said Yahng Yi, reaching for the envelope. I'll tell you.

Gabriel jerked it away quickly and stood up.

–Jesus, Patch, she said. It's just a letter. Lemme see it.

–Not yet, he said.

–What's going on, Patch? If you don't know what the hell the letter's about, then why you actin' so fussy about it?

–Just let me think for a second.

Yahng Yi looked into his eye and saw the iris dart away quickly. –You were lyin', Patch, she said. You know damn well what that letter's about.

Gabriel nodded. –I've got a hunch, he said.

–What kind of hunch?

–My hunch is that it's about something bad I did that I don't remember doing. Something to do with your mother.

Yahng Yi stepped forward, and that made Gabriel step back, both hands still on the envelope's edges.

–Then throw it out, she said and reached out again, this time holding out her hand and leaving it there, palm up. Give it to me. I'll get rid of it for you.

–I've thought about it, said Gabriel, but still kept the letter close to him and Yahng Yi at a distance.

–Then what you waitin' for? she asked, advancing on him.

–I can't explain it, he said, backing a step with every one of hers, and the two of them dancing a strange waltz around the barn.

–Hand it over, Patch. Something like that shouldn't be messed with. You been given a gift. Given a chance to start over. It's a blessing that you can't remember the terrible things you done. You should thank your lucky stars. Why would you wanna go and ruin it?

–Because we are made of our pain, Yahng, he said and breathed deeply the stench of the barn, the moldy hay and wet wool and dung, holding in the air as he closed his eye and tried to find some memory, some good memory that he could prime for further remembering. But nothing came to him. No images. No faces. Just darkness and a chill that started from the inside, spreading out from the torso to the limbs and diffusing to the skin and the hairs to make them stand forth with the follicles raised. He slipped his finger in the flap opening and ran it down the length of the envelope and held it out to her.

–Read it, he said.

Yahng Yi backed away from him until she reached the door of the last paddock under the loft, staring at the letter in his hand as he approached her. She hung her chin low to her chest and shook her head, tossing her thick hair back and forth and letting it curtain forward over her face.

A part of her wanted to read the letter, wanted to know its secrets and what those secrets would reveal about her mother and her mother's place in the world, and from that place her own place. But she knew those same secrets would darken the good man before her. No, she thought. She would not take part in that. He was Gabriel, and she knew him as he was now, and she did not want him changing.

–No way, she said, waving her hands at him. I ain't gonna have any part in makin' you live your nightmares again. And if this is about me, then forget it. I don't need you to suffer to make me feel better.

–I'm suffering already, he said.

–What if it makes you wanna kill yourself again, Patch? You wanna take that chance?

–It's different now, Yahng. I've got you in my life. And your mother. Got plenty to live for.

–And that ain't enough?

–I wish it was.

She paused for a moment, trying to think of some irrefutable argument that would make him see things her way. –God forgives, she said, shaking her head. You told me so yourself. You gotta move on. Forget about it and move on.

Gabriel sighed and appeared to shrink as the breath left him. She looked into his eye and saw that it did indeed look smaller, and she knew that for all he talked about forgiveness and walking in the light of God and tasting of the living water and the salvation that he foresaw upon his death, he knew no peace. She remembered seeing him asleep, seeing his dreaming. Always the sweat appearing around his crown and the warping of his face as he dreamed of things she wished she could see, when he reached up to clutch his wounded eye or down between his legs, and then the relief that came over his body when he was no longer dreaming.

–My mind's made up, he said.

Yahng Yi bit her bottom lip as she took the letter and then slumped down along the support beam to the barn floor. –You gonna sit? she asked.

Gabriel walked to the beam and leaned his left shoulder into it and put his hands in his pants pockets. –No, he said.

Yahng Yi looked up at him standing above her, somewhat angry that he had placed her in this position, that of the reckoner. She glanced at the face of the envelope. There was a return address in the top left corner. A Billings address. And a mailing address just off center. Kansas City. She said nothing about the addresses, removing the contents from the envelope and then folding the envelope once across the middle and stuffing it in her back pocket.

There were three pages altogether, trifolded, and written front to back on lined white paper. The body text was scrawled somewhat sloppily, revealing the haste in which it was written. She folded the papers against their creases so that they would stretch flat and then raised her knees up to press the pages of the letter against her thighs. And then she began reading.

I don't really know where to start, but you wanted my war experiences, so I guess I'll just write things as they come to me. They shipped us out from Tokyo in the middle of the night. Something wasn't right about it. They rounded up some guys from the apartments they kept for their panpan girls and from the whorehouses all throughout Ginza. Nobody knew what the hell we were doing once we got to Korea.

When we got near the Yongdong front, the roads were already packed with refugees heading south. Old women and men and children right in the thick of the artillery fire and antitank mines. *We stood there and watched them marching like it was happening in a movie. They told us to keep our eyes open. Treat all gooks like they was the enemy. They said the North Koreans had infiltrated the refugee columns. Said they were moving supplies in their pushcarts through the front line, hiding radios in their shirts to transmit our positions. Some officers said that whole units of the North Korean army traveled among the peasants, picking off our guys under cover of nightfall. It was all talk, though. Of all the guys I talked to from the 24th, none of them actually saw anybody hiding radios or bombs.*

We were there to give support to the retreat of the 24th. To dig in among the hills to cover the dirt highway and the rail line. Take out the gooks if they chased the 24th east to where the rail line turned south again. Seemed easy enough. But all those people made for problems. I remember hearing the officers talk about what to do with all of them. It was a mess. We were just a bunch of seventeen- and eighteen-year-old kids. Just did what they told us. Those people weren't really human to us anyway. And we weren't old enough to know any better.

On the third night there, we were bunkered on a hillside. It was dark. Quiet. And then we started hearing machines moving toward us. Big trucks or tanks or something. And then all hell broke loose when the machines came closer. Guys started taking off running. M-1 fire all over the place. Some guys started firing at the convoy coming through the valley. I waited in a dry streambed until things settled down. Spent the night there. In the morning, I started walking back to camp after the sun came up. I remember there was a bunch of bodies on the road. Dead people who had been walking in front of the convoy. I found out later that the convoy was ours. It was the 24th.

I caught up with the rest of the 7th near No Gun Ri. We were shooting the crowd huddled under the rail bridge. Probably a few hundred in there. I asked one of the sergeants what was going on and he yelled to get down and engage. So that's what I did. I started shooting. I shot the people at the edge of the tunnel and the people running out of the tunnel, trying to escape. I watched them slump to the ground as I popped them. Kill shots to the head. Just like I was back in the mountains bagging elk. Just lined them up in my sight and kept squeezing off rounds. Saw their heads jerk back, bits of their hair and skull blown off. I must have killed at least a dozen. None of them armed. I can still see them dying. As clearly as the day I killed them.

Then I saw this girl come out of the tunnel. She started walking toward our line, hands by her sides. Not in any kind of hurry. Just walking at us like she was waiting to be shot. I lined her up and was about to fire when I recognized her. It was a girl I'd seen back near Chu Gok Ri. Just a little peasant girl who had been running away from the fighting up north. And that's when it dawned on me that what we were doing was wrong, orders or not. I left my gun and ran after her, and kept running until I caught her and covered her. I remember the mortar explosion behind me and the shrapnel burning into my back. Then I passed out from the pain. That was the last I saw of a battlefield.

The whole five months I was in the hospital in Pusan, that peasant girl waited for me. She told me we were linked by fate and that she didn't have anybody else. She was pregnant too. After what I did, I knew I had to bring her home with me. I figured it would grant me some kind of forgiveness.

I thought Emily would understand. Thought she might like having a little one around. She'd always wanted a baby herself. When I got back to the ranch, I told her the baby wasn't mine, but I don't think she fully believed me until after he was born and she saw the baby had no white blood in him.

I never could bring myself to tell Emily exactly what I did, and because of that, she never truly understood why I brought the girl home with me. I think she put together some of the pieces. That I did something pretty bad over in Korea, and was trying to make up for it. But she could never imagine just how bad it was.

We tried to make a go of it. To pick up where we left off. Even talked about getting married and having some babies of our own. I kept telling her to wait. That I wasn't fully healed, but as soon as I got better, we'd get married the proper way.

That day never came. I just couldn't shake the memories from the bridge. Seeing all those people I killed, over and over again. The faces of old men and women. Faces of kids barely old enough to run. I couldn't do hardly anything. Couldn't sleep. Couldn't eat. Couldn't work.

The only thing I could do was watch over that Korean girl. It was the only thing I thought was worth doing. The only thing that made me feel any good. Just taking care of her, keeping her safe. It didn't take long for me to think I loved her, and for her to think she loved me.

Emily eventually realized that I wasn't the same man that had left her for the army. The Gabe she loved was dead. I remember her face in those days, after she came to accept that things would never be like they were. I remember her sad eyes. Like a widow's.

I got to be a mess. Too much guilt. Too much regret. I couldn't bear to watch Emily mourning me like that. And it got to the point where I couldn't look at the peasant girl either. Every time I saw her face, I saw the faces of the dead, her people. So I left them. Left them both. Left my home and my life, and everything that made me who I was. I thought

206

by leaving everything behind, that someday I'd forget. That day never came either.

I haven't been back to the ranch in almost forty years. Sometimes I wonder about that Korean girl. I wonder if she made a go of it in this country. Or maybe she went back to Korea. In the long run, bringing her back didn't make me any less guilty. If I would've left her over there, I'd be in the same place I am now.

Yahng Yi folded the pages and held them up to Gabriel. He shook his head. She stuffed them back in the envelope and put the envelope in her pocket.

Gabriel did not cry. Did not show her anything. Everything she read had always been there, and it was more psychology than physiology that had blocked those images out. They were still unclear, as if seen through wet glass— the sounds of dying muted, as if hearing them through water. But they were there. And the emotions were there too. The fear, the anger, the confusion.

He had expected something monumental, a moment of catharsis, something celestial. But he realized that he was still the same man.

–You okay, Patch? asked Yahng Yi, looking up at him.

He rolled his hand across the top of her head, the gesture like the passing of a secret, the wiping away of memory, the burying of sins in the snow. She wanted to say something comforting, something compassionate, but could find no words. She only looked at him, and he saw her looking and did not look away.

HAM FINN WAITED in the boarding zone of the Gallatin National Airfield, watching the edge of the storm drop snowflakes atop a 727 docked at the gate. In the northern sky to his left, a half moon hung just outside the reach of the storm clouds, near some dimmer stars in the expanse at the valley's end.

He stared at the airliner and thought about his childhood in Casper, and how he and his best friend Birdie would spend their idle hours building model planes and listening to Birdie's older brother, Dean, tell stories about being a bombardier in the Pacific during World War II. Dean told them about flying the skies over open ocean water, and the thrill of spotting the island enemy on the horizon. Dean wasn't like the other somber boys who came back from the war, not like the ones who had fought on the beaches of France or the North African desert. He was livelier, a caricature, the kind of larger-than-life figure who reveled in his own heroism. He said he could convince girls to let him feel their breasts because his hands had killed so many Japs. *Screwing and killing go hand in hand,* he'd said. *Breeding and Dying.*

After high school, Birdie joined the navy to become a fighter pilot, and Ham went into the army, his weak eyes unsuited for military flight. He spent his first year in Tokyo for occupation duty, most of his time there dedicated to cards, panpan girls, and drinking at the clubs on the Ginza strip, bankrolled by the profits from his black-market affairs.

He eventually chose one of the panpan girls he frequented to be his *onrii wan,* his kept woman, and rented her a place in the city. At the time, he thought it was love, but after his company was shipped to Korea, he never saw her again, despite his best efforts to reach her.

He thought about Yahng Yi's Mother, and how easily she had rebuffed him at the diner. He thought about how she had worked him over the years, using the prospect of her company to barter—not unlike his *onrii wan* in Tokyo. He thought about how she had made him promise to never tell Yahng Yi that he was her father, at risk of losing her company forever.

Now that Yahng Yi's Mother had denied him completely, there was one last thing to do before he left the valley for good—mend the bloodline that she had forced him to sever.

The storm had reached the tops of the Spanish Peaks and now covered the sky from horizon to horizon. There would be no flights in or out until the snowfall dissipated, and he slouched in his chair and closed his eyes, trying to clear his mind so there would be none of their faces in his dreaming.

–WE BETTER ROUND UP THE BAND and take them up to the barn, said Gabriel. I don't think they're seeking shelter on their own. Can the dogs cut sheep?

–No, said Yahng Yi.

–We'll have to round them up ourselves then.

Gabriel walked along the row of paddocks, taking tally of the animals.

–Five lambs in here, he said. How many down in the valley?

–Just four.

–How many yearlings?

–Ten.

Gabriel nodded and the two of them put on gloves that were tacked next to one of the support beams, and then Gabriel took a coiled rope off the wall and looped it around his arm.

–We'll take the lambs and mothers up first, he said. I'll carry the lambs and you lead the ewes up by rope. Shouldn't be too hard after we get a trail blazed, but the first one's gonna be hell.

–What about the yearlings?

–We'll see what the snow does. They look to be big enough. I don't think they'll smother unless the snow comes down like this tomorrow too. We'll see. Might have to just try and herd them all into the gully. Maybe borrow a couple horses from Finn. Will the dogs be all right out in the snow?

–Sure.

–Make sure they stay out overnight then. Coyote might be prowling around looking for an easy meal.

Yahng Yi nodded.

–Let's get on with it, said Gabriel. Quicker we move, the easier it'll be.

–You sure you're up for it, Patch? Just last night you were sicker than a dead dog.

–Sure I'm sure. You?

Yahng Yi grinned and the two of them stepped out of the barn and back into the silence of snowfall. There was a foot and a half down on the plateau, but the wind had built drifts near the fence line and there looked to be swells and undulations by the band's loitering spot.

Gabriel walked the lead, shuffling his feet to clear a path. He headed down the incline at an angle, trying to minimize the gradient of the path for the return trip back to the barn. Yahng Yi followed him, shuffling her feet as well.

It took them several minutes to reach the valley floor. The band was in their usual place and there was a flat spot among them where they'd trampled the snow. The lambs and mothers hung around the middle of the band, the lambs butting and playing together, having their first experience with snow. The grannies bordered them, hanging around the periphery, some of them lying on the ground and the snow blown up to their backs so they were half buried. They watched as Yahng Yi and Gabriel entered the circle, and Yahng Yi went to one of the lambs and picked it off the ground, its legs writhing. The lamb's mother came out to claim the lamb and Gabriel tied the rope around its neck.

–Give me the lamb, said Gabriel.

Yahng Yi handed him the lamb and Gabriel traded her the rope and began walking back up the incline, his steps slipping and wasting energy from the lack of friction. He turned around and saw that Yahng Yi was not far behind, the ewe following closely at her heels.

Gabriel stopped halfway up and squatted down and tucked his chin into his chest to catch his breath. Yahng Yi squatted down next to him. The snow did not let up and even as they squatted for a minute the trail ahead of them had already filled halfway with powder.

–We gonna make it three more times? asked Yahng Yi in between deep breaths.

–We have to, said Gabriel and got to his feet.

The wind had picked up and white darkness descended upon the valley. They lowered their heads and trudged up the incline through the ground fall and made it to the barn in ten minutes. Gabriel entered the barn and turned on the lights and placed the lamb in an empty paddock. The ewe followed him in and lay down in some loose straw and the lamb came to it and settled at its ribs. Gabriel leaned his weight onto the paddock door and rested for a moment. Yahng Yi untied the rope from the ewe's neck, her hands trembling.

–You okay? asked Gabriel.

Yahng Yi nodded, a trickle of drool coming down from her mouth. Gabriel came over to her and patted her back. She motioned him away.

–Let's take turns, he said. I'll go down and get a lamb and bring it up here while you rest. The ewes will follow. No sense in doubling our trips.

−We'll both go, said Yahng Yi in a weak voice. Both bring up lambs then.

−Okay, but if you can't make it carrying a lamb, just leave it and go back on up. I'll pick it up later. You understand? Don't go acting like a hero.

Yahng Yi nodded and walked quickly to the door and out into the snow before Gabriel could coil up the rope. He dropped it on the floor and went outside, following Yahng Yi back down the path. They made it to the valley floor and each picked up a lamb and headed back up the incline. Gabriel insisted on trailblazing again and Yahng Yi followed, struggling with the extra weight of the lamb.

The ewes followed them dutifully, and they stopped at the halfway point as they'd done on the last trip. Yahng Yi sat down in the snow this time, her mouth open and eyes half closed. Gabriel reached out with his free hand and shook her. She looked up at him with only her left eye, her face still angled toward the ground.

−I'm sorry, she said, drifting away. For what I did.

−I know you are, said Gabriel. You got to get ahold of yourself.

−Gotta move on, she said, her voice thickened with slur. Gotta keep goin'.

There was no pain in her anymore and she stared at Gabriel and his face became Jihn's, his hair full and dark, and then his eyes ripening to brown, and the smooth skin of his cheeks and the bed between his jawbone and neck where she wanted to rest her head.

−Forgive me, she said and she closed her eyes and fell to her back and let the snow come down upon her, let it come down and bury her so she could be born again with the thaw, when the melt was done and the rivers ran fat and the wildflowers bloomed, and life began again, and all her sins forgiven.

Gabriel set the lamb on the ground and knelt down next to her and tried to rouse her. She did not wake. He moved behind her and squatted down and hooked his forearms under her armpits and hoisted her up. He heard the falling of a dead tree near the edge of the forest, and he looked behind him and saw as the house lights flickered off. He turned Yahng Yi around and lifted her onto his shoulder, fighting the wind as he carried her slowly up to the plateau.

TWELVE

Five hours later, Yahng Yi awoke on her bed, in the same clothes that she'd worn earlier and her boots still on. The night hour had come, the bedroom containing only darkness and a low white glow from the window. She sat up in bed, her head pounding and her body aching, and nearly toppled over from her weakness. Her mouth was dry and she pursed her lips together to make saliva and swallowed what came out. The snow still fell and the ambient light from the heavens lingered, trapped between the whiteness of the sky and the ground, some soft pinkish light coming through the unobstructed windows.

She reached over toward the bedside table and turned the switch on the lamp, but no light came on. She got out of bed and tried the light by the door, but that didn't come on either. She sighed and thought of the remaining sheep down on the valley floor, no doubt buried again in the drifts blown high by the north winds, and she went to the window and opened it. The cold air and the snow in the air came through as if they'd been waiting for her. She looked out and saw the smoothness of the snowfall down the incline to the valley, squinting her eyes in the dull light and looking for movement on the valley floor.

She left her bedroom, walking unsteadily, and wondered if Gabriel had managed to round up the other lambs. The house was empty, so she walked through the kitchen to the back door and exited the house into the falling snow. She went straight to the barn, stepping high in the fresh powder, the tracks from earlier in the day already buried. There were some newer tracks leading past the barn and into the forest and she knew that her mother had recently made the trek up to the mountain shrine. She worried about her mother for a moment, but decided against following the new tracks, her legs sore from moving the sheep and also the fever that had come upon her. The snow was packed against the barn doors and she swept it away with her foot and swung open the barn doors.

She checked the paddocks and saw that all the lambs were penned. Gabriel had finished leading them up. She breathed deeply, relieved that she wouldn't need to haul any more lambs up from the valley floor.

There was still a couple of days of hay left piled next to the barn, and she decided she would feed them in the morning. If the storm continued, even at moderation, the rest of the band would have to forage the snow-covered ground, the hay reserved for the new mothers to make milk. She hunched over to regain her bearings and then walked back to the barn door. She closed the doors, making sure the latch was tight, and then went around to the side of the barn and retrieved the shovel that Gabriel had used to bury the dead ewe from the afternoon. Then she walked back to the edge of the plateau where the barn and house rested and peered down into the valley. The snow had been letting up, the flakes sparse and smaller, and she saw the band was huddled by the fence line, buried a foot deep already, higher in the drifts.

She took a few steps down the incline, holding the shovel, and her legs grew wobbly and her head began to throb and her knees buckled. She stayed like that for a moment, on hands and knees, her face a few inches from the two feet of ground fall, so her warm breath reflected off the snow and back to her face. She lifted up her head and let the cold reawaken her, and then pushed herself back up to standing. She left the shovel on the ground and retraced her steps back toward the house, the breaths harder to find and her legs grown numb from cold and muscle acid.

As she came upon the tracks that led to the back of the house, she saw a low yellow light coming up from the gully. She stopped and watched it, and saw Jude Finn appear in the clearing next to the barn, an oil lamp swinging limply at his side.

Jude saw her and the set of tracks leading to the back of the house and he angled toward them and stepped into the holes already made, lifting his feet high and walking toward her, watching the ground until he was within a few yards. And then he stopped and stared at her, at her thick black hair covered in patches of white.

–What the hell you doin', Jude? asked Yahng Yi. You know you ain't welcome here.

Her hair looked pretty, brambly and flattened from meltwater and cold enough that the flakes clung now and maintained their angles, crystalline and carrying the colors of a prism from the faint yellow light of the oil lamp. Jude reached up to touch her face, her eyes looking cataracted through the haze and ghostly.

She pushed his hand away and turned her back on him and began walking toward the house. He jogged through the snow to catch her, grabbing the crook of her arm and pulling her. She slipped and fell lightly to the snow and turned up to face him.

–Come with me, he said. I'm gettin' outta here. Leaving for good.

He held his hand out to her, but she denied him, standing up on her own and then brushing the snow off her arms and legs.

–No, she said.

–Come on, Yahng. We'll take that drifter's money and get out of here.

–No, said Yahng Yi. I don't want to see you no more.

Yahng Yi began walking toward the house again. Jude came up quickly behind her and pushed her in the back. She fell to the snow and lay there and laughed.

–Quit laughin', said Jude.

She didn't. She kept laughing at him and he spat at her.

–I never loved you, he said. I was lyin'.

Jude began kicking her in the snow and she rolled over onto her back. He tried to stomp on her belly but she moved her arms down to block him so he stepped down on her forehead with his boot heel. She lay there still, and he knelt down and shone the lamp on her face, that face so pretty with its blood rushed up to warm her from the cold, her lips blood-filled and pouty.

–I'm sorry, he said and knelt down next to her. I love you. I'm beggin', Yahng. See me here on my knees.

–You're an ass, she said.

He rose to his feet and dusted the snow from his knees. Yahng Yi rolled to her side, the pain in her ribs and forehead slowed by the cold, and she got to her knees and began playing there in the snow like a child, moving the snow around with her bare hands. Then she made a small snowball and threw it at his face.

Jude wiped the snow away from his nose and cheeks with his forearm. –Come on, Yahng, he said. Let's get. We'll go back and get my truck and just head off.

Yahng Yi sat up, legs crossed, and swept the snow to her lap, burying it in a mound. She turned her head and stared off blankly into the former emptiness of the valley. Jude stood above her, watching the snow come down to coat her hair, the flakes collecting there in the tangles and building upon themselves nearly to fleece.

–Come with me, said Jude, softly now. Please, Yahng. Come with me. I ain't got nobody.

Yahng Yi looked up at him and she held out her hand and he took it and hoisted her to her feet. She felt dizzy from the head rush, and her muscles ached as she stood, the fever clouding her head and making the whiteness of the world go to red.

–Thought you wanted to leave this place, he said.

She looked at him for a moment and thought of his handsomeness, and how she had once lusted for him, his strong limbs and jaw, and the blossoming masculinity once so seductive that she could not see past it. But things were different now. She saw him as he was. A boy who offered nothing more than strong symmetry of body and face.

–Ass, she said and turned away and trudged through the snow to the kitchen door, opening it and entering without looking back.

Jude watched her disappear into the house and then collapsed to the ground, still holding the oil lamp. There he sat in the snow, staring at the house and holding the lamp between his knees, the heat of the flame coming barely through the glass and touching his inner thighs with the hinting of warmth. But still cold. Still cold, and he stared into the lamp, into the flame, and then back at the house, and pictured it burning. All of it burning.

YAHNG YI STRUGGLED TO MAINTAIN HER BALANCE as she entered the house. Her head pounded hot and she went to the sink and ran cold water from the faucet and cupped her hands under the flow and leaned down and drank heavily from it, the water still aerated from the faucet and bubbling as she swallowed, but unable to satisfy her thirst.

She took her coat off and for a moment felt chilled as the last of the water evaporated from her face. She lay her head down on the kitchen table and closed her eyes, letting her heartbeat slow, and thought of the sheep down on the valley floor, by now poking their muzzles out from the snowdrifts and struggling for breath.

Sleep called and she raised her head and shook it firmly and then pinched her thigh, knowing that soon she and Gabriel would need to dig the drowning sheep out of the snow to keep them from smothering.

She thought of her brother, and how they'd found his body buried in a drift near the fence line almost three years ago to the day. He was just sitting there, facing the valley, his chin tucked into his chest and his arms wrapped around his knees, like he was relaxing, enjoying the beauty of the storm. Auntie's body was found farther down the road, almost to the gully. Hers was sadder. She had been crawling toward the Finn compound, as if trying to go home.

JUDE WALKED QUICKLY through the house and into his grandfather's study. There he removed a small key from beneath a clutter tray in the top drawer of Ham's desk, and then went to the gun cabinet and retrieved a Mossberg 14-gauge and a box of bird shot. He did not notice the big shadow hunched down in the corner near the bay window.

–What're you doin', Jude? asked Val, who was sitting by the window in one of Ham's huge leather chairs.

–Jesus, said Jude, jumping back.

–Just me, Jude, said Val in a soft voice. Ain't no reason to be scared.

–What the hell you sittin' there in the dark for? asked Jude.

–Power's out.

–No shit, the power's out. Ain't you never heard of a flashlight or a candle?

–Sorry, Jude. Don't know where nothin' is in this house. Went down to the compound, but you already took the lantern. So I been sitting in the dark.

–Shit, man, said Jude, his heart just coming clean from its racing. I'm glad you're here. Come with me across the gully. She knows where the money is, Val. I'm gonna get it.

–What you need the gun for? asked Val, pointing lazily with his right index finger.

–I guess it's for you now, Val, said Jude and walked to Val and pressed the stock of the shotgun into Val's chest. You're gonna be keepin' watch.

–I don't know, Jude, said Val as he sat up from his slouching.

–Quit being a pussy.

–Don't want no part of it, Jude. I told you that messing with that man's gonna be bad luck.

They stared at each other by the lantern light, Jude's hair wet from the melted snow and his white face flushed and a madness in his eyes. Val ever stoic, sitting there passively, his long black hair shiny and his skin coppered and looking more so by the light of the small flame.

Jude made a slow grin. –You know it's all sold, Val, he said. What you gonna do? Go back to the rez?

Val stood up from the chair, standing tall and his shadow taller yet, and both his shadow and himself much bigger than Jude and his sinister posturing. Val held the shotgun out, barrel forward and out to eye level as if to gauge its meter.

–Thought you said Granddad was gonna take care of everything, he said as he lowered the gun and held it back out to Jude.

–I lied, Val. Granddad ain't gonna have enough to do much more'n pay off what he owes. He's takin' what's left over and moving to California or some shit.

–I don't believe you.

–Wise up, Val. Granddad don't care a lick about no one but himself. You're just another prairie nigger to him. That ain't never gonna change. What you think he brought you back here for? Ain't from the goodness of his heart. It's cause you was the biggest goddamned Injun on the rez and he didn't want you for an enemy. Didn't want you standing in the way of tappin' the fresh squaw over there. *Me Big Ham Finn. Me hit Injun pussy all me want. Me like'm redskin.*

–No, Jude, said Val. I don't believe you.

–Believe it, dumdum. Ham Finn's a no-good sonofabitch.

Val stared at him, still holding the shotgun, but the barrel lowered and limp and the mouth of it pointed toward the earth, Jude's eyes even wider now and looking crazy.

Val did not know if Jude spoke the truth, or if there was still an allegiance between them. While he was pondering on it, Jude took the shotgun away from him and went quickly behind the desk and pulled on one of the locked drawers. Then he pumped a shell into the Mossberg and fired at an angle so as to blow the face of the drawer away, splintering wood upon the both of them and pocking their faces with slivers and the beginning of bleeding.

–Sonofabitch, said Val, picking the splinters from his face.

–Goddamned right, sonofabitch, said Jude and reached into the hole left by the shotgun blast. He pulled out a stack of papers, and on the top was a copy of a letter to the Bureau of Indian Affairs.

–You know what that is? asked Jude, holding the letter to the lantern and pointing at the top right corner of the page.

–Yeah, said Val. That's the seal of the BIA. What's it say?

–Says *I, Ham Finn, request the bureau of Injuns to admit one Val Rey back on the rez starting next Tuesday.* That's what it says.

Val took the paper and stared at it, and though he could not read, the words looked to be about the same length as what Jude had said and he recognized his own name and that of Ham Finn. He crumpled it up and tossed it over his shoulder.

–Now get your shit together and come with me, said Jude, handing Val the shotgun again. We'll get the money and cut out. Screw Granddad and the rest of the fuckers around here.

–Then what? asked Val, his heart feeling shrunken and his left hand gripping the barrel of the Mossberg so hard that he felt like his fingers would melt metal.

–We'll split the money half and half. I made up my mind already. I'm leavin' tonight. You can come with if you want, take half the money if you want.

–Where you goin'?

–Mexico, said Jude.

–What's in Mexico? asked Val.

–Shit, man. Cheap beer and cheap pussy. Sunny and warm all the time. I can't take this cold no more, Val. Tired of having to pull my balls out my ass nine months out of the year.

–Mexico?

–Shit yeah, Mexico. Just come with, Val. Ain't no big deal. She's all by herself over there. Ain't no one gonna stop us.

Val nodded and clutched at his ribcage, trying to paw out the pain.

Jude smiled. –I'll tap her one last time and you can tap her too, he said. I seen the way you look at her. We'll hit it one last time, you and me both. Then we'll take the truck and get the fuck out of here. Granddad'll be gone till Monday. By the time he gets back we'll be in Texas.

Val said nothing, and Jude took his silence as agreement and the making of a pact. He went to his grandfather's liquor cabinet and grabbed a bottle of bourbon and tossed it to Val. Val caught it with one big hand, the other still holding the Mossberg.

–Drink up, said Jude.

Val opened the bottle and took a good pull, coughing when the whiskey found his windpipe. Jude laughed and slapped Val on the back, and Val took another good one and then one more before handing the bottle back to Jude.

–Good, said Jude and pulled one himself. You feeling brave?

Val nodded and Jude went and retrieved the crumpled letter to the BIA. He took a lighter from his pocket and lit the paper—a letter dated two years earlier that Ham Finn had returned to the BIA accepting the title of Val's legal guardian.

Jude tossed the burning paper to the floor and took the bourbon from Val and poured it around the flame until the floor was lit, and then they were off, Jude with the lantern and Val with the gun, outside the burning house and under snowfall.

Val watched the snow fall as he walked, so pretty as it fell in large flakes and the world all quiet except the two of them walking together through the powder, the whiskey good and hot in his belly like mother's milk. He wanted to speak of how pretty it looked, how beautiful it all was, all that white and all that silence like a great downy blanket to offer sanctuary from the darkness. But he would not tell Jude. There was only one other with whom he would share such a thing, and she lived across the gully and had yet to learn of his affection.

YAHNG YI'S MOTHER KNELT BEFORE THE SHRINE, watching the snow falling upon the platter of sweet red bean and rice cakes. She wore Emily's old wool shawl wrapped around her shoulders, and below it one of Emily's flannel shirts rolled three folds to the wrist, and a pair of her daughter's jeans and only wool socks and slippers to protect her feet. She was numb at the extremities, but did not shiver, and she blew hard through her mouth to watch her visible breath, watching its body taking shape and thinking of her homeland and the cold on the island, wet and invasive, her clothing never thick enough to shield her. She and the other children would run to keep warm, making games out of nothing, chasing each other around the village and peeking into the huts to spy on their mothers. When their bodies grew warm they would breathe hard into the air to watch the steam come forth. The boys would hold fingers to their mouths to simulate the way their fathers smoked.

It had been forty years since she'd fled her village to the mainland, stowing with her two sisters aboard a fishing boat. The communist invasion had just begun and she remembered taking the bus all the way to Seoul and then joining the evacuation south, the roads jammed to the train depot at Osan, businessmen and laborers fleeing together, overflowing onto the farmers' lands, and walking for days until boarding the overpacked cars as the monsoon rains opened up all through the ninety-mile trip to Chu Gok Ri.

That small village had quickly overflowed with refugees, no one believing the war would reach that far south. The villagers had welcomed them, though. More people to pull weeds in the rice fields. She remembered fondly those days before the fighting reached them. At the time she had no inclination of what her future held or that she was with child, reveling only in the known and immediate freedom she felt since leaving her island home with her sisters.

She would sometimes go out to the paddies to help with the cultivation, sometimes play with the children after they came running home from the small village school, but she still felt out of place in the valley, the mountains walling her in like the ocean had done on her home island. The poverty was as bad among the farms as in her fishing village, the small huts huddled closely in community, the gravesites nearby on the steep inclines of the low mountains with worn dirt paths from those tending to the dead.

In Chu Gok Ri, they would see the trains moving south all day long, packed so full of refugees that they spilled from inside the cars and onto the roofs. And then Tae-Jon had fallen and the Americans arrived, the convoys of trucks hauling artillery and men, and the children would wave at them and cheer, hoping they would not have to abandon their lands and the graves that held the remains of their ancestors.

The valley became engorged with the Americans and their war supplies. Thousands of men to man the artillery, taking positions around the road and along the mountainsides. They would spend the days milling around the valley, some playing cards in their camps or playing with the village children who were brave enough to confront them.

As the days passed, the army men became more inquisitive, venturing through the rice fields and to the village where they called out laughingly that they needed women, that they had cigarettes to trade. Some of the girls, including her and her sisters, had cut their hair to make themselves look like boys. Some dressed themselves in ragged clothes and smeared their faces with mud and walked around with hunches in their posture, pretending to be elders. Sometimes they smeared themselves with dung to make their scent repulsive.

She remembered the cruel day that took away her sisters. That gruesome day when she saw enough dying to corrupt a hundred lifetimes. She remembered walking out of the tunnel into the firefight, and how Gabriel had run through the gunfire to save her. She remembered the days she spent waiting for him in the forest outside the hospital in Pusan, waiting for him to recover and to bring her with him to America. She remembered their first months in Montana, and how he had cared for her after Jihn was born, sitting by her bedside during all her feverish nights, during the pains in her abdomen and the bleeding. She had loved him, and then he had left her, disappearing from her life like the morning fog.

The memories still burned inside her, the hotness radiating, burning hot like the sun-baked roads that led south from Seoul after the monsoon. Hot like the blazing muzzles lighting up the hillsides with their fire in the night.

–Umma, she said. I was never a girl.

The voice did not answer, the first time that the *mulsin*, her mother, did not answer.

She stood up and let the stiffness in her legs loosen a bit before she began the descent back down the mountain. It would be the last time she would visit the shrine, and she knew it, but did not make good-byes or ask forgiveness. She walked slowly down the mountain, enjoying the white silence of the snowfall, all the trees and rocks layered already and looking peaceful, like the satisfied dead. She would leave this place, let it be buried with the fast-falling snow, waiting to be reborn like all things needed to be reborn now and then in order to truly live.

Halfway down the mountain she saw Gabriel walking up the path, following the filled footprints from her ascent, his outline blurred by the light snow and the radiant light reflecting from the ground, approaching her like the birthing of a man within a dream. She smiled and stopped, waiting for him.

When he reached her they embraced and he kissed her lightly on the mouth.

–Brought you some tea, he said. Figured you could use something hot.

–That was not necessary, she said.

–I wanted to.

She touched him lightly on the face, his loose skin having grown hard with the cold and making his weathering even more pronounced. –You look tired, she said.

Gabriel smiled and then unscrewed the thermos he was carrying and poured the steaming tea into the lid and handed it to her. –Pretty out here, he said.

Yahng Yi's Mother took the tea and brought it to her nose. –What kind of tea is it? she asked.

–Don't know, said Gabriel. Found it in the pantry. Bag wasn't marked.

Yahng Yi's Mother emptied the cup onto the snow and took the thermos from Gabriel and dumped the rest of the tea as well. –Did you drink any? she asked.

–Not yet, he said. Why?

–It is a special tea. Used in the *kut*. It helps the *mansin* to channel the dead.

Gabriel nodded. –Is that the tea Yahng gave to Emily and your boy that night . . . ?

She pressed a finger to his mouth before he could finish and then stepped into his arms. He held her and felt her warmth. The connection was there again, returned with the return of his history. But he would not tell her his secret, would not tell her that rounds from his rifle rang in the hollows under the bridge, that his gun had felled the innocent, and that it was out of guilt that he brought her with him to America, that it was out of guilt he fell in love with her, his self-hatred fueling his devotion to her, his love for her, in a futile attempt to assuage that guilt, to expiate him for the wronging of her and those who shared her skin.

He would not tell her that after realizing the impetus for his love for her, he would never be able to establish that same emotion again on those same grounds. He could not rebuild that love from something so perverted. To love her again would be to start over again. But he would not tell her that. That much he owed her.

–Where is Yahng? she asked him.

–Still sleeping.

–She is okay?

–Fine. Just feverish. She needs rest.

–The lambs?

–In the barn.

–When shall we leave?

–When this snow melts.

–Where will we go?

–It does not matter.

And she smiled, and as she smiled he brought her into himself, kissing her hard and grabbing her hips and bringing them tighter to his own. Bringing her in and pressing and then moving his face away from hers and into her neck and letting those heavy locks fall down upon the back of his head and his nose in the nape of her neck and moving in circles and smelling her open skin and the ready pores, his face still buried and still bringing her into him and pressing, and her humming softly in his ear. His face moving against hers and the snow all upon them and their heat together hotter than the cold was cold.

THIRTEEN

It feels like a dream to Yahng Yi and she awakens with her head resting sideways on the kitchen table, a puddle of saliva at her mouth and her vision blinded momentarily as she opens her eyes and looks directly into the burning flame of the lantern in front of her, the flame in stasis even though there is a stiff draft blowing through the barely open back door and some loose flakes broaching that crack and swirling a bit in the eddy of the kitchen enclosure.

But it is not a dream.

The initial shock of the resonant light fades and she sees Jude sitting next to her, watching her. She looks past him at the window and the firm light coming through, the snow still falling and flakes clinging to the panes, and she feels an aching all through her body and the heat of her hair has her sweating though the room is cold. She reaches up and feels her forehead with the back of her hand and feels her skin, hot from the fever and the lantern heat.

–You still here, Jude? she asks and then notices the madness in his eyes and the lantern light illuminating his face from below and casting shadows that angle upward, making him look unrighteous.

–What the hell's goin' on? she asks and looks past Jude and sees tall Val standing in a shadow, holding a shotgun and looking unstable.

–Val? she asks. That you?

Val nods and steps into the light and Yahng Yi sees that his countenance is not as she has ever known it, his eyes drooping and the angles of his face all lost, just a dumb blank stare. He wobbles a little and she can smell the whiskey in his big breathing.

She turns to Jude. Jude reaches over and tries to stroke her hair. She does not let him, moving back and pushing his hand away.

Jude stands up and walks behind her. –Where is it? he asks.

Yahng Yi turns her head around to track his movement. –Where's what? she asks.

Jude sighs and then backhands her across the cheek. Yahng Yi falls to the floor. Val tries to help her, but Jude holds out his arm to block him.

–Where is it? asks Jude.

–Don't know, says Yahng Yi, trying to crawl toward the back door.

Jude kneels to the floor and begins crawling alongside her.

–You wronged me, he whispers to her and then turns her over and sits down on top of her and she feels all of his weight pinning her there. She struggles for a moment, but the fever has her weak and she tires quickly. She looks over at Val.

–Val, she says. Help me.

–Val, says Jude. Go look around outside to see if anyone's comin'.

–Val, says Yahng Yi. You know this ain't right.

–Go on, Val, says Jude.

–Help me, Val, says Yahng Yi.

–Goddammit, Val, go outside!

–Get him off me, Val. Come on. I ain't done nothin' to you.

–Val, I'm gonna count to one.

–Val, whatever he's told you, don't believe him. He ain't never said a word to no one that ain't been a lie. You know that. He's using you. He don't care about you.

–Shut up! yells Jude and punches her in the mouth and then stands up and walks to Val. Go, he says and grabs Val's arm. Val does not move.

–What the hell's the matter with you? says Jude. Go on.

Val looks over at Yahng Yi, sees the blood coming down her nose and her eyes unfocused. Her dark eyes, dark like his and glossy, and the eyelids folded at the inside corners, the epicanthic fold, a trait shared by their ancestors. She is like him in so many ways. Her face, her skin, her hair.

He shakes his head drunkenly. –No, he says. I ain't gonna let you do nothin' to her.

Jude purses his lips and nods. –You ain't comin' with me to Mexico, then, he says.

Before Val can answer, Jude turns and strikes him square in the gut, and as Val doubles over, Jude wrenches away the shotgun and then comes down with the stock onto the back of Val's head, knocking him out before he hits the floor.

Yahng Yi gets to her knees again and begins crawling away, toward the front room this time. Jude sets the shotgun on the kitchen counter and walks to her quickly and kicks her hard in the ribs and she flips over, gasping for breath. Jude grabs her feet and pulls both her boots off and then yanks down her pants and pries her legs apart.

As Jude drops his own pants and drawers, Yahng Yi reaches down quickly and grips his scrotum and squeezes. Jude rolls off her, howling.

Yahng Yi stands and lunges for the kitchen counter. She grabs the shotgun, and swings around and as she aims, Jude comes toward her, his pants still around his ankles. He stumbles as Yahng Yi squeezes the trigger, but the safety is still on and no shot is fired.

Jude head-butts her and Yahng Yi falls to the ground again. Jude retrieves the shotgun and puts it back on the counter and then clutches his aching groin. Yahng Yi moans, semiconscious at his feet. Jude pulls his pants back up and then steps on Yahng Yi's throat.

–Just tell me where it is Yahng, and I'll leave. I'm done screwin' around.

–Don't know, she says, struggling for air. I swear. He never told me.

–Liar, says Jude and kicks her again in the ribs, and then goes around the kitchen, opening the cabinets and emptying their contents to the floor, pots and pans and glasses.

–Ain't in here, says Yahng Yi.

–Ain't lookin' for money, says Jude. Need a drink.

–Hell, there's plenty to drink. Look in the pantry.

Jude goes to the pantry and opens the door. Yahng Yi waits until he is out of her sight line, and then gets to her feet quickly and runs to the kitchen counter and grabs the gun again. As she toggles the safety this time, Jude rushes at her, and she manages to discharge a shell, but the shot is wide and blows out the refrigerator.

Val awakens from the noise and as he regains his bearings, he sees Jude and Yahng Yi wrestling on the floor, their arms entwined and strained and their faces taut and teeth clenching deeply into gums. Jude gains the advantage and wraps his hands around Yahng Yi's neck, trying to choke her. Val crawls to them and curls his big arm around Jude's head and pulls him off.

–Get the gun, says Val to Yahng Yi.

Yahng Yi crawls for the gun. Jude ducks under Val's arm and elbows him across the head, knocking Val back. Jude lunges for the shotgun, reaching it before Yahng Yi, and then holds the gun in front of him, pointing it at Val.

–Tough luck, Val, he says, laughing.

The back door opens and Gabriel bursts inside, having heard the gunshot while emerging from the forest. Jude turns and fires a shell hastily, the blast blowing out the corner of the kitchen and sending Gabriel to the floor. Gabriel scrambles on the ground to his knees and picks up the iron skillet nearest to him as Jude pumps out the empty shell. Jude fires another shot at Gabriel and it misses as well, shredding the kitchen table and exploding the gas lantern, sending flames upon the wall.

Gabriel throws the iron skillet at Jude, but Jude side-steps and the skillet hits Val in the chest. Gabriel reaches down to pick up another weapon and Jude fires again, and misses again, blowing out the dry wall behind Gabriel and splintering a beam so that the ceiling bows.

Jude looks at Gabriel and then at the shotgun, dumbfounded. –Lucky sonofabitch, he says.

Yahng Yi jumps onto Jude's back as he is loading another shell into the gun chamber. She beats on his head, and he stumbles all around the kitchen, tripping over the pots and pans on the ground. Jude throws Yahng Yi off him and aims the shotgun at her chest. Yahng Yi retreats backward on all fours, then sees her mother to her right, standing in the doorway a few yards away.

–Jude, says her mother as she walks toward Yahng Yi. You are a bad seed.

Yahng Yi's Mother stops in front of Yahng Yi, blocking Jude's sight line of her daughter. A second passes and then another, Jude holding the shotgun in front of him, pointed at Yahng Yi's Mother, the fire growing thicker and now crawling up two walls and across the ceiling. There is only the sound of the flames as the seconds pass, another and another and another, and then suddenly Jude pulls the trigger and it cuts into Yahng Yi's Mother's right hip and explodes the window behind her. Gabriel makes a move toward Jude, but Jude pumps another shell into the chamber and steadies the barrel on his chest. Gabriel stops.

–That's your last shell, Jude, says Val in a wheezing voice, rising from the floor and clutching his shattered sternum. Put it down. You hurt enough people already.

Jude trains the barrel on Yahng Yi.

–Put the gun down, Jude, and we'll all just walk away, says Gabriel.

–You heard him, says Val. Just walk away. We'll sort things out some other time.

–We're supposed to be brothers, says Jude, glaring at Val. Supposed to go to Mexico.

–Come on, Jude, says Val. We gotta get outta here. Fire's gonna take us all down.

Jude lowers the shotgun and holds his hand out to Yahng Yi. –Come with me, he says.

Yahng Yi shakes her head. Jude snarls and then raises the gun toward Yahng Yi's head. He holds it there, gripping it hard and his arms shaking. –Last chance, he says through a clamped jaw.

From the corner of her eye Yahng Yi sees Gabriel sneaking behind Jude, holding a skillet and his movements muted by the roaring of the fire. –Okay, Jude, she says and holds out her hand.

Jude's face relaxes and his shaking stops. As he lowers the shotgun to meet her hand, Gabriel brains him in the back of the head and he crumples.

Yahng Yi goes immediately to her mother and places her hand on the wound at her mother's hip. She sees her mother's teeth clench and her eyes close tightly and the muscles wind around the facial bones, twisting the prettiness out of her. Then her mother goes limp for a moment, and her eyes become perfect and round again, the amber in there reflecting the light of the spreading fire, and her lips near one another, the distance between them finger-wide and fleshed out in their fullest, as in a kiss.

–Daughter, she says lovingly.

Yahng Yi hooks her hands under her mother's arms and tries to pull her toward the back door.

–Leave me, daughter, says her mother.

–You get outta here, says Gabriel to Yahng Yi. I'll get her.

Yahng Yi does not move, gripping her mother tighter, and the two of them stare at each other, the first time in Yahng Yi's years that she has ever truly stared within her mother's eyes, and Yahng Yi sees the gesture as her mother had wanted, as a gift. She sees her mother for what she is, a lonely old woman in need of affection, and she leans in and kisses her mother on the cheek.

–Get her out, says Gabriel to Val.

Val goes to Yahng Yi and tugs lightly on her arm. Yahng Yi's Mother slips from her daughter's grasp as Yahng Yi follows Val to the back door and into the snow, leaving the last exchange between mother and daughter unfinished.

It is only the two of them now, and Gabriel lowers himself to the ground and moves Yahng Yi's Mother's arm around his neck to hoist her up. They stand up together and walk slowly to the door, the heat tremendous and the smell of melted plastic and char, their steps small and slow and the fire all around them and the sounds of the ceiling joists creaking. Then part of the ceiling collapses, blocking their egress.

They both fall back to the floor, and lie there together, the fire all around and the smoke like island fog, everywhere and inside them. They lie there, but not with any fear, not with any sadness.

–Will you leave me again? asks Yahng Yi's Mother, blood pouring from her wound and her lungs thick with soot.

–No, says Gabriel.

–I want you to leave me, she says.

–No, says Gabriel. I will stay.

Gabriel strokes her hair and they hold each other the way they should, like lovers, sleepy from the heat and enjoying each other's arms.

Yahng Yi's Mother goes first, and Gabriel sees her go, sees it in her eyes, and he thinks upon his life, thinks it strange that it should end like this, with him at peace and waiting for the memories to come, the death memories, hoping the holes in his history will be filled and the images will be slow, so he can see them and relish them and know for certain that the stories he has lived are his and his alone.

–Forgive me, he says as he leaves his body behind. He can see them burning, both of their bodies burning.

VAL HELD YAHNG YI IN HIS ARMS, kept her from going back inside the house, and she screamed and pounded at him, but he would not let her go. They watched the house burn and the walls collapse and then she dug her nails into his hands, but still he did not release her.

When her screaming was done she raised the crook of her arm to wipe away the tears, and when she looked again, the sun had begun its ascent behind the cloud cover.

They sat down together, and Yahng Yi scooped some snow up with her hands and held it out to Val and Val took it and held it to the burned skin on his forehead. She watched him wince and reached over and rubbed his back, the ashes of his shirt flaking upon the snow and his skin exposed in the holes where the embers had burned through. She asked him if he was cold and he said no. She asked him if he was hurt, and he told her he would need to see a doctor about his chest and she nodded, and then she lay back in the snow, the warmth of her fever warming the snow beneath her and reflecting her body heat back and her hair covering the sides of her face and warming her as her tears warmed her as well.

The snow had stopped falling and she heard the barn swallows clamoring against the dying grumble of the fire, and then the familiar blatting coming up from the valley floor. She sat up and cleared the moisture from her eyes and looked over her shoulder toward the band's feeding spot and saw the dogs hopping in the snowdrifts, climbing upon the backs of the half-buried ewes, who were staring up the incline at the burning house.

The last of the load-bearing walls collapsed and the house folded inward to silence the fire. The birdsong from the forest and the blatting ewes grew lucid, and she closed her eyes to listen for the creek hidden in the gully. The sounds of the water were barely audible, coming only in the quick moments between heartbeats, her head still cloudy with fluid and sorrow, and the snow having dampened the ground-level noise and the creek itself too viscous and lazy with the cold. She got to her knees and rose atop the matted snow, breathing in the cold clean air not corrupted by the ash, and then walked into the sunlit valley to free the animals of their bondage.

FOURTEEN

Yahng Yi had hitched a ride in the bed of a pickup with some Blackfeet who were heading north toward reservation land near the Canadian border. They rode along the creek-lined, single county road that ran north-south between the town of Leeth and the interstate. The truck moved slowly, a few vehicles passing them in the opposite direction—trucks hauling stacked hay bales and boxed leghorns, and a horse trailer in front of them, the horses' muzzles pointing out from the portholes to taste new air and their stench streamlining over the cab and caught in the dead spots within the perimeter of the truckbed.

She clutched Gabriel's pack to her chest. There was much work to be done back at the ranch, but she had work of her own to finish first. Her father and the sheep could wait.

After the roads were cleared following the storm, Ham had made his way back to Harter from the airport, where he found both his grandson and beloved dead. Warm weather had followed the snowfall, and the dump of the storm melted on the mountains while he mourned, flooding the valley's waterways and the compound on the valley floor.

Ham, Val and Yahng Yi stayed in a motel in town while funeral preparations were made and paperwork was filed and the sun dried up the floodwater. After the funerals, Ham decided not to sell the ranch after all, using the insurance money to rebuild the log cabin and deeding everything to his heir, Yahng Yi.

Only Val Rey had stayed on among the cattle hands, having found out that Ham had not betrayed him after all. The sale of Ham's cattle had grossed enough to pay off the ranch's remaining debts, and the whole of the land was devoted to sheep again, as it had been through its stewardship by the Cottages. Ham added to the Shetland herd and left it up to Yahng Yi and Val to tend the ranch while he watched over them, as he'd once watched over Jude.

The Blackfeet truck slowed and then came to a stop next to the creek at a thin wood post jutting out from a cluster of willows, and Yahng Yi jumped out over the bed and then nodded her head and waved to the driver as the truck sped off. She adjusted the pack on her shoulder and walked east from the road where the post dug into the ground, following a pair of ruts that headed straight off toward an old tin-roofed house, the roof reflecting the light of the noonday sun. The house stood in the middle of a parcel of meadow covered with spring grass. Undulating mounds curved behind the house as the land sloped gradually to a small butte. Yahng Yi stepped over a packed dirt bridge intersected by drainage pipe and ran her hand across the leaves of the serviceberry bushes that were clustered near the creek.

The house was in need of whitewash, the exposed wood looking hoary and the lattice around the crawl space bro-

ken away in gaping holes. Yahng Yi walked the path toward the house, waving at the yellow jackets going back
and forth between the lavender prairie flax blooms and
her neck sweat. In front of the house was a yard goat tied
by rope to a metal pole on the left side of the porch. The
goat was nibbling at the ground in search of grass roots,
the area of the goat's reach bare to the brown dirt.

The goat looked up at Yahng Yi as she approached and
the tuft of its tail wagged and it baaed. Yahng Yi saw the
hanging udders underneath it, looking sad and dry. She
petted the goat on its head and let it lick her hand as she
approached the three steps going up to the porch. There
was a hinged gallon jar of sun tea brewing on the bottom
step. The boards were split, and as she stepped upon the
first it gave near the center. She stepped the next one over
to the side where it was braced and then skipped the top
step up onto the porch.

The gray floorboards of the porch were caked in dust
save for a direct path to the door, and there was debris
lined up along the railing—tin cans and a couple of
moldy-looking burlap sacks that hadn't yet dried from the
last rain. A short-haired gray cat came out from the screen
door and Yahng Yi looked at its cataracted eyes. The cat
came up to her and brushed itself against Yahng Yi's legs
and then went under a rickety porch swing, where there
was an old bird carcass, tail feathers scattered around the
body to mark the spot of its death. The cat picked up the
carcass and trotted slowly down the porch steps and
sprinted away into the grass, the goat following it to the
end of its tether.

There were two windows juxtaposing the screen door,
both boarded with plywood. Yahng Yi stared at the windows, at the cracks between the wood planks and then at
the door, the mesh torn from the frame near eye level and

the bottom hinge not attached to the frame. Beyond the door was blackness.

She walked to the threshold and set the pack down and pulled gently on the door handle. It creaked loudly and a voice came from within the house.

–Branch? a woman called out. That you?

–No, said Yahng Yi.

–Who is it then?

–Name's Yahng. I'm a friend of Gabe's.

–Well come on in, then. Maybe you can tell me where the hell he's been.

Yahng Yi stepped through the door. The inside of the house was dark except for a few slivers of sunlight coming through the gaps in the boarded front windows. Her eyes were not yet adjusted to the darkness, and she saw only the slivers of light and what they showed her. A dusty plank floor and an armless pine rocking chair against the far wall. A stovepipe in the corner and a section of the black iron heat stove. An older woman stood in the center of the room, lines of light running horizontally across her body.

–Dark in here, said Yahng Yi.

–Can't stand the bright light, said the woman. Hurts my eyes.

The woman stood with a slight hunching, a purple wool shawl over her narrow shoulders and a patchwork skirt hanging over her hips. Her hair was all gray but full, and her skin wrinkled and still holding some remembered remnants of sun.

–Lemme see you, said the old woman and squinted.

Yahng Yi set Gabriel's satchel next to the door and walked toward her, the floor joists creaking as she stepped.

–You're just a girl, said the woman. What business you got with Gabe?

–Him and my mother was friends, I guess, she said, looking around the room and smelling the old woman's not unpleasant scent, lye soap and line-dried laundry.

–That where he is? the woman asked. Visiting your mother?

–He was, yeah.

–Was? He dead or something?

–Yeah.

–I figured something happened to him. It's been a couple years since he's been home.

–This was his home?

–For twenty years.

–Who are you, then?

–I'm his wife.

Yahng Yi shook her head and then heard meowing coming from the door. She turned around and saw the cat there, pawing at the screen and then trying to wedge itself in the space where the mesh had torn away from the frame.

–That's Emily, said the woman. Gabe's cat.

Yahng Yi went to the screen door and pushed it open. The cat backed away and then scampered into the house and went immediately to Yahng Yi's legs, purring. The woman sat down on the rocking chair and clasped her hands together in prayer. Yahng Yi watched her rocking back and forth and saw that the old woman's lips were moving though no sound came out.

–Did he suffer? asked the woman when she was done with her prayer.

–Can't say, said Yahng Yi, and then went to a wooden stool set near the heat stove. She sat down on it gently, testing it with weight before letting it support her completely. She looked over at the wall and a plywood shelf there with three thick books set upon it, one of them a leatherbound Bible.

–My name's Millie, said the woman. You want something to drink?

–No thanks.

–Where you from?

–Harter.

–You come all this way to tell me about Gabe?

–Didn't know what I'd find here. All I had was an address from a letter Gabe wrote.

–Was it the letter he was writing to the newspaper man? asked Millie.

–Newspaper man?

–Gabe didn't tell you about that?

–To be honest, ma'am, Gabe didn't remember much of anythin'.

–Why? What happened to him?

–He had an accident.

Millie breathed deeply and let the air come out fully, her small body collapsing like a bellows blowing out into a fire. She nodded in understanding. Then she smiled.

–So he didn't remember what it was he was suffering for?

Yahng Yi shook her head. –He found out again, she said. From the letter.

Millie nodded. –Sounds like something he'd do. I used to tell him, *you tasted the living water, Gabe. It's awful arrogant to think you know who's deserving of forgiveness better than Jesus. You asked forgiveness and it came upon you the day you did so. Now quit fretting and recognize how good a man you are.* I used to tell him that all the time. But the man was stubborn as a mule. Headstrong.

–I know it, said Yahng Yi and stood up from the stool and went to the plywood shelf and removed the leatherbound and ran her fingers along the worn creases in the spine and then flipped through it.

244

–Who was the newspaper man he was writin' to? Yahng Yi asked.

–Just some Korean fellow writing a book about the war. Said there was some people got killed under a bridge. Women and kids. I guess he found out Gabe was one of the soldiers there, so he tracked him down. Kept calling all the time. I finally had to unplug the phone. I thought that was the end of it, but after that, Gabe started changing. Got to be where I didn't even know him anymore.

Millie sighed. –We lived here seventeen years, she said. Happily. I always knew he had some stuff in his past. Sometimes he had nightmares. But he hid it well. After that reporter came into his life, though, the nightmares got worse. He was moody, too. Would just start crying from the middle of nowhere. Then he started getting angry. Started drinking again. He went seventeen years without a drop, and then all of a sudden he was drinking a liter every two days. Started having fits of rage. Breaking stuff. That's why the house is as bare as it is. Gabe broke about everything in it.

–Why'd you put up with it? asked Yahng Yi.

–I loved him, said Millie and then her eyes watered and she started rocking faster and turned her head away from where Yahng Yi was standing and kneaded her hands within her lap.

Yahng Yi saw the chain of it all. Starting with Gabriel, linking to all he touched, and to those whom those had touched. So much death. So much suffering. And the loneliness. She wanted to say something meaningful. Something Gabriel would have said, with all those aphorisms he always had at hand. But she could think of none, and the woman's rocking made her uneasy, her looking so much like Auntie. What was it that Gabriel had once said?

That most things were perfectly like something else, and at the same time perfectly different.

Millie stood up and walked toward the back wall and through a doorway. Yahng Yi followed her into a bare kitchen with no furniture and just a few items in the cupboards. She watched as the old woman stood on her tiptoes, reaching into one of the high cabinets for a glass.

–Lemme get that, said Yahng Yi and reached it easily.

–You're tall, said Millie and poured sweet tea from a plastic pitcher sitting on the counter. Get yourself a glass too.

Yahng Yi did so, and Millie poured hers as well, but not as full. Yahng Yi took it and drank fast, the chill of the dark house keeping the tea cool. It was weak in tea taste and oversweet, the opposite of her mother's. She set the empty glass on the counter.

Millie walked past her and went back to the front room and sat down on the rocking chair. The cat stepped to her quickly and leaped up on her lap and Millie raised her glass as the cat landed. She stroked it across the back with one hand and held the tea with the other.

–So Gabe finally ended up writin' to that newspaper man? asked Yahng Yi as she sat back on the stool near the heat stove.

Millie made baby talk with the cat, smiling wide and then letting the cat sip a little from the sweet tea. –I guess, she said. Don't know for sure. He wouldn't tell me anything. Man went a whole month without talking. Not saying a word. You know how much bitterness it takes for a man not to talk for a whole month? Not even to his own wife. Then one day he was real calm, like he'd had a weight lifted off him. I guess he decided he'd talk to that reporter after all. Said he'd write him a letter or something. Day after that he was gone. Just up and disappeared. Didn't say good-bye.

Didn't write good-bye. Just disappeared. To be honest with you, I'd had enough by then. Now don't get me wrong. I never blamed Gabe for what he did. He was a good man. Soldiers become soldiers because they believe it's the right thing to do. And they become good soldiers because they listen to what they're told. That's when you get good people doin' evil things, and good people just can't live normal knowing they done evil.

–He ever talk about my mother? asked Yahng Yi. Or Emily Cottage?

Millie furrowed her brow and her mouth turned down at the corners.

–No, she said. He never talked about what happened before we met. Said the past was the past and that we are made of our hopes, and not our regrets.

–He said that? asked Yahng Yi.

–Yeah. But I always suspected he didn't believe it.

Yahng Yi nodded and waited for her to continue, but instead the old woman stood up and glanced at the door, announcing her desire to be left alone.

–Well, I appreciate your time, said Yahng Yi and pointed at Gabriel's old leather satchel on the ground by the door. Guess that's yours now.

–Keep it, said Millie. I've closed that chapter in my life.

Yahng Yi took the satchel and slung it over her shoulder, somewhat pleased that she would be keeping it, but also annoyed. A man like Gabriel didn't deserve to be forgotten like that, just thrown away when the time came for the turning of pages. There was never love here, she decided. And she understood why Gabriel never remembered Millie. She was like the scenery to him. Like the short-lived perennials of the foothills in summer.

She waved her hand and Millie smiled and waved back, and then Yahng Yi walked quickly out the door and down the porch and across the ruts back toward where she came from, patting the goat on the head as she passed it. She turned left where the ruts reached county road and walked south beside the creek and along the ditch grass and wild violet, back toward Leeth, where Val Rey would be waiting for her. She glanced over her shoulder one last time at the tin-roofed house, and saw Millie standing in the doorway with her left hand perched across her forehead above her squinted eyes, fighting the light as the light shone upon the meadows and buttes and all the good things that she no longer saw.

Almost like home, thought Yahng Yi as she waved away the yellow jackets and took in the airborne sweetness of rendered nectar. She felt a light misting on her skin from the slow creek breaking on rocks and roots and sensed her mother in there, in that broken water that longed to move with the wind. She glanced at the wildflowers along the ditch, the pink and purple blossoms looking perfectly like the flowers back home and at the same time perfectly alien, and she remembered what Gabriel had told her about the bitterroots, how they were called the resurrection flower because even after they'd been picked and dried, you could revive them with water. Make them live again.